T0343525

THE
HERMIT

Advance Praise

"A Tom Wolfe for the Instagram age! Katerina Grishakova writes with the assurance of a seasoned novelist even as her pages sing out with the exuberance of a newcomer. *The Hermit* is a stylish, sophisticated story of how internal turmoil can ravage the soul even as external success can nourish the ego. Ruthless, funny, and dazzlingly sharp-eyed on the details, Grishakova is a thrilling new voice."

– Meghan Daum, author of *The Problem With Everything*

"This is an extraordinary book, rich in observation and keenly attuned to the inner world of its spiritually impoverished protagonist. The mosaic-like accumulation of physical detail—much attention is paid to food, houses, shoes, and clothes—and the author's deep understanding of and affection for her wryly comic but wholly credible cast of eccentrics cohere over time into a portrait of a troubled psyche that doubles as an indictment of a troubled nation, one consumed with technology and profits, plagued by demagogues and charlatans, and driving at full speed towards something dark. The final fifty pages—an extended sequence that is at once ominous, dream-like, and achingly sad—is some of the finest writing of the year, calling to mind the films of Martin McDonagh and the Coen Brothers."

– *U.S. Review of Books*

"I admire the dexterity and keen eye Grishakova shows, and her ability to deftly craft a social novel that captures fraught, and always intriguing, class dynamics."

– Ross Barkan, author of *The Night Burns Bright*

In *The Hermit*, Katerina Grishakova crafts a compelling character study of one man's midlife journey to rediscover purpose and meaning beyond his outwardly successful but soulless career on Wall Street … Grishakova excels at slowly building Andy's inner turmoil while never sacrificing keen observations and penetrating cultural criticism.

– *IndieReader*

THE
HERMIT

A
NOVEL

KATERINA
GRISHAKOVA

UNBOUNDED CREATIVITY
HERESY
PRESS
FEARLESS EXPRESSION

Heresy Press books may be purchased in bulk at special discounts for sales promotion, corporate gifts, fund-raising, or educational purposes. Special editions can also be created to specifications. For details, contact the Special Sales Department, Skyhorse Publishing, 307 West 36th Street, 11th Floor, New York, NY 10018 or info@skyhorsepublishing.com.

Skyhorse Publishing® is a registered trademark of Skyhorse Publishing, Inc.®, a Delaware corporation.

Visit our website at skyhorsepublishing.com.

HERESY PRESS
P.O. Box 425201
Cambridge, MA 02142
heresy-press.com

Heresy Press is an imprint of Skyhorse Publishing.

10 9 8 7 6 5 4 3 2 1

Library of Congress Cataloging-in-Publication Data is available on file.

Jacket design by Elizabeth Cline

Hardcover ISBN: 978-1-949846-66-9
Ebook ISBN: 978-1-949846-67-6

Printed in the United States of America

Contents

I: Soiree at the Pierre   1

II: On the Trading Floor   15

III: Madeline and Ava   27

IV: Birthday Party   39

V: It Takes a Special Understanding   55

VI: Lauren   65

VII: Between the Primal and the Cerebral   73

VIII: A Night on the Town   81

IX: Misidentification of Evil   95

X: Madeline's Fears   105

XI: New Mexico   113

XII: Vegas   123

XIII: Zombies, Fat Tails, and Teddy Bears   131

XIV: Summer Doldrums   147

XV: Gradually, Then Suddenly   159

XVI: At the Wellness Center   169

XVII: Can't Identify the Disease   183

XVIII: We're Special, But Nobody Knows That   197

XIX: Presence at Dusk   203

XX: Oleg's Barbeque   209

XXI: The Ends   223

XXII: A Good American   231

XXIII: A Man in Flux   239

XXIV: Ava's Disappointment   249

XXV: The Hermit   255

20 +0.98   ZAR $7.02 +0.24   WUP $228

MN $7.02 -0.14   QUO $118.48 -1.23

KT +118.48 -1.44   VCX $22.10 +0.MWP

1.98   MER $7.02 -0.14   WUO $118.48

+2.25   RZC $22.20 +0.98   ZAR $7.02

Q $118.48 -6.22   PLM $22.10 -0.33

MC $22.10 +0.98   MER $7.02 +0.14   WUO

MER $7.02 -0.14   WUO $118.48 -6.22

MER $7.02 -0.14

I: Soiree at the Pierre

To be in full character for tonight's performance, Andy Sylvain, a managing director at Keating Mills Capital, ate junk food, skipped exercise, and neglected grooming for a whole month. This regimen had added a doughy softness to his otherwise well-defined frame, and that morning, when he looked in the mirror, he was satisfied with what he saw: a working-class English lad, pale and cocky and ready for a brawl.

Later that day, on a warm October evening, Andy took a taxi from his office on Park Avenue to the Pierre Hotel for a closed-door, invitation-only industry event. A fleet of taxis and limos discharged the partygoers in front of the hotel's white-and-gold awning, stalling the traffic on Fifth Avenue and on the adjacent streets. Some guests who got out of the arriving cars were dressed in formal wear—tuxedoes and evening dresses—while others seemed to have prepared for a masquerade. From one black town car emerged a middle-aged man clad in a leotard and a tulle tutu, followed by another, older gentleman dressed in a cartoonish purple jacket with green lapels, a top hat, and swinging a cane.

Andy stepped out of the taxi on 61st Street and Madison Avenue and walked one block west, maneuvering between the honking cars. He wore a baseball cap, gray Champion sweatpants, a T-shirt, and a hoodie. He carried a dry-cleaned tuxedo on a hanger in one hand and a gym bag emblazoned with his firm's logo over his shoulder. In the bag there was a change of clothes—a costume for his skit.

A velvet rope guarded the hotel's doors. Two young women dressed for a night out stood in front of the entrance with disappointed looks, blocked from entering by the hotel's polite but unyielding doorman.

Andy smiled at them.

"Could you get us in?" one of the girls asked him, sensing an opportunity.

"Any other party I could. But not this one," he replied.

"What is this? Some secret society?" the girl asked, bulging her eyes in exasperation.

"A *pretend* secret society," Andy remarked, raising his eyebrows and pressing his lips into an all-absolving can-you-believe-it? scowl—a handy expression that every New Yorker deploys to quickly and without consequences convey a range of emotions from amusement to helplessness, to apology, to skepticism.

The girls pouted. Andy dove into the hotel's revolving doors.

The cool, marbled foyer of the Pierre, with its regal interior and its ceremonial staff, was a far cry from the chaos and expediency of the trading floor, Andy's usual habitat. Gold-framed mirrors and meticulously polished floors reflected the dim light of the crystal chandeliers. Fresh white lilies in vases that sat on the lacquered side tables along the wall smelled of dust and the past, like a rich old widow's boudoir. For a Street guy like Andy, the tranquility and otherworldliness of this place could be a bit intimidating, and when he walked in and inhaled the floral air, he told himself that all this grandeur was a mere façade, an inflatable magic castle for adults. This palatial stuffiness and old-fashioned sentiment simply begged to be occasionally debased by mischief and juvenile frolicking, paid for with money made in a bawdy, foul-mouthed pit.

The gilded lobby bubbled with a frat-house atmosphere. There were wigs and sequins and platform shoes. Wall Street titans in drag sought to discard their mature front, as if maturity was a handicap, greeting each other with jolly yells of endorsement. Andy patted and gladhanded his way through the motley crowd.

"Andy," he overheard someone. "You gained a few pounds."

"It's for the role," he responded.

A floor sign that read The Seventeenth Annual Street Bohemians Jamboree directed the guests toward the ballroom. Inside the ballroom, the planners, sparing no cost for preparation, had hired a Broadway theater crew to install a temporary stage and equip it with a concert-grade metal truss with professional lighting. A large canvas banner with the Street Bohemians coat of arms—a blue-and-gold wedge-shaped shield crisscrossed into four sections, two of which featured tragedy and comedy masks, the other two a bull and a bear—and its motto, *Ars Longa Vita Brevis*, spanned over the stage. Multiple round tables covered with white tablecloths dotted the audience area in a checkered pattern. Offstage, behind the curtains on the left and right flanks, the performers unloaded their props and costumes.

Andy found his table and sat down. A polished waiter hurried to fill his glass with ice water and put a small porcelain bread plate with a dinner roll and butter in front of him. The pat of chilled butter was styled into an equilateral triangle with an eye—a totem of no meaning but inviting infinite projections—in its center.

Andy looked around the table. To his left he saw a salesman from a small, aggressive broker-dealer whom he had run into many times at industry gatherings. He never remembered the salesman's name but acknowledged him with a curt nod.

"Hey, Andy," the salesman said. "What are you working on these days?"

"Eh. A wait-and-see approach. There's no yield out there," Andy said languidly.

"I hear you. Can't squeeze water from a stone," the salesman commiserated with a grim chuckle. "Trust me, we're scouring all kinds of arbitrage opportunities, all kinds of niche products. There's no premium out there at all. I heard of some guys who are earning five percent leveraged three-to-one and are happy to get even that."

"Yeah." Andy shook his head and gave the salesman the same all-purpose pressed-lipped frown he had bestowed earlier upon the unsuccessful party crashers.

The emcee—the elderly man in the purple-and-green jacket who, by day, was a board member of several public companies—walked on stage. "Ladies and Gentlemen," the emcee announced. "Welcome to our Seventeenth Annual Street Bohemians Jamboree. Today, we leave our competitive spirit outside. Today is not about deal-making and one-upmanship, but about art and fun and camaraderie. This is our annual cleansing, a truce. We gather here to take a lighthearted dig at ourselves and at our daily battles, indecipherable as they are, to which we shall return tomorrow."

There was a limp round of applause.

"As the rules say, all the phones inside this room should be turned off and no recording or photography is allowed. Your compliance is mandatory, and those who disobey will be asked to leave. But enough with the formalities." The emcee spanned his arms and gazed at the room with a wide, wily smile. "Look at this crowd. If anyone from outside stumbled in here they'd think we're a bunch of fags. Excuse me, L-G-B-T-Q. Plus."

Mischievous laughter rolled over the room.

"And we'd rather keep it that way!" a man in a mullet wig and a mesh top shouted from the audience.

"A-ha!" The emcee pointed a finger at the wigged man. "I see what you're trying to do here. You want to be a persecuted minority."

There was satisfied laughter again.

"And since we're on topic, what did the caddy say when a foursome landed their balls really close together?" The emcee paused and darted his eyes left and right as the audience held their breath for a risqué punchline. "I haven't seen four balls that close together since *Brokeback Mountain*."

Ba-dum-tiss, a drum from the deep end of the stage impressed on the resolution.

"Ahh, I kid the gays. They're nice people. Nice neighbors."

Andy scanned the room for his co-star, Zeke Klein. Klein wasn't anywhere to be seen. Andy excused himself, stood up, and made his way to the bar counter. He ordered a scotch on the rocks and sipped it as he watched the first sketch of the evening.

The room darkened, and an Elvis impersonator, the head of macro strategy at a large bond fund, came onstage. His thickly gelled bouffant, his sequin jacket, and his white silk embroidered cape glistened under the projector lights. He assumed a wide-legged stance and glided his palm over his left temple. An instrumental part of "All Shook Up" came on the speakers. The macro strategist jerked his knees to the tune's rhythm in a signature move and began to sing. The things that made this Elvis all shook up were: "Bernanke put," "running presses," and "bond-market liquidity."

His voice was deep and rich, and his timbre bright and playful. As he concluded the song, encouraging everyone present to "go coach a Little League," he turned on his heels, and his cape swirled along behind him. He pointed at the ceiling, kissed his bejeweled finger, then lunged his left leg forward in a sturdy karate stand and spun his right arm.

"Thank you. Thank you very much," the macro-Elvis muttered in baritone.

"What a voice. What a talent," the emcee hailed, clapping his hands. "And we are a talented bunch. I often think about what we could've accomplished if we didn't have to do what we do. What we could've been. Imagine the kind of songs or books we could've written if we didn't have to watch the Fed chairman's every move. In my youth, I wanted to be a stand-up comedian. But I became a salesman instead. I rue that day." He sighed theatrically. "This is our cross to bear. We will live and die by complexity."

A raffle vendor holding a glass jar filled with paper tags stopped by Andy. "Would you like to participate in the raffle, sir?" the vendor asked. "Part of the proceeds go to the children's cancer fund."

"Sure," Andy said after a brief hesitation.

He bought five tickets, paying two hundred and fifty dollars. The raffle vendor tore five small tickets with numbers from the roll he wore on a string around his neck and gave them to Andy.

Andy went back to his table. A waiter put a plate of roasted chicken breast and a side of steamed broccolini in front of him. Andy took a bite, then put down his fork. He wasn't hungry. Subtly, under the tablecloth, he checked his phone for a message from Klein. Klein hadn't responded to his last three texts, and Andy was beginning to worry.

Meanwhile, Andy's old friend Doug Caldera, clad in a white shirt, black trousers, and a thin black tie, with a black fedora on his head and black Ray-Ban sunglasses, cartwheeled onto the stage. "I'm a soul man, I'm a soul man," he bawled for the first two beats, kicking his legs forward in fast succession, like a dancer from the Red Army dance ensemble, and then broke into a potpourri of well-known tunes laden with his own, impenetrable to a layman, lyrics. He sang about yield drought, and hidden value, and cash on the sidelines, and people worrying about bond-market liquidity—a puzzling set of sentiments to put in a song by the standards of any other spectator but flattering and funny for the present crowd. The majority of the people here had come to their current station through the trenches, through the low-ceilinged, loud, crowded, anarchic trading floors; their worldview was shaped by heuristics and not rules, and Caldera's bluster was a fitting homage to their combative, maverick spirit.

Andy had known Doug Caldera for more than thirty years. They met in college, at the University of Buffalo, then parted ways when Andy went to Wharton Business School and Caldera to a second-tier law school in the Midwest. They reconnected in New York while forging their paths in the corporate world. Unlike Andy's steep rise, Caldera's professional start, in a small no-name law firm, had been slow and unremarkable, but due to his blowtorch-flame energy and what he called an ability to feel the terrain, he had worked his way up to an opaque but prolific capacity at a large activist fund. His business-card title said legal counsel, but, depending on his mood and the audience, he called himself a bankruptcy lawyer, a recovery specialist, or a lobbyist. Caldera's firm managed a smorgasbord of conventional and esoteric assets ranging from corporate bonds to holdings in private prisons, vineyards and wine collections, a portfolio of hospitals, and a disaster-recovery operation.

Normally, Caldera's stage specialty at these annual gatherings was renditions of beloved industry tropes—random scenes from Scorsese or Coppola movies. Last year, he and a group of rowdy traders had done a pun-filled interpretation of the "How am I funny?" bit from *Goodfellas*. A year prior to that they did the iconic final scene from *Apocalypse Now*, where Caldera played Colonel Kurtz and an M&A lawyer played Captain Willard, with combat face paint and all, and they altered the haunting final dialogue to sound like they were talking about leveraged buyouts and not about the horrors that lurk beneath the thin veneer of civilization, and the clever, culturally aware spectators connected the two sentiments with knowing, grieving laughter. Recently, Caldera had complained to Andy that he was running out of material. "I'm scraping the bottom of the barrel at this point," he said. Now, looking at his friend, immersed in verbal and physical acrobatics, Andy admired his bottomless versatility.

Andy's phone rang, and, with a guilty smile, he muffled the device and quickly crouched out of the ballroom into the hallway. On the other line was Zeke Klein.

"Are you far?" Andy asked him, annoyed. "We have to be on stage in, like, twenty minutes."

"I'm stuck in traffic on the FDR. You'll have to improvise," Klein said.

"Stuck on the FDR?" Andy exclaimed. "Like you didn't know there would be traffic on FDR?"

"I'm sorry. I had to take care of something. I fucked up. I owe you one."

"For sure," Andy said tensely and hung up. He looked around the empty lobby. "Fuck."

Back in the ballroom, Caldera, now with a bandanna on his head, was finishing his act. He clasped the mic stand and swayed left and right and engaged with the audience in a spirited call-and-response. "All we need is just a little patience," he crooned.

"Yeah-yeah-yeah," the giddy crowd replied, aware that *patience* in the current context referred not to a love interest but to the bonds bought at a fire sale.

When Caldera finished and left the stage, Andy picked up his gym bag and tuxedo and went to the bathroom. The bathroom of the five-star hotel featured a furnished foyer with an upholstered sofa, fresh flowers, and a male attendant in a burgundy uniform. A large mirror in a golden frame hung on the wall. The attendant acknowledged Andy with a "sir" and offered to take his bag. Andy handed him the tuxedo and asked him to hold on to it.

He put the bag on the sofa. A toilet flushed, and Caldera, red-faced and rubbing his nose, walked out of the stall. The attendant hurried to extend to Caldera a folded linen hand towel. Caldera washed and wiped his hands and returned the used towel back to the attendant, who tossed it into a weaved basket in the corner.

"Feature request!" Caldera exclaimed, raising his index fingers. "A standing cock bidet. It's high time we had an elegant way to wash the cock and the balls while standing without taking a full shower."

"I'll relay it to the management, sir," the attendant said. Caldera put a five-dollar bill in a tip bowl on top of a marble side table.

"You gained a few pounds," Caldera said to Andy. "You want a bump?"

Andy glanced at the clock, then at Caldera. Caldera was already high, his pupils dilated either from the drugs or from his performance or both.

"I gotta ask you for a favor," Andy said. "Klein can't make it here on time. You can totally do his part."

"Oh yeah?"

"It's a nonspeaking part. All you have to do is chase a guy around the stage for, like, two minutes. That's all," Andy said. "I have all of your props here. You'll dress as a sea captain."

Andy unzipped his gym bag and took out a fake white beard, a blue captain's coat with golden buttons, a white yachting cap more suitable for a leisure cruise than for an epic sea adventure, and a wooden prosthetic leg fashioned out of an old chair, with leather latches that wrapped around one's knee.

Caldera looked at the props.

"Arrr. I'm game," he said. "What's the scene about?"

"It's called *Hunting for Alpha*. Hoffman is the whale. And you'll be the captain."

"You mean like *Moby-Dick*?"

"You got it!"

"Are you kidding me?" Caldera yelled. "Me as Ahab? That's awesome. And who is the whale?"

"Hoffman."

"Hoffman from Rockbridge?" Caldera's eyes lit up.

"Yep."

"You're kidding! I've wanted to get that schmuck for a long time."

"Hold on. Is there a beef between you two?"

"Long story. I'll tell you later."

Andy sighed and rubbed his forehead with his palm. "Okay. You have to be extremely gentle. Hoffman specifically wanted a fellow member of the tribe out there. Said he didn't want to be roughed up by a goy. I had to beg Klein to do the part."

"He's in for a big surprise now!" Caldera said.

"No." Andy held up his hands. "Just chase him a bit, but don't catch him. You're not supposed to catch him. That's the whole point."

"That's a big ask. But I will do my best," Caldera said, grinning. He fastened the prosthetic leg to his knee and leaned on it, balancing. "And, uh, who are you?" he asked. "Ishmael?"

"You'll see."

* * *

In the ballroom, the emcee came out on stage.

"Our next performance is called *The Hunt for Alpha*," he declared with a smirk and a raised eyebrow. "We can all relate to that."

The lights dimmed. A man in a whale costume glided onto the stage. It was Hoffman, a hedge-fund manager from Greenwich. Hoffman's bespectacled face showed through the oval-shaped cutout right underneath the whale's painted mouth. His arms were lodged into the mesh fins, and his skinny legs, clad in black leggings, stuck out from the hole at the bottom of the gray rubbery cocoon. The audience welcomed him with sporadic cackles loaded with anticipation.

Hoffman the whale was accompanied onstage by a man with a guitar who was dressed in a black silk shirt and black bell-bottom pants embroidered with a colorful pattern that coiled from his hips to his ankles. For the first few seconds, the guitarist played a standard blues progression but then quickly veered into a dark and heavy riff. This new, foreboding refrain—the effect of a special dropped-D tuning that graduated listeners from merely being entertained into being enthralled—now oscillated between high and low octaves in a stirring arpeggio, prompting some in the audience to cut their conversations and redirect their attention to the stage, where Hoffman bounced around in a structureless, wanton interpretative dance. As the riff progressed, it bulldozed over the remaining table chatter until all the lingering conversations stopped midsentence, and some men, recognizing the iconic "Moby Dick" intro, began to slide their fingers along invisible guitars, their faces strained with fake agony. By this point, even the few women in the room became quiet.

Hoffman shook and flapped his fins, and did a series of bizarre shimmies and twirls, and made clumsy attempts at both a moonwalk and Irish step dance—so far as the bulky costume allowed—for about a minute. The mysterious guitarist finished the rousing opening and bowed out from the stage, and the light beam shined onto a drummer who was quietly waiting his turn in the shadows.

Behind the imposing drum kit sat Andy. He wore a red tank top and a black bowler hat. His bare arms looked soft and pasty, deliciously deceptive of the hidden potential, just like the arms of his idol Bonzo, the greatest drummer of all time. For better effect, between his teeth he squeezed a lit cigarette. Now he brushed the cymbals and, with a few delicate taps, established the rhythm. The drums responded with an uneven but distinct tempo, like the first, shy drops of a summer rain on a tight tent top. The drum solo—a masterpiece impervious to imitation—was prerecorded, but Andy hoped that he could fool enough people in the audience into believing he was for real. For the last two months he had been practicing synchronizing his moves—the speed, the intensity, the triplet licks—to the original Led Zeppelin classic. He had memorized it all to an impressive accuracy.

Caldera, in full captain gear and with a demented grimace, careened onto the stage on a wooden stump tied to his bent left knee. Hoffman interrupted his pas de chat and squinted at Caldera to briefly reassess the situation and recalibrate his strategy. Caldera used the pause to ram Hoffman in the stomach with his head, but Hoffman dodged the frontal assault with a deft pivot to the right. Caldera, however, was able to grab Hoffman's fin and tear it off, which, he seemed to quickly realize, was a tactical mistake, for this move liberated Hoffman's arm. Without wasting any time, Hoffman grasped at Caldera's prosthetic leg and pulled it toward himself. The leg came undone, and Caldera lost his balance, falling backward. Hoffman seized his chance and straddled Caldera, pounding him with the stump.

The smoldering cigarette in Andy's mouth began to scald his lips. He waited for a brief slowdown, around two minutes into the instrumental, when the taps became more discrete, and spat the butt out, just as the solo was about to gather speed for the final buildup.

"Sylvain, you fuck!" Hoffman screamed and jumped off the stage into the audience. He zigzagged between the tables, pulling

at tablecloths, leaving broken plates and glasses in his wake, and
Caldera followed him. Caldera had maneuverability, but Hoffman's
costume made him impenetrable, and he had a weapon, the stump,
in his hand, which he deployed every time Caldera came near.

Andy's raindrops became a downpour and then a monstrous thun-
derstorm. He was now on the upswing, headbanging, pounding the
drums with primeval gusto. The bowler hat flew off his head. The
sweat shone on his face, and his jaw slacked in ecstatic abandon. His
eyes were closed, and his hands moved without effort, on pure muscle
memory. The signature triplets—right hand, left hand, foot, snare
drum, snare drum, bass drum—gained in velocity and rolled off like
rapid fire from a machine gun.

For a millisecond he felt as if he were floating, suspended in the
air, like a particle in superposition, defying gravity and noise. He saw
himself in slow motion, with beads of sweat flying off the tips of his
hair and stopping in midair, sparkling under the projector lights. He
wished at that moment that filming were allowed in the room, that
there would be a record of him in this glorious, magical state.

The crescendo was nigh.

Hoffman now ran back toward the stage, hopped on a chair, then
on a table, spilling wine glasses and stepping on plates. Under his
weight, the table careened. Red-faced, cheering guests jumped from
their seats, knocking over chairs, as Hoffman let out a high-pitched
yell and leaped from the table onto the stage, landing on the drum set
and crushing it beneath his bulk. He dislodged Andy from his seat and
pinned him to the floor. Caldera, not far behind, piled on them both.

The drum solo continued on its own, now approaching its dramatic climax. Caldera and Hoffman wrestled on top of Andy as he
struggled to liberate himself from under their weight, shielding his
head from their jabs and blows. He smelled smoke and saw that the
curtain near him had caught fire.

"Fire, you idiots! We're on fire!" he screamed, but Caldera and
Hoffman ignored him.

"Move!"

Andy heard a cry above him. A stocky man in a janitor uniform with a fire extinguisher, jumped on stage. The curtain to the right was ablaze, and the janitor released a foamy torrent from the red canister. He sprayed the foam all over the curtains, the stage, and the wriggling heap of bodies, until his canister was empty. He was thorough and doubly successful in his task, putting down the fire and breaking up the fight. Andy, Caldera, and Hoffman sat on the floor, coughing, wiping their faces, shaking off the foam.

The black-clad guitarist, unfazed by the calamity, reappeared on the trashed stage. His spidery fingers ran over the guitar's neck in a D-major arpeggio, bending the strings with an aural flourish, and he closed the act by ripping the farewell three-chord send-off—the E, the C, and the cathartic A.

The emcee walked onto the stage and stood, silently observing the wreckage, for about a minute, in the pose of a lost, confused man, his arms apart, palms facing upward. "Moby Dick seeks thee not," he finally said with theatrical diction. "It is thou, thou that madly seekest him."

A crew of firefighters poured in, only to witness the aftermath, and the partygoers began to stumble out from the ballroom into the lobby. The raffles man stood by the doors and shouted the winning numbers.

Andy, still breathing heavily, his face flushed, stopped and checked his ticket. The numbers matched. "Here!" He raised his hand.

The raffles man verified Andy's ticket and handed him a sealed envelope.

"What did you win?" Caldera asked. "Let's see."

Andy unsealed the envelope. Inside was a voucher for a three-day stay at a high-end meditation resort in New Mexico. "Seriously?" he scoffed.

"I'll take it if you don't want it," Caldera said, reaching out for the voucher.

"Fuck, no!" Andy held his hand high. "Lauren might want it. It's her kind of thing."

Outside the hotel, on the sidewalk, some partygoers demanded the continuation of the festivities and were ushered either by hotel personnel or by their more sober friends into the awaiting town cars and limos.

"Next year I'm sneaking a camera in here," Caldera said as they stood outside, hailing taxis. "The world needs to see this beauty."

"After today we won't be able to rent any ballroom in Manhattan," Andy said.

"Grand Prospect Hall will take us," Caldera replied.

II: On the Trading Floor

Midtown Manhattan, Andy's playground, was more than a geographical location. A square mile that stretched several blocks north from 42nd Street to around 57th Street, and east to west from Lexington to Sixth Avenue was an anthropological site, a vertical-slice exhibit of the stages of human potential. The naive, steeped-in-pop-culture eye of a tourist would be searching for visual markers of the hierarchy, for pinstriped suits and hair gel, only to find a seascape of discretion and conformity. That uniformed fleece-vested blandness, however, skillfully disguised a vast spectrum of niches, each with its own tonality, each with subtle traits and tics, and if our tourist was of the determined and inquisitive type, he could use one foolproof technique to place a Midtown specimen on the scale: to focus on the faces, not on the clothes. And the faces would tell a tale of a three-tiered ecosystem.

The members of the first tier that populated the streets of Midtown were still young and fluid, they still had their idiosyncrasies that they cherished, but they had already been stamped by having glimpsed at what was possible. They crowded at the threshold of that possibility, determined to get in. Their outside world—relationships, family, friends—was quickly diminishing, and the weight of the choice before them was visible on their ashen, preoccupied faces. They were extra-attuned to the surroundings, always weighing and analyzing various opportunities that tugged at them from different directions, figuring out whether a particular option was worth the time and effort. And they still had the option to escape.

The next, smaller group looked at the world with an emotionless, vacant stare. There was turmoil behind that blankness, for they were already in the middle of the battle. By this point, the members of this faction had lost all outside interests; they had discarded all the unnec-essary mental ballast. They moved through the streets like shadows, quick and stealthy, guarding their time, rationing their attention only for matters of importance. Their eyes skimmed emptily over every-body and everything they considered fallow, and when they talked, which was rare, their vocabulary was so restrained and so calcula-tedly lifeless that even when discussing their niche subjects between themselves, that conversation would appear to an outsider as a string of sterile, meaningless words and phrases that could mean at once everything and nothing: *In size. Felt a little soft. I covered it. Macros came in. Algos kicking in. Offers lifted across.*

Despite their jadedness, however, members of this group still had the ability to be impressed, to feel joy. They were impressed by the catastrophic and the furtive. The catastrophic—like the sudden col-lapse of a large rival hedge fund—let them gauge their own standing in the grand scheme of things, and the furtive—like the option of a first look at that failed hedge fund's inventory—pointed at their mem-bership in the exclusive club. The blood in the water meant game, and if they could make it to the carcass before anyone else, it could mean the trade of a lifetime, the making of a name. One endured the everyday drudgery for a day like this.

Out of that already narrow population slice, a few years down the road, emerged yet another cohort, smaller and more elite. These men led a hermetic existence. They were rarely seen in public, and if they ventured outside, they protected themselves from unwelcome eye contact and from occasional press cameras with the help of curbside town cars and low-slung baseball hats with an innocuous US Open (either tennis or golf) logo. On their faces one would find neither bravado nor predation but, inexplicably, a hint of acquiescence, a reluctant acceptance of their place as permanent dwellers in the Midtown's black hole. By now they were too far beyond the event horizon, beyond escape. Their acquiescence also pointed at the possession of a grave insight into the futility and wickedness of human effort, and into the absence of the appropriate cure. To cope with this awareness and not go insane, they had developed the peculiar property of strategic unseeing, the state of an immanent, almost childish helplessness, a PTSD of power. They sought friends in the art world. They started charitable foundations. And they longed for simplicity with a mind that had evolved to not understand simple things.

If anyone asked Andy where he stood on this totem pole, he'd say he was still hustling. Andy's trading station, or "the rig," as he liked to call it, was located on the far side of Keating Mills's expansive trading floor, the last one in the row of window-adjacent desks. He sat with his back to the window, and when he stood up to stretch and to take a mental break from the screens, outside he could see and hear the Park Avenue bustle. Such proximity to the ground, for someone of Andy's rank, was by design. The slow business of lawyers, compliance, IT, and investment bankers allowed them the time for a long elevator ride, thus assigning them to the highest floors. But the prime producers of the firm, the traders, always pressed for time, always living by minutes and seconds, commanded the nether regions of any Midtown office tower. The preciousness of time, however, wasn't the only factor in the distribution of the company's vertical real estate. A potential six-sigma catastrophe of the sort that seemed to visit New York with increasing regularity was always in the back of management's mind, granting this inverted hierarchy even more license: a shop will shrug off the loss of a lawyer or a compliance officer; it will be crippled if it wastes an investment banker; if it loses its trading team, it's as good as dead.

The rig had four monitors, two on top and the two on the bottom, and the trading turret phone, a switchboard-like device with blinking buttons and a heavy black handset built for abuse. On the two upper monitors there were black and orange Bloomberg screens: the one on the right with constantly updating newsfeed; the other, on the left, with a contrivance called Corporate Bond Pricing Tool—a Tetris-like interface with a multitude of small rectangular data fields to be filled out. The two lower screens featured an opened company email inbox with most of the messages unread and destined for the trash bin, and an elaborate Excel spreadsheet with multiple open tabs that read Baseline, Best Case, and Worst Case.

Three months ago, Keating Mills had absorbed a small regional bank and with it its entire balance sheet. Andy and his team were sifting through the bank's holdings, which ranged from US Treasuries to illiquid esoterics, in order to reassess the risk. Today on Andy's radar was a fifty-million-dollar position in Concordia-Walden, a midwestern oil-and-gas equipment manufacturer, an industry Andy knew nothing about. But in his line of work, he didn't really have to. All he cared about was how Concordia-Walden bonds behaved under different scenarios. The trade was illiquid—CW bonds didn't trade much, but in the meantime that position earned Andy and his team a steady yield of 350 basis points.

Andy typed the bond's CUSIP, an eight-digit identification number, in the search field on the top of the Bloomberg screen and pressed the Corp button. The screen's orange rectangles filled out with CW bond data—name, maturity date, coupon. Some rectangles appeared empty; those would have to be filled out manually by a portfolio manager, based on his assessment of the market conditions. It was this arbitrary part of the analysis that turned the investment craft into art.

In the Spread field, Andy entered 350 bps—350 basis points, or 3.5 percent over a 3-month LIBOR index. He glanced at the maturity date—10/15/2020, six years from today—and paused. *I will turn fifty-six then,* he thought.

He looked around the floor. *Let's hope no one remembers. I don't want any hype around it.* Fifties is a great age for a man. There's an auspicious convergence of wisdom, ability, and access to resources. *I probably have three or four more good decades ahead of me most likely doing the same thing ten, twenty years from now.* He sighed.

Four more decades sounded problematic for someone already on top of his game. Andy's upward, forty-five-degree-angle career trajectory that he got accustomed to in his twenties began to flatten in his thirties and, finally, stalled in his forties, stunted by a shrinking field of suitable conquests, locking him, just as he achieved mastery, into a torturous, idle limbo. The charged, ambitious potential of his muscular mind, restless will, and the intricate, powerful levers at his disposal were condemned to lie fallow, withering with every passing year into obscurity. The epic battles that he fought and won would remain niche industry lore told by insiders at private dinners and conferences, accursed by the uncinematic complexity of his craft. The lay public would never understand and celebrate the ingenuity and heroism of a fixed-income trader whose most climactic moments amounted to shouting jargon and expletives into his phone while staring at numbers on his Bloomberg screen.

Andy bounced in his chair. He checked once again the filled data fields and pressed on the Calc Price function below; the screen printed out the number into the Price field: 101.2. He leaned back. He rubbed his chin and played some more with the Spread field, trying the sequence of increasing numbers: 400, 450, 500. The Price field displayed correspondingly: 100.3, 99.5, 96.7.

There's no way CW would ever trade at 500 over, Andy thought. Not in this environment. One would have to get lucky to get 350 over LIBOR today for a solid debt like CW.

He switched to his Excel spreadsheet on the lower screen. Keeping the 500 spread on the Bloomberg screen, Andy went to the Worst Case tab on the Excel sheet and pressed the Price Portfolio button. The spreadsheet, linked to the Bloomberg machine via a complex code, froze in silent calculation, running the invisible algorithm behind the model, and then spat out the number into the P&L estimate cell: $230,544.

Andy stared at the result. *Even if CW ever trades down to the price of 96.7, we'll still be two hundred and thirty grand in the black.* He twirled the pen between his fingers like a drumstick. Where the fuck is Scotty, he thought, looking at the adjacent empty desk.

The sharp sound of bagpipes punctured the monotonous humming of business. The glass doors leading from the elevator lobby to the floor opened, and a bagpiper trio, in full Scottish dress—tartan kilts, high socks, fur crotch pouches, and black feather bonnets—marched inside. They walked solemnly in file, squeezing "Scotland the Brave" from their pipes. Fuck, not this, Andy thought. Must be Scotty's idea. Indeed, behind the bagpipers, matching their pace, walked Scotty, Andy's direct subordinate and a loyal right-hand man. Scotty held a remote-control panel in his hands; before him a four-legged yellow Boston Dynamics robot, the Big Dog, goose-stepped squarely on the gray carpet, its steps synched to the tune by an invisible command. Some traders stood up and watched the procession, happy to be distracted from their routines.

The bagpipers' function was to put on a spectacle. On any given trading floor, on important enough occasions, any important enough managing director, no matter the heritage (Andy identified as a mutt), got treated to the same ceremonial Highlander pomp.

The extravagant convoy made its way to Andy's desk and stopped. The music stopped, too. Scotty looked at Andy with a searching smile.

"You like it?" he asked, pointing at the robot. "It was my idea. We thought for months about what you could possibly want, and I've concluded that you absolutely must have a robot. How cool is that?" Scotty played with the remote, and the robot obeyed with a little dance.

"What else does it do?" Andy asked.

"Uh, it can run and jump."

"Oh."

"It can synch itself to any melody."

Andy looked at the bagpipers. "What else can you play?" he asked the musicians. "Do you know 'She Moves Through the Fair'?"

"Of course," the bearded, heavyset chief of the band said, surprised. "You are the first person who ever asked us to play it though. Everybody wants Aerosmith."

He turned to his crew and gave brief instructions. They segued into a slow, melodic Irish folk ballad about a tragic love story. Scotty poked on the panel's buttons, but the robot stood still, either unable to detect the rhythm or on the verge of passing the Turing test.

Scotty gave up. "But really, it just shows you what's possible," he said. "This is just a taste of the future."

Dave Pinkus, Andy's boss, stuck his head out from his glass office, intrigued by the commotion. He caught Andy's attention and gestured for him to come in.

Pinkus was on the phone, and Andy sat down, waiting for him to finish the conversation. Pinkus listened to the other line, playing impatiently with a rubber stress ball. He looked at Andy and rolled his eyes and pressed his tongue into his lower lip, suggesting a boring, vomit-inducing exchange.

Andy waved his hand, encouraging Pinkus to take his time. He stared at a piece of finance art on the wall: a sheet of one-dollar bills, still attached together like they came out from the US Treasury's press, inside a protective glass case. On the glass surface a red sticker, the kind one might find next to a fire extinguisher, read: "In case of a margin call, break glass." A set of golf clubs, ready for an emergency, stood in the corner.

"Yeah, yeah. I hear you. But I gotta run," Pinkus said and hung up. "What's that about?" he asked Andy, pointing outside.

"Nothing big. It's my fiftieth birthday, and Scotty decided to bring in the circus."

"Fiftieth already? Why didn't you tell me? We'd have booked Avra. Ahh, I remember when I turned fifty. I was at Cubbs Harding. I almost retired then. Can you believe it?" Pinkus sighed. "Anyway, just wanted to get some color on CW."

"Why, you hearing anything?"

"No. But we're long credit. It's a fifty-million-dollar position. Just trying to get a feel."

"I think that we'll do just fine marking it to model for now," Andy said. "It widens, it tightens back in, and we still collect the three hundred fifty running to maturity. Aside from that, everything is trading at par today, all kinds of junk."

"Yeah. Did you check where the CDS on it is trading? Could we buy some protection?"

"It's kind of illiquid. I can reach out to some guys to give me some quotes, but I don't think we'll get anywhere under three hundred. It could be points upfront. It just doesn't make sense from the P&L standpoint."

"Uh-huh. Could it jump to default?"

"I mean," Andy mused, compressing his lips into a pensive sphincter, "these days you can't rule out any possibility. But to take a ten-thousand-foot view on this, it's unlikely to default, because it's a heavily subsidized industry with a powerful lobby."

"Yeah," Pinkus said, bouncing his rubber ball off the wall. "Anyway, I just want to make sure it doesn't get out of hand. Keep an eye on it. It's a sizeable position."

"Frankly, I think that we're in such a bizarre interest rates environment that the Treasuries could widen before CW. If I were to unwind anything, it would be the Treasuries."

Pinkus chuckled. "I don't disagree. But it's your call, Andy."

On the way out, Andy stopped in the doorway and turned around. "Madeline is organizing a garden party for me this coming Sunday in Westchester. You should come," he said, trying to sound casual.

"Aren't you guys separated?"

"We are. I guess this … this is her parting gift for me," Andy stuttered.

"How refreshing it is to see civilized people handling their affairs in a civilized manner," Pinkus said. "I saw some ugly divorces in my time. Ugh."

"Madeline was always old school."

"You're a lucky bastard," Pinkus said. "I'll check my schedule. I might be able to make it." He put his feet on the table and picked up his phone. "Close that door."

When Andy returned to his desk, the traders had gotten bored with the robot and left it sitting on its bent hind legs in his chair, its front paws on the keyboard. Scotty was waiting for him, waving an upscale lifestyle magazine.

"I know what I'm getting you for your next birthday," Scotty said.

"What?" Andy mumbled, hiding his annoyance.

"Immortality," Scotty declared with a solemn cadence and poked at a glossy article. "They can download your brain now."

Andy skimmed it. The article peddled digital simulation software tailored to well-heeled clients who wanted to continue to function as themselves in cyberspace after their physical death. "Why do you want to live forever, Scotty?" he asked.

"Why? Don't you?"

"What will you be doing?"

"Taking advantage of the compounded interest," suggested a snippy trader a few seats over.

"There. Good idea." Scotty turned on his heels, aiming his index fingers at the trader.

"But will you be able to do this?" Andy masturbated the air with his hand.

Traders brayed. Andy wondered whether Scotty would have made it this far if he hadn't hired him back in the day.

Scotty was dumb enough to do what he was told and just smart enough to understand the end goal of all the spreadsheet drudgery—a

P&L in the black at the end of the month. He joined the desk certain that it was all about buying low and selling high and expected that he would be given the phone and would start calling clients on day one, and was at first confused about why he was instructed to learn how to build a macro function in Excel. But Andy saw the potential in him. There was energy behind Scotty's flat, round, freckled face. He oozed enthusiasm that could be channeled productively, and, crucially, he did not question Andy's orders.

Andy rose from his seat and looked around the sprawling, light-filled, humming floor. Here, at the initial and the final point of all the world's commerce, death seemed like a distant afterthought. Screens blinked in red and green, desk phones rang, and on the flat-screen TVs, mounted on the walls, an endless tape rolled and the talking heads, switched to mute, agonized in affected mimicry. A trading floor was a paradigm of perpetuity. It was a permanently lit, buzzing, deliberately optimistic place, a refuge from the sentimental and the unmeasurable, a shrine to logic and action. Death only existed in the news, as an abstract event, a running headline at the bottom of the screen. If death ever dared to visit a trading floor, then it was only in the form of a fine-print clause of a derivative instrument that eager young analysts, unfazed by the ridiculousness of the assignment, would structure, and the resourceful, cackling traders would price and trade away to a regional bank. Traders, the high priests of verve, long on material but short on vocabulary and time, told their stories with numbers. And if traders spoke numbers in life, they could speak numbers in their death. Maybe Scotty was right, in his own perverse way.

In late afternoon, after the markets closed, someone brought wine and beer and plastic cups to the desk. Pizza and sandwiches had also arrived. Trade support and back-office people—the ones who happened to be in the vicinity, for no special invitation was sent out—joined the small party. There was a young woman from compliance, a smart Asian girl with a bright future if only she could figure out how to navigate the delicate gray areas of asset valuations and off-balance sheet reporting, if she could differentiate a speculation from a suggestion, if she could detect and appreciate a joke. There was Sandeep, an Indian IT consultant, who worked on fixing bugs in the inhouse pricing model, and who, by Andy's estimate, often exceeded the daily allotted number of communications with traders. There was a stern-faced Russian quant who never talked but always, miraculously, delivered.

A drunk Scotty told an Obama joke, something about a black man holding a steady job, a stupid joke that only someone like Scotty would find funny, the kind that wasn't meant to be heard by anyone outside the small group of traders—all white, all comfortable in each other's presence, and Sandeep laughed the loudest. Andy glanced at him with amusement, and Sandeep met his gaze, still laughing, as if seeking a connection.

"Andy," Sandeep said. "I finally resolved how to fix that aggregation function."

"That's great," Andy said.

"Yeah, you won't have to run it twice anymore."

"Sounds good. Good job."

Sandeep refilled his plastic glass with Coke from the can. "Do you, by any chance, happen to have an opening for a trading assistant?" he asked, lowering his voice.

"Um, not at the moment, no."

"Could I send you my resume, just in case? So that you have it on file for when a position opens up?"

"Sure," Andy said, looking at his phone.

"Thank you, Andy."

Andy told everyone to continue the celebration without him and excused himself. He went downstairs, where, in front of the building's main entrance, a black town car waited to take him to his Westchester home. In the car, he kept thinking about the hustling Indian consultant, wondering why he'd laughed at that stupid joke. Did he find it funny, or was it a ploy to become chummy with Andy? And if it was a ploy, did he think Andy was a racist? Andy's thoughts veered in an ugly direction. There's a point at which ambition becomes toxic, he thought. A man of color eager to debase himself before a white man, elbowing peers to get into the club. The underprivileged, the minorities, just want access to the trough like everybody else. Everything is a racket, he bitterly concluded as he yawned and slouched in the limo's back seat.

III: Madeline and Ava

Last year Andy had separated from Madeline, his wife of eighteen years. Madeline and Ava, their teenage daughter, moved to Madeline's late father's house in Connecticut, ten miles away from their old house in Westchester. They could've stayed in Westchester, as Andy offered to move out to his pied-à-terre in Manhattan, but Madeline rejected his magnanimous gesture. Since it was she who initiated the separation—and although she never explicitly articulated it—Andy knew that she felt like it would be rude to kick him out. Over their nearly twenty-five years together, he'd learned that Madeline was guided by a set of archaic, chivalrous principles, a result, perhaps, of her sheltered, bookish life. She never worked a day in her life; she could afford to indulge in proprieties.

One day, two years ago, Madeline told him that she had come to the conclusion that they should give their union a "reassessment," because of "palpable mismatch in temperament and sensibilities." When Andy asked her to be more specific, she replied that at this juncture she wanted to be alone and focus on her writing and on

Ava's college applications. "It's like a switch went off after forty," she said. Bullshit, Andy thought and hired a private eye. The PI came back empty-handed. He sounded a little apologetic that he didn't have the goods. The fact that Madeline really didn't have anybody on the side was an even more disturbing discovery.

Now Ava spent most weekdays in Connecticut with her mother, and weekends at Andy's apartment in Manhattan. The Westchester home stood mostly empty, except for some occasions when Andy entertained guests from the city. One such occasion was coming up: his fiftieth birthday party. He had tried to whistle past it unnoticed, but Ava insisted on a celebration.

"What do you mean 'not a big deal,'" Ava told him when he mentioned he'd rather not celebrate it. "Don't be silly. I'll help organize it."

Now that Ava had gotten herself involved in planning and managing the guest list, Madeline, too, had joined the party committee, and it would be petty and small-minded to exclude her.

Two days before the party, Andy waited for Madeline and Ava at a diner, not far from the riding stables, where Ava owned a pony.

What's your ETA lol, he texted Ava.

10 min. Pls stop saying lol after every message you send. Nothing you write is laugh out loud, Ava texted back.

He sent her back a sad emoji.

She didn't reply right away.

He waited a few more seconds and wrote: *Cut your old man some slack.*

Stop being so insecure, old man, she wrote back.

Lol.

Not funny, dad.

He fidgeted and checked the yield on a ten-year Treasury bond on the Bloomberg app on his phone—a ritual that began years ago as a casual glance at the current bond market conditions but by now had evolved into a reflexive tic. The yield hovered somewhere around 1.5 percent, as it had for many years. He put the phone down.

Ava and Madeline walked into the diner minutes later dressed in riding chaps and boots, dusty and sweaty and content. Madeline greeted him with a pursed-lipped resemblance of a smile. Ava hugged him and then slid into the booth's seat with her mother. *Not on my side*, he noted. His mental situational radar was always on alert, permanently set on reading any room, any social setting, for subtle rankings and slights. There's nothing to it, he told himself. Maybe I am an insecure old fool. Ava is family.

"Happy birthday," Ava said, smiling. From her backpack she took an envelope and gave it to Andy. Inside were season tickets to the New York Philharmonic.

"There are two tickets," Madeline said. She tilted her head and wrinkled her forehead in a show of sympathy. "We'd hope you have company," she added sweetly.

"This is wonderfully thoughtful."

"They have an interesting schedule this year. There's Schumann and Brahms in the fall, and Berlioz in January. You should like that one," Ava said knowingly.

"I should."

Ava had developed a certain swagger and assuredness in her moves and words—the kind girls usually acquire during a Goth phase, from which Ava was slowly emerging now, at seventeen. Several years ago, after an unfortunate Instagram debacle, Madeline deleted all of Ava's social media accounts and made her join the school's debate team. Ava complained but complied with her mother's orders. Spared from distractions, she soon became the team's captain, and under her leadership they won several regional contests. Andy noted how quickly she had transformed from a little girl to a young adult. She seemed to have skipped over the difficult, rebellious stages of adolescence, and Andy was pleased to see that her demeanor lacked the usual teenage entitlement and unearned weariness. Ava spoke in thoughtful, well-constructed sentences that she delivered with a straight face and a measured, and even a bit pedantic, voice.

He imagined how she would deploy this inscrutable, cruel mode against lascivious, smirking jocks on campus. Boys will lust after her, but not knowing how to approach her, will date pliable, giggly, credulous blondes instead. They would lose their heads over his Ava, and she wouldn't even know about it or care.

Madeline was like that when he first met her. The same default stone front, the same probing eyes. He remembered that he, too, wanted to learn what was behind that cryptic deportment. He wanted to know what excited Madeline—what things or experiences besides her horses. But two decades in, she was still a puzzle, still a stranger whose primary concern was manners.

"So. We have thirty guests, a five-person catering crew, and a three-man band," Madeline said after they all ordered coffee and eggs.

"What kind of band did you get?"

"Seventies and eighties cover band, of course."

"Wonderful. Is Misha coming?"

"Misha is coming. Caldera is coming. Scotty."

"Did Pinkus confirm?"

"He's a maybe."

"What would I do without you," Andy said, shaking his head. "Anyway, I hope you won't mind if I bring Lauren."

"Of course not. It's your birthday," Madeline said. Too eagerly, he thought. That snotty, impenetrable, blue blood posture of hers, that WASP-y propriety. Oh, she'd make a whole show out of being overly courteous and welcoming to Lauren, his new girlfriend. If there is a scene between Madeline and Lauren, he thought, it will be one of icy nothingness. Why couldn't she be like other guys' wives, emotional and messy and fun?

Andy always felt like Madeline knew something he didn't. Inexplicably, she sabotaged his perfect plans for becoming a power couple on the scene by eschewing the necessary markers of New York social life, a life that was hers for the taking, where she could shine at charity galas, where her friendship would be sought, her benevolence and beauty celebrated, preferring instead the company of horses and books. In addition to her equestrian hobby, she took six years to write an indulgent master's thesis on early nineteenth-century Russian history. Those six years she spent traveling all over Eastern Europe, scouring and translating old manuscripts. Madeline's rationale remained a mystery to Andy, who, finding the question too heavy for casual family chatter, acquiesced to her eccentricities and her pastoral mind, and it lingered unasked and unanswered. And now, in a final masterstroke, she'd left him for nobody.

How promisingly it had all started. They'd met at a Manhattan Young Economists Club luncheon where Madeline—a thin, preppy, rose-cheeked brunette—managed the welcome table. Andy, then a rising young star at Cubbs Harding, a premier investment bank, got his name tag and struck up a conversation. Madeline wasn't in finance. She was there to help her father, Charles, a famed Chicago School economist who was headlining the event. Excited, Andy told her how much he revered her father, whose papers on rational choice theory and utility optimization he'd referenced heavily in college. When they began dating, Andy was so eager to meet him that Madeline grew suspicious. To disabuse her of doubts, he had to buy the biggest stone he could afford. Girls like Madeline—with famous fathers, humanities degrees, and expensive hobbies—expected, and usually received, an old-fashioned courtship.

On their wedding day in 1996, right after the exchange of vows, Andy left their lavish two-hundred-guest party in Montauk to race back to the city to steer recalcitrant parties back to the deal table. He was slated to get an MD (managing director) title that year, and he couldn't afford any career mishaps. His client—the billionaire owner of a European shipping company looking to issue dollar-denominated debt, whose trust Andy had earned through months of negotiations and handholding, and who was now on the verge of walking away over a minor clause—demanded his presence. Accompanied by an entourage of drunk, howling groomsmen, Andy dashed to Manhattan in a speedboat; he burst into the conference room still in his tux shirt, disheveled and sunburnt, with sand in his boat shoes, and smelling of the sea. He closed the deal.

And Madeline? Well, what was Madeline going to do? Throw a fit and cancel the wedding? She wasn't stupid. Andy was one of the city's most eligible bachelors.

He did make managing director that year. He was thirty-two years old.

Now in the diner he stared at Madeline. Could it be that she was bitter about *that* for the entire eighteen years of marriage? She must've understood what it was all about. His career would have taken a different, stunted course if he hadn't closed that deal. Sure, it wasn't very romantic, but it was a *rational* thing to do. It showed the kind of lengths he was prepared to go to provide for his new family. His father-in-law, Charles, would certainly understand and appreciate it. How could Madeline not see that these are the kind of sacrifices someone in his business had to make? And why couldn't she just turn it all into a joke, why couldn't she use this incident—a really funny one, if you think about it, and not at all tragic—as a people-pleaser story, told lightheartedly at parties to make everybody laugh? *Ah-ha-ha, that stupid jackass Andy, com'ere, bro, let's drink to that*, people would react to her little anecdote. *To our patient wives who endure our adolescent stunts.* Why couldn't she do that? Every trader's wife has a story like that. They put up with much worse than this.

"Will you stay for the whole party?" Andy asked her.

"Only as a curator. I'll leave the mingling to you," Madeline replied.

"You were never a schmoozer." Andy sighed.

Madeline shrugged. "I understand that some find it to be a useful social skill, but it takes a lot of mental energy. That I'd rather spend on something else."

Andy sipped his coffee. "You could've been a staple of the social chronicle," he said. "Just imagine what you could've been. Glamorous pictures of you all over the local press. People seeking your friendship, your favors."

Madeline smiled and tilted her head in her signature "Are you serious?" angle that had always foreshadowed a spikey response. "Have you seen those pictures?" she said. "The forced smiles, the calculated poses, the exposed cleavages. Fifty-year-old women pretending to be thirty. They're all trying too hard."

"Maybe, then, you could've shown them how it's done. How to be a grand dame."

Madeline scoffed. "Grand dames are grand precisely because they do not parade themselves gratuitously."

"In this day and age, if you don't parade yourself, no one will know you exist."

Ava was listening to their exchange quietly but glanced at Madeline after he said that. He must've scored a point here with Ava.

"I don't want to be a part of that exhibitionism," Madeline said. "There's nothing there. Those people always insist on being friends, they're grasping for my attention like a clingy street vendor, and I have run out of polite ways to say no thanks. My attention is a limited commodity. You want my attention? Show me something beautiful and meaningful and serene."

For Madeline, aesthetics were the foundation of all goodness. It was a heuristic that she used to assess events, ideas, people.

"It's all too vulgar," Madeline continued. "One wonders whether those people are moved by charity or by something else."

"Well." Andy sniffed. "At least they're moved by something." Even now he was still needling her, poking boundaries, probing her disposition, fishing for a reaction.

Madeline and Ava stared at him like two owls. Calm, clever eyes. Their irises, light gray, the color of fading bonfire smoke, dissolved into the surrounding white, giving their gaze a hypnotic, bottomless quality. Ava had inherited her mother's unblinking stare too—questioning, merciless. Andy felt judged.

"Just kidding," he said.

And what is it with girls and horses? Could it be sexual? No, there must be something else. Girls become obsessed with ponies long before they have any concept of sex. And then they grow up, but the affinity remains. What was the nature of such a lifelong bond? What was the appeal? A mental refuge, perhaps.

He once gave horsemanship an honest try. A colleague, a New York banker, was getting married in England, and he and Madeline got invited to the wedding. The ceremony was held at a sixteenth century castle, and he took care to look appropriate. Aside from the tails for the formal part, he bought a nice Barbour jacket, and a pair of Hunter rubber boots, should an opportunity to explore the English countryside come about. On the plane to London, he fell asleep imagining himself on a horse, galloping through the foggy moors like some medieval lord.

There was no nobility at the wedding, just a lot of bankers from London and New York, yet everyone, especially the Americans, behaved like they were characters in an English novel. On arrival Andy caught himself (and noticed the same linguistic metamorphosis happening to other Americans) altering his vocabulary to include words and phrases like "I beg your pardon," and "lavatory," and—with a downward smirk— "'m'fraid so, old chap." A couple of Etonians, in the spirit of hospitality or, more likely, as a prank, indulged the overseas guests in their pastoral fantasy and invited them on a country ride. Most Americans jumped at the opportunity. That would be *splendid*, they said.

Andy blamed Madeline for not warning him about the pitfalls of riding. She just watched him get on the horse, told him "to focus on your balance," and with a masterful subtle move commanded her white mare into a feisty gallop. Andy banged on the gelding's sides under him with his heels and jerked the reins. The phlegmatic animal refused to move until the last horse left the courtyard, and then broke into a brisk canter to catch up with its stable buddies. Andy bounced on the gelding's back and held on for about ten seconds and then fell like a sack of rocks in the mud. He broke his arm. Later, back in New York, when asked by concerned coworkers about his arm cast, he got to playfully reply that he "went on a fox hunt in England."

Now the boots, with British mud still stuck in their corrugated soles, were consigned to the basement, but the stitched Barbour jacket was in frequent use. Andy wore it to work like the other financiers, and he cherished the fact that *his* was once used as originally prescribed—amidst fog, rain, and manure.

If Andy had to single out one catalytic event that had set in motion the unravelling of their marriage, he'd blame the financial crisis of 2008. Professionally, he was at his peak: the short position in various mortgage products that he had built gradually since 2006 and that he gleefully unloaded, in large chunks and at huge profits, during the worst, panicky days of 2008, made him a wealthy man. Madeline's father, Charles, however, went through a bitter identity crisis in the wake of that debacle. After the markets collapsed, he watched Alan Greenspan's muted, grudging confession before the Congress on TV, where the Fed chairman acknowledged in "shocked disbelief" the irrationality of markets, and the entire conceptual foundation on which Charles had built his life's work crumbled in a matter of days. His old textbooks still sold for a hundred and twenty dollars in university bookstores, and he still had friends in academia and in libertarian think tanks, but the more they tried to assure him that the crisis was a one-off, a fluke brought about by bad actors, the more annoyed he became, sensing the dishonesty, however benign, in them and in himself. His son-in-law's wealth came from a bet that his own textbooks would classify as irrational. What does it say about *Homo economicus*? "The tools were there, Charlie," Andy would say. "I'd be a fool not to take advantage of it." Madeline sensed that Andy's usual reverence for her father had dissipated into pity, and that he tried to hide that pity. Charles became withdrawn, rarely venturing out in public, and shunning all his former acolytes. The reclusion weighed on his mental health, and he declined quickly.

Eventually Madeline decreed that economic and political discussions should be off-limits, and Andy complied. The last time Andy saw his father-in-law, at a Thanksgiving dinner, the old man shook his walking stick at him and called him a fool. At that point, Charles's mental decline was so advanced that Andy wasn't sure whether he'd been labeled a fool for his professional occupation or simply for being there. Charles died a month later, a lost and confused man.

Madeline watched the news and read the newspapers, and even though she didn't have a background in finance, she could grasp the essence of the whole fiasco. "But if the act of putting on a short exacerbated the very problem it sought to expose," Madeline wondered after the details of what had happened began to seep into the broader public discourse, "and if there are no operational or legal boundaries to the scale of that short, then how can a man know when to stop?"

Andy didn't have an answer for her. The answer that would satisfy her would have to cross into philosophy and morals, a field beyond his expertise and lacking any tangible measures. "We always self-correct," was all that he could say.

Madeline didn't press him to elaborate. But she began to drift away.

"I'll see you on Saturday," Madeline said now, getting up. "They're coming to install the tent on Friday. I gave them your number just in case."

"Okay," Andy said.

Madeline left. Andy and Ava watched her get into her Mercedes and drive away.

"You gotta stop picking on Mom," Ava said. "That's who she is."

"I guess I'm somewhat entertained by her unorthodoxy."

"I'd say it's orthodoxy," Ava deadpanned, and both of them giggled. His Ava was so smart.

The diner's payment system was down, and Andy didn't have any cash. The cashier apologized and asked him to use an ATM across the street.

"Can I just PayPal it to you?"

The cashier smiled. "We're not there yet."

Andy went to the ATM. Ava stayed behind, saying that she needed to use the restroom.

When he came back with cash, he found Ava sitting on the diner's steps. She told him that she had found two twenty-dollar bills in her backpack and paid the bill.

"Ah. Clever," Andy said with a sly grin. He split two twenty-dollar banknotes from the cash wad and gave them to Ava.

"What do you mean 'clever'?" she asked.

"You know, how you triangulated between me and the cashier and made forty dollars."

"What are you implying? That I didn't pay the bill?" Ava said, indignant.

"I'm sure you did," Andy backpedaled, sensing Ava's opprobrium. "But all the conditions for misconduct were there. Think about it. It was a great setup, if—*if*—you were capable of impropriety. I mean, you could have. If you wanted to. Never mind. Forget I said it. I was just kidding."

The stare that she gave him could have curdled a glass of milk. "You're embarrassing yourself, Dad. I hate that now I know how your mind works," Ava said and fished out a wrinkled piece of paper from her pocket. "Here's the receipt."

They got into his black Escalade.

"Sorry, love," Andy said. "Life teaches you to assume the worst about people. This way you'll never get disappointed."

"Is this the world you want to live in?"

Andy sighed. "I'm just playing my hand the best I can."

IV: Birthday Party

On the day of his birthday garden party, Andy and Ava drove to Westchester from Manhattan. Andy's six-bedroom colonial in Bedford Manor, a quaint, leafy, old-money community a forty-minute train ride north from Grand Central Terminal, was concealed from the unwanted gaze by five-foot-tall hedges of thick, geometrically trimmed boxwood shrubs and a long, private gravel driveway that, after a hundred yards, wrapped in a perfect circle around an ornate, multilayered fountain in front of the main entrance. Four limestone Ionic columns supported a triangular awning above the heavy, custom-carved doors, with ivy crawling, in a cultivated pattern, over the mansion's red brick walls up toward the second-floor windows. Countering the regal front-yard symmetry, a wild pine and birch forest in peak October colors encircled the estate on all the other sides, extending uninterrupted, as Andy believed, all the way to Canada.

Andy pulled up the driveway and saw two dust-covered contractors that he had hired earlier to touch up the drywall in the upstairs bedroom after a small leak. The duo was headed by a burly, thuggish-looking Russian, a former boxer named Oleg. Oleg's partner had a long Slavic name that Andy never bothered to remember. They stood on the driveway next to their van, smoking, looking a little lost amidst all the party-related commotion of arriving and departing delivery trucks.

Oleg was happy to see Andy. Andy remembered that he owed Oleg the next cash installment for his work, and that Oleg had texted him, mentioning that he'd stop by to collect it today. Andy had forgotten about it until now.

Seeing Oleg's smiling face, Andy was overcome by a sudden bout of hospitality. "I'm fifty years old, can you believe it?" he said. "Come and join us! There will be food and drink."

The Russians looked at each other in silent agreement.

"Just for a little while. Very nice of you, Andy," Oleg said, scratching the back of his thick neck.

"Follow me," Andy said.

They stepped inside the house, into an airy foyer with a curved staircase and a polished baby grand piano in the center. The baby grand was a decorating decision of Andy's interior designer, as no one in the family played the instrument. Vases and family photos crowded the piano's surface. There were pictures of both Madeline and Ava on their horses, and with their equestrian prizes, pictures from Madeline and Andy's wedding, and pictures of Madeline's parents, both now deceased. Andy's parents were absent from the photo collection.

To the right of the foyer was a cozy sitting room with a stone fireplace, dark wallpaper, a Persian rug, four leather armchairs facing each other, and heavy built-in bookshelves featuring picture books, travel mementos, and economics textbooks written by Madeline's late father. The intriguing potential of the room would enthrall, if only for a moment, any distracted New Yorker visiting Andy's estate. Slow, intellectual, face-to-face discussions of weighty matters of the world could be held here, with a group of intelligent people, into the wee hours of the night, fueled by eighteen-year-old Scotch and a crackling fire. In practice, however, the room was the most dead-end space of the house, both architecturally and functionally. In the age of texting and snark, it was condemned to languish unused, its promise unfulfilled. A guest would enter, imagine the possibilities, and walk out to dive back into the bustling party.

To the staircase's left was a much lighter—in mood and color—dining room. It was equipped for a full twelve-person affair, with a long table and fine china sets in the glass closets along the wall. The dining room had a bigger fireplace of white marble, a higher ceiling, and its windows faced both the front yard and the backyard.

The dining room converged with a large kitchen that led, via sliding doors, to the deck and, down the steps, to the backyard lawn.

The contractors followed Andy, carefully treading in their dusty boots through the polished foyer and the dining room to the deck.

A big white tent was stretched in the middle of the freshly mowed lawn. Madeline was already there. She was dressed in an oversized white knit sweater and light beige linen pants. On her feet she wore her old riding boots that she kept in the basement, while the delicate suede mules that she'd come in with (she loved everything suede) had been left on the mat by the deck's sliding doors. At the moment, she was busy coordinating the catering and entertainment crews, criss-crossing the large green lawn, which was soggy from last night's rain.

Andy waved at Madeline and pointed at Oleg and his comrade. "They will be joining us," he shouted.

Madeline came over. With an impenetrable expression, she looked at the workers, then at Andy, smiled and said: "The drinks bar is open, the snacks will be served soon. Please make yourself comfortable. I'm Madeline. If you need anything, please feel free to find me." There was not a hint of surprise or condescension in her voice.

The Russians walked to the bar, cautiously asked for a beer, received two canned beverages, then went to the far corner of the yard, at the very edge of the forest, and placed themselves on wooden lawn chairs.

The guests started to trickle in. They were mostly couples—traders and portfolio managers with their wives and girlfriends. The men were dressed casually, in polo shirts and khakis and sports jackets, one indistinguishable from another. The men's ranks, out there in the real world, could be discerned from their female companions, whose image consciousness and anatomical aspirations varied in range and intensity. Some pursued the tight, curated look of a female TV anchor, with long blond hair abused by the curling iron, loud-logoed purses, too much exposed skin, and visible augmentations to their lips and noses. Others, a less numerous group, sought to conceal more than to reveal. Their faces were skillfully preserved to look exactly the same as they had twenty years ago, their hair was made to appear slightly unkempt, and their expensive light lambswool coats of indefinable color and *nameless* handbags pointed to the kind of wealth that wished to remain anonymous.

The men were chronically unamused people who had seen and done everything but could, in certain social situations, discard their default indifference and conjure up amusement on cue. Right now, on the lawn, there were cries of delight and chummy conviviality.

Andy zigzagged between the groups of people, glad-handing the men and complimenting the women. He halted a busy waiter with a drinks tray to get a refill and scanned the crowd. He spotted his old friend Misha Pomerantzev, who stood alone by the bar, with a forlorn expression, clutching a can of Coke.

Misha was currently in a career transition. He was a former quant turned star credit trader. Last year, Misha made his company, a large hedge fund, two hundred and fifty million dollars by betting on a basket of corporate-debt contracts. After a dispute with his firm's management about the size of his bonus, Misha wrestled a 12.5 percent payout of the total profit, about thirty-one million dollars, but still resigned, saying that the dispute had left a "bad taste in his mouth." He was now a free agent. Any credit desk on the Street would snatch up Misha in a second, and he already received several high-seven-figure offers, but he was biding his time. Industry insiders speculated that he was thinking of starting his own shop.

Andy scooped a glass of champagne from a passing tray and walked toward Misha. Misha was unshaven and dressed in an odd combination of cargo shorts, a white business shirt with a couple of missing buttons on the belly, and a sports jacket. A green baseball cap with an Ace Accounting logo covered up his longish, unkempt hair. On his feet he wore white tube socks up to midcalf and old black sneakers.

"If I saw you on a street corner, I'd give you a coupla bucks," Andy greeted Misha, handing him the champagne.

Misha chuckled and ran his fingers across his throat, signaling that he had quit drinking. Andy put the glass on a nearby table. They slapped their palms bro-style and patted each other.

"Why didn't I see you at the Bohemians' party?" Andy asked Misha.

"I, uh ..."

"You should've come. I did a killer John Bonham impression. We totally trashed the place."

"It's bullshit," Misha said. He spoke with a very slight accent, but the earnestness and the urgency of his delivery betrayed his Russian roots. "That whole thing is bullshit. My first time there, they didn't tell me it was gonna be a roast. They just told me to prepare a talent bit. So, like an idiot, I practice a piano piece for two months. I show up there and see all those people dressed like clowns, and I realize that I fucked up, that I was expected to come up with some stupid joke. But it was too late. So I go and play my classic piece, a mazurka, play it badly, and everybody is expecting some kind of punchline or some joke at the end, like I'm gonna jump and strip naked and dance to 'YMCA' or something. And then I finish and stand up and everybody's quiet. I'd rather got booed. Never forgot the feeling. I felt so stupid. Someone in the bathroom later asked me: 'Misha, I didn't quite get your sketch, what were you trying to say?' I told him to fuck off. I never went again." He scoffed. "Don't want to partake in that simulacrum of rebellion."

"Anyway, it was wild," Andy said.

Misha took a sip of Diet Coke. "The wilder the party, the bigger the grief that they're trying to assuage," he said.

"Huh." Andy patted him on the back. "Whatever you say, bro."

"Misha!" Madeline chimed affectionately, walking toward them. There was a genuine ring of delight in her voice. Madeline and Misha air-kissed each other's cheeks two times, European-style.

Madeline had liked Misha from the first time she met him years ago at the Keating Mills Christmas party. At the party, a drunk analyst, trying to be cute or to ingratiate himself with portfolio managers, made a crude joke with a punchline that revolved around a sexual innuendo, the kind of joke that's not really funny but is simply used to gauge the rottenness of a listener's imagination. Everyone laughed, except Misha and Madeline. An instant bond was born. They started talking, and Madeline told Misha that she was writing a thesis on nineteenth-century Russian history. They talked the entire evening, and afterwards she consulted him about some difficult Russian-to-English translations.

"Are you here with a date?" Madeline asked Misha. "I put you as 'plus one.'"

"No. Just me." Misha slouched and looked down. "We broke up."

"What a pity," Madeline chirped.

Andy's phone buzzed. It was Lauren. She was here, she said, in front of the house. Andy excused himself and went to meet her.

Lauren got out of her BMW SUV, looking chic in a body-hugging gray wool turtleneck dress, gray puffy vest, and knee-high white leather flat-heeled boots. Her hair and half of her face were concealed by a silk scarf and large square-shaped black sunglasses. Not underdressed, not overdressed, just perfect, Andy thought. He liked that about Lauren. They hugged and kissed. She smelled of expensive freshness.

She took off the sunglasses and squinted. "How does it feel to be an AARP member?"

Andy paused, trying to come up with something witty. "Liberating," he sputtered.

Lauren's face could have been described as pretty if not for a slight overbite and a weak chin. This type of face looks angelic in youth, but it does not age well. Andy didn't care about that. Lauren had an ideal body, slim, flexible, with long limbs, capable of arousing him naturally—an important detail for a man his age. Besides, she knew how to look gorgeous in pictures she took with her phone, rendering that minor handicap irrelevant.

Lauren was a bit jittery about Madeline's presence. Andy placated her with a dismissive "She's ten years older than you!" and that seemed to do the trick. When she saw Madeline, she relaxed. Lauren had a keen eye for a fellow woman's status and mindset, and she was pleased to see a fortyish woman who looked and acted like she had moved on from—or never even participated in—the rat race. She did not detect a suppressed spring of accumulated frustrations hidden behind a cheerful front. There was a tiredness, perhaps, but no cattiness.

When he introduced them, Andy made sure to register both of their reactions. Lauren radiantly greeted Madeline and complimented her on her sweater.

"Andy told me that you organized all of this," Lauren said. "This is wonderfully planned. Trust me, I know some professional party planners who can screw up a kids' matinee. But this is well done. I'd love to get your catering contact."

Madeline smiled and thanked Lauren, and Andy noticed in her fleeting expression and in a slight bend of her lips that she approved of what she saw, and that approval made him uncomfortable.

He left Lauren at the mercy of Madeline and went to get drinks. As he was walking back with the drinks, he overheard Lauren telling Madeline about a charity for inner-city children that she was currently active in. Lauren was always active in something. He saw Lauren open her crossbody Chanel bag, take her business card that he knew described her as "philanthropist, filmmaker, entrepreneur," and hand that card to Madeline.

"You're multitalented, Lauren," Madeline said after politely examining the card.

"And we have an annual gala. You should definitely come," Lauren said.

"I think what you do is admirable," Madeline replied. "However, modern-day philanthropy is not something I would want to encourage with my participation."

Lauren doesn't know what she got herself into, Andy thought.

"I totally understand," Lauren said. "But this charity has been in business for forty years."

"Oh?" Madeline raised her eyebrow. "For forty years? They seem to be doing something right."

She's so good and so cruel, Andy thought.

"Call me anyway," Lauren said. "We should do lunch when you're in the city."

"We definitely should. Let's stay in touch."

The Boston Dynamics robot, powered by Scotty with the remote, passed them by, and Lauren squealed in surprise. Madeline smiled at her, excused herself, and went to greet other guests.

In the far corner of the garden, Oleg and his stern-faced partner were still sitting on the lawn chairs, now observing the guests with a quiet, dogged interest. They were smoking, and even though the party was understood to be smoke-free, neither Andy nor Madeline wanted to enforce the code.

Oleg's eyes were glued to the robot. Scotty directed the metallic creature at groups of people, bumping it into the back of people's knees and then, when they turned in confusion, making it do a shimmy. Oleg observed Scotty's shtick with intense opprobrium, jaw muscles flexing. He leaned in and said something to his friend, and they bobbed their heads in grim, silent agreement. When Scotty finally got bored and left the robot near the gazebo at the other end of the lawn, Oleg stood up from his vantage point and slinked across the lawn to the abandoned machine. He examined it with great interest and care, cleaning its metal legs from the pieces of grass and soil stuck there from all the human encounters. He went to the bar, got a glass of vodka, took a table napkin, dipped it in the alcohol, and wiped its metal carcass free of all the crumbs and debris.

"Tough day, huh, buddy? *Nichego*, we'll get you out of here," he kept saying.

Andy spotted Dave Pinkus talking to Misha and two hedge-fund guys and walked toward them to say hello. Misha had somehow scored a cigarette from his working-class compatriots and was smoking it, quietly listening to Pinkus.

"Anyway, I almost retired at fifty." Pinkus spun a yarn of his failed retirement. "I had enough money. My kids were out of college, two houses paid off, a comfortable conservative portfolio." Pinkus scoffed. "And you know what? I felt castrated. By the lack of access to the tape, by not knowing where the spreads were for this or that. That informational void was debilitating. I missed Midtown and the crowds and the shop talk and the afterhours. People stopped calling me after a few months. A few more months in the wilderness and nobody would even remember that there was this guy Pinkus, and he did some crazy shit in his heyday." He looked wistfully at the woods and sighed. "So I came back. That was fifteen years ago."

"I guess it's not about the money then," a bald hedgie in jeans and a puffy vest said.

"I guess not." Pinkus shrugged.

"It's about our limited imagination," Misha inserted.

Scotty, with a plate full of snacks, elbowed himself into the circle. "Did you land anywhere yet?" he asked Misha.

"Not yet," Misha replied.

"Hey, I always wanted to ask you," Scotty said and paused to bite into a mini hotdog, "if your full name is Mikhail, why did you shorten it to Misha? It sounds kind of effeminate."

"First, it's a custom abbreviation," Misha said. "And second"—he puffed smoke into Scotty's face—"it is interesting how you

Americans evaluate everything on the degree of masculinity. Says a lot about you."

"Is it different with the Russians?" Scotty asked, grinning.

Misha didn't respond. Instead, he stopped a passing waiter with a tray full of wine glasses. "You have any hard liquor?"

"What would you prefer, sir?" the elderly waiter asked with crisp diction.

Misha dipped into his pocket and found a ten-dollar bill. He slipped it to the waiter. "Grey Goose. No ice."

"Right away, sir."

After gulping down the vodka, Misha wandered into the nearby woods. He reemerged half an hour later carrying several large, spongy, porcini-like mushrooms. His red face brimmed with joy. "You can't get these in any store," he exclaimed. "Only in the woods."

"What kind of mushrooms are they?" Andy asked playfully.

"Not *that* kind," Misha said. "These you eat. Fry them with potatoes. You have a plastic bag I can use?"

"Go ask Ava. She's in the kitchen."

Andy scanned the lawn to check on Lauren. He found her immersed in some chit-chat with a trader and his wife. She was giving the trader's wife her business card. A party photographer snapped their picture. Andy went over and ran his hand over Lauren's back and squeezed her butt. "I'm glad you're not wasting any time," he whispered in her ear. He thought that maybe it had been a mistake to bring her here.

He went to the kitchen, where he found Misha midspeech, drawing invisible schemes in the air, and Ava listening to him, cradling her chin in her palms.

"Reason gave a man a guillotine and an atom bomb. One cannot be an industrialist, a techie, and build a pristine, harmonious community, unspoiled by ambition, a Shire, so to speak, as those two are antithetical, mutually exclusive notions," Misha rambled. "Even if one spends the money building a replica of that kind of community, it will only resemble it visually, but its essence will be missing. It will be an ersatz copy. Potemkin villages. Look it up. I can send you a link later. You have to familiarize yourself with these terms."

Andy sat on a stool and signaled to Misha to continue his thought.

Ava leaned toward him and whispered: "We started with the mushrooms."

"I had a VC friend once who bought several hundred acres in Colorado with a river and a giant rock cliff," Misha continued. "He made a big project out of turning those big rocks into these fifty-foot-tall statues, standing with their hands athwart, as if guarding the property."

"Like the Argonath," Ava said.

"Yes. Like in a movie. They carved one statue out of the existing rock. The other, on the other bank … They had to transport large boulders there, then carve them into building blocks, then assemble them. There wasn't a road big enough for the trucks to come in, so he built a road just for that. Had to cut down trees. It was a protected habitat, but he went around the law somehow. The funny thing is, he spends about one week a year in that place. He doesn't even go look at those rocks. He just wanted to have them, so that he had a cool story to tell. Anyway, then the arm on one statue crumbled to the river below. Couldn't hold its weight."

"Life imitates art," Andy said.

"The manner in which he went about it mocks the very purpose of art. He couldn't see a disconnect between the visual attributes and the essence those visuals claim to represent." Misha sighed. "We're all drowning in irony. Nothing we do is serious anymore."

"Yeah." Andy leaned toward Misha and poked him in his pasty belly showing through the hole in his shirt. "That's why you dress like a schmuck. An ironic schmuck."

Misha fell quiet. "Maybe we are all just poseurs," he said after a long pause. "We don't know what else to do."

"He-hey! There you are."

They heard a loud, clownish voice and saw Doug Caldera coming in from the dining room. Caldera wore a black Catholic priest frock.

A three-foot-long ragdoll dressed as an altar boy was attached to Caldera's trousers, its face buried suggestively in his crotch.

"How the hell did I think it was a costume party?" Caldera said.

Madeline stepped in the kitchen from the deck. She stared at Caldera and his blasphemous wardrobe, wincing, but did not say anything.

"Sorry, Madeline," Caldera said. "I thought it was a costume party. I must've read the wrong email. I get so many invitations."

It was getting dark. The electric garlands that hung along the edges of the white tent and on the deck railings lit up. On the lawn, a hired cover band began to play feel-good oldies from the 1980s, and Scotty and a couple of drunk traders were dancing. Lauren swayed along, drink in hand. She saw Caldera walking toward them, and, upon seeing his getup, she bent with laughter.

Madeline gave Andy an exasperated glance, then took scissors from the kitchen drawer and went outside. Andy watched her through the kitchen window as she marched across the lawn toward Caldera and gestured at the unfortunate ragdoll. Caldera resisted limply at first then complied with her orders. He lifted his arms and, as Madeline fiddled around his crotch with the scissors, grimaced in mock horror. Scotty and the traders watched the impromptu wardrobe surgery and laughed. When she was done, Madeline pointed the scissors at them sternly and said something, and they straightened up, saluting her as if she were a military officer. Holding the ragdoll under her elbow, she went up to the party photographer and ordered him—or so Andy discerned from her uncompromising hand signs—to delete the problematic images from the camera. She watched the photographer as he obediently clicked through his reel.

"Come on," he said when Madeline returned to the kitchen. "People are having a bit of harmless fun."

"It's atrocious," Madeline said. She turned to Ava. "Are you ready?"

"Are we leaving now?" Ava asked, sounding disappointed.

"Let's allow Dad to have some quality time with his barbarian horde," Madeline replied.

Andy chortled and looked at Ava with a helpless smile.

Ava collected her backpack, came by, and kissed him on the cheek. "Have a good time, Dad. See you next week."

Madeline gave Misha a hug. "Keep an eye on this saturnalia for me," she instructed before leaving.

"I'll make sure everything is up to par," Misha replied.

"So, you broke up with Joanna, huh? What happened?" Andy asked Misha when Madeline and Ava had gone.

"She's impervious to introspection," Misha said. "She's always in elevated mood."

"Is that bad?"

"It's unnatural. I guess, for anyone but an American." He scoffed and looked at Andy. "We had some good times though," he added wistfully.

"We will find you a nice Russian girl then. So that you can brood together. And go mushroom-picking."

"No," Misha said grimly. "I want nothing to do with the Russians. They're a lost people."

Andy and Misha went back to the lawn and joined a cluster of chatting traders.

"A commercial space tourist jaunt," the chubby, pink-cheeked trader was saying as they came near. "That's what I want for my birthday. I often imagine how it would go. I'd probably have to go through some training and get on a special diet and stop dining at steakhouses."

"You'd have to give up your coke habit," Caldera inserted, unsolicited, to a round of rowdy chuckles. The trader mock-wrestled Caldera, locking his neck in an arm vise and knocking his knuckles on Caldera's head.

"You can just jump with a parachute," Scotty said. "Then you won't have to give anything up."

"Nah," the trader replied. "A parachute is different. You don't actually experience any weightlessness. But in space you do. And there, for a brief moment, nothing matters. Not your positions, not your P&L, not your counterparties. All is meaningless dust. Even what you do doesn't matter. 'Cause you can't do anything. All the controls are back on the ground. And that, I guess, is the beauty of it. The total helplessness. The letting go. Like in a song. *'I'm floating in the most peculiar way.'*"

"If you like feeling helpless you can go to a dungeon and get yourself a dominatrix. She'll float you in a peculiar way," Caldera said, causing even louder hoots and cackles. He sipped his vodka-cranberry.

"I'm staying here, on this shitty earth," Caldera concluded with a sniff. "I have everything figured out here."

The guests began to disperse around nine o'clock. Caldera enlisted Scotty to help him search the house for his ragdoll, a costume accessory that he planned to use at several upcoming Halloween parties. They found it on a chair in the sitting room, its ropy arm wrapped around a glass of melted ice. Caldera offered to give Scotty a ride back to town.

The caterers were cleaning up. Andy and Misha got a bag of marshmallows from the kitchen pantry and went to the stone fire pit near the gazebo. They found Oleg there, sitting alone, staring at the flames.

"Do you mind if we join you?" Andy asked.

Oleg shook his head. "Please," he said.

Misha scored another cigarette from Oleg and stretched out on the garden chair, puffing, gazing at the night sky.

"What's your take on Concordia-Walden?" Andy asked Misha.

"CW is kind of opaque," Misha said and sighed. "Where do you have it marked?"

"Three hundred and fifty over."

Misha bent his lips. "I think it's way too optimistic. This is where investment grade trades now."

"Everything trades at investment grade right now."

"They could trade at IG levels without being IG. But if you rely on spreads, you are mispricing the risk. CW valuation models should be based on the quality of the collateral, not on spreads."

"Yeah, it's too labor intensive though. I just don't have those kinds of resources right now. I'd have to have an oil and gas specialist on hand to get that kind of granular analysis. All I have is Scotty."

Misha shrugged. "The easiest way for you to do it is to assume the worst will happen and focus on what can be recovered. I think the risk there is very asymmetric, and you should be prepared for all kinds of externalities. If you can, you should run some stress-tests for credit, duration, and event risk. If you can't do that then recalibrate your model to focus on recovery values. If it happens, at least you'll be prepared. And if it doesn't happen, you book a profit."

"Too bad you're too expensive. I'd hire you for this project," Andy said dolefully.

"Caldera would be more useful. He's, shall we say, a recovery specialist," Misha said.

They both looked at Oleg, who sat quietly, listening to them, fixated on the fire.

"Did we bore you yet, Oleg?" Andy asked.

"Problems at work." Oleg bobbed his head. "I understand." He turned to Misha. "Are you in accounting?" he asked, pointing at Misha's hat.

"I guess you can say that," Misha said. He gave Andy a quick "let's not disappoint this poor guy" glance, and Andy kept quiet. "Here, try this." Misha handed Oleg a stick with a marshmallow. "It's like *pastila*. Roast it first—it's tastier this way."

"Andy." Oleg used this moment of attention to broach a pressing topic. "What do you plan to do with the robot?"

"I haven't really thought about it yet."

"Maybe I can buy it from you," Oleg probed.

"Let me think about it."

"Thank you," Oleg said. He exhaled with a mix of awe and

gratitude. "America is a great country. You open business. Work hard. And become a rich man."

No one responded to Oleg's observation. Oleg held the marshmallow over the fire until it darkened on all sides, pulled it out and bit a small piece. He chewed it with a cautious, distrustful expression. He looked at Misha. "This is not really *pastila*," he said wincing. "This is crap."

Misha laughed.

Andy smiled, looking at Oleg, but his mind was now elsewhere. How touchingly innocent it is to still want to acquire new things, to be excited by owning them, he thought.

He smacked his forehead.

"Damn. The money. You've been waiting all this time? Why didn't you remind me?"

Oleg shrugged and mumbled something about "your birthday."

"Come. Let's get you paid."

Andy, Oleg, and Misha went back to the house. Andy brought cash from upstairs and gave it to Oleg, who said that he'd stop by next week to check if the wall had dried properly.

"I might be in the city. I'll leave you the key," Andy said.

Oleg left. Andy looked around for Misha and found him slouching in an armchair in the library.

"I have a wide selection of accommodations," Andy said. "There's my office with a couch there. There's Ava's bedroom. There's Madeline's study. There's the old nanny's room."

Misha said that the office couch would suffice. Andy went to fetch a pillow and a blanket, and when he came back, Misha was already asleep and snoring.

Andy went to his bedroom. Lauren was waiting for him there, reclining in a feline pose on the bed, wearing a set of lacy black underwear. There was a faint smell of weed. He stepped back, gasping theatrically, as if smitten by the sight of beauty.

"You're the hottest date in town," he said. "I'm a lucky guy."

V: It Takes a Special Understanding

Andy's father, Erwin, was a motivational speaker. He fashioned his seminars after the big names of the talking circuit of the late 1970s. "Everyone goes an extra mile, but you *run* an extra mile and get there first" was his signature phrase. He had modest success, booking a few events across the Rust Belt towns, and later he branched out into recording the speeches on video and selling the VHS tapes for $19.99 a pop at midwestern dentists' and real estate agents' conventions.

Motivational speaking isn't a bad occupation in itself, until one begins believing one's own schtick. At one of his seminars, Erwin met a timeshare salesman who invited him to give a speech, for a good fee, to a retirement community. Erwin rebranded his spiel from "Everyone goes an extra mile" to "Build value while you sleep" to tailor the message to a new audience. The timeshare sales went up, and Erwin was booked for more events, and pretty soon he got an offer to join the business as a partner, with some money down but a guaranteed income. Erwin mortgaged their Washington Heights apartment to come up with the money. The whole scheme turned out to be a fraud when his partner took all the money from the customers and fled the country. Erwin, although a peripheral member of the whole operation who wasn't allowed anywhere near the finances, was convicted on a series of wire and mail fraud charges and got sentenced to fifteen years in prison and a fine of a hundred-thousand dollars. Others involved in the scheme walked free or got smaller sentences. To Andy, the fact that Erwin had allowed himself to be the fall guy meant that not only was he reckless, but he was stupid.

Erwin showed up in New York after his release, two weeks before Andy's wedding. He got off a Greyhound bus at the Port Authority Bus Terminal and walked three blocks east straight to Andy's office, carrying all his belongings in two plastic Walgreens bags. Andy met him at the downstairs atrium of his office building.

"Look at you, my boy. A serious man. A businessman." Erwin put down his bags and shook Andy by the forearms.

"I'm not a businessman," Andy said, unclasping his dad's hands.

"Who are you then?"

"It's not important."

"Well, you work in an office, and you wear a suit, and you make big decisions." Erwin smiled. He had missing teeth. "Doesn't matter what you call it. I hope the money is good."

Andy asked him if he had had lunch and, ignoring Erwin's meandering answer, walked him quickly outside, to a nearby coffee shop.

As they sat at a table, he said, "I'm getting married, Dad—"

"Ooh, who is the lucky girl?" his father interrupted with an excited grin.

"—and you can't come to the wedding. I just wanted you to know that I'm starting a family, and I don't plan for you to be any part of it."

Erwin deflated and ran his hand over his thinning, sweaty hair. "Okay, I understand. I don't blame you. I did my things. I wasn't planning on staying here anyway. Thinking of going down to Florida. A new opportunity opened up there."

A flock of traders Andy was friendly with stepped into the coffee shop. They noticed him and looked with bemusement at his father.

Andy thought that he'd have to come up with a plausible story when he got back to the office.

Erwin dipped into one of his plastic bags and produced an old VHS tape. "Here, I think this one has some good marriage advice in it. If you skip forward toward the end, I think. I remember recording it when I took Mom on a cruise. The idea is that one should spend more time planning the marriage than planning the wedding. A wife should always be treated like a queen."

"You seem to know a lot about that," Andy scoffed. "As a matter of fact, I plan to do just that. And do it in a way that I don't end up in jail."

With his hands shaking, Erwin peeled off the top from a Cof-fee-Mate cream capsule and poured its contents in his coffee. He picked up a spoon and stirred it. The spoon jingled unevenly against the ceramic surface of his mug. He put the spoon down and played with the paper napkin, rolling it into a strap, then flattening it back out. "I loved your mother. I wanted her to have a good life. Sorry it turned out this way."

Edna, Andy's mother, quit her job as a secretary when Erwin's speaking career took off, and she did not bother herself with the de-tails of the family's finances. Erwin bought a summer house on Fire Island, and the family vacationed in Florida every winter. After Er-win went to prison, they lost the house and the Manhattan apart-ment and had to move into a one-bedroom walk-up in Newark. Edna went back to work as a department store cashier. She never recovered from the shock. She died when Andy was in college. Her autopsy showed a mix of alcohol and sleeping pills.

Before parting ways, Andy took Erwin to the Times Square Marriott and paid for a one-night stay. He asked the concierge to help arrange a one-way ticket to Orlando for Erwin and then, after a moment of hesitation, wrote Erwin a check for two thousand dollars. He left his father in the hotel lobby, walking quickly outside without looking back.

He never saw his father again. Madeline and Ava both learned that Andy's family was something he didn't want to talk about, although Madeline knew Erwin's story, rehashed in a more benign light for her consumption.

Sitting at his desk, with his chair turned toward the window, Andy stared at Park Avenue traffic and thought of Erwin. How insufficient it is to go an extra mile without making a proper assessment of the direction and of the shifting landscape, he thought. How easy it is to miss the point at which unexamined zeal becomes self-destructive. And how many bright, ambitious people fall into that trap, confusing enthusiasm with efficiency.

Twenty feet away, a group of young traders gathered around someone's desk for a brief recreational activity: watching a video on YouTube. The sound of a human voice in severe distress came from the computer's speakers, and the traders mimicked the sound, braying and laughing. Andy stood up and walked over to the neighing crowd. On the screen he saw a video compilation of farm goats that bleated with a shockingly anthropomorphic candor. "Aaah, aaah," the goats shrieked like a jump-scared person. "Aaah, aaah," the bros echoed. Upon seeing Andy, the group dispersed. The traders went to their desks but continued to randomly re-create the chilling sound, tying their high-pitched wails either to the market quotes on their screens or to the Tinder images on their phones.

Andy went back to his seat. And how rare it is to see a person who possessed an ever-present sense of urgency and an inhuman level of focus, and, at the same time, an almost artistic mastery of the craft, attuned to shades and whispers and pitfalls. Because there's no formula; one has to tread a new path every day.

Andy searched for this kind of mindset in all of his hires. He monitored the flocks of summer interns, hoping to find a delicate mix of rote obedience, curiosity, and initiative but quickly found that he could get obedience, and he could get initiative, and he could get brains, but that those rarely came in the same package. Andy once hired a young analyst, a nerdy kid with a PhD in applied physics. Andy had misgivings about the kid's concave chest and bad breath but wanted to give him a chance. Taking the advice of watching and learning too literally, the young nerd spent most of his time standing behind Andy, gawking at the numbers on his screen, eavesdropping on his phone conversations, and then pestering him with stupid questions: Why is this bond priced at this level? What's the point of being long and short at the same time, isn't that a net wash? The kid thought that he was entitled, perhaps on account of his PhD, to stand there and receive answers from a head trader when all the other analysts were busy jacking off—as they should!—the VLOOKUP function on their Excel spreadsheets. Annoyed, Andy told him to get lost, but the kid didn't budge. Maybe he thought it was some kind of loyalty test. Eventually, Andy's patience snapped; he turned around and punched him in the face. The poor kid was marked for death after that. He had to go back and apply his physics in academia. And for what? For a lack of *understanding*. With all his scholarly brilliance, he failed to figure out that sometimes there's no context, no secret test, no initiation ritual, and that if you're told to fuck off, you should just comply. After this incident, Andy gave up on quixotic attempts at proselytizing and reconfigured his hiring bias in favor of duller, meatier in flesh and attitude, and thus more reliable business school graduates.

The only person in Andy's entire career who displayed a rare divine spark early on was a young intern named Joanna. Back in the summer of 2003, Andy's team and their lobbying firm were working on an amicus brief for an upcoming piece of legislation on prepayment penalty guidelines. The interns were collecting and combing through gigabytes of prepayment data on the pools of residential mortgages. Joanna sat quietly during the morning meetings, eschewing the bravado and idle performative posturing of the gang of Wharton bros, listening to instructions, taking notes, and then completed the boring, numbers-crunching task with no errors and before the deadline.

Andy took a mental note of Joanna's auspicious blend of skills. She spoke up only once, when they were discussing the impact of the penalties on homeowners and their likelihood of default.

Joanna raised her hand in charming overachiever fashion and inquired, "They're punished for responsible behavior?"

Scotty, the brattiest intern on the team, with a school ring on his pinkie, rolled his eyes and let out a dramatic sigh. Scotty saw dollars, an admirable quality, while Joanna's seemingly naïve question hinted at her systemic understanding of how the whole sausage factory operated. Scotty opened his mouth, but Andy shut him up with a raised hand. He then went on to explain to Joanna that early prepayments by homeowners carry a risk, an optionality that the bondholders would like to be compensated for. He could tell that she was not satisfied with this explanation. It's not that she didn't understand the rationale; it's that she, correctly, concluded that his answer did not address the question she asked.

"I understand that," she said impatiently, "but they're not making any mistakes to be charged those fees."

Andy made a steeple with his fingers, leaned back, and bounced in his chair, thinking of how best to address the dilemma without alienating this bright young woman. She was too smart to be placated with jargon and platitudes. "It's possible to commit no mistakes and still lose," Andy mused. "That's life."

Joanna stared at him. He caught an impudent glint in her eyes. "But we can, uh, reprogram the simulation, no?" she probed with a grin.

Andy perked up: the girl had received and returned a sci-fi reference only a Trekkie would know. "No, because we don't like to lose," he replied, gratified by this unexpected back-and-forth. He wondered what she might be like in the sack, what kind of clever wordplay they could have engaged in between the sheets, but pushed that thought away.

Scotty fidgeted, nervous that he had lost track of the conversation. As they walked back to their desks, Scotty whispered in a conspiratorial tone: "Does she know what's going on, what we're doing out here?"

"Better than you," Andy replied loudly enough so that Joanna could hear him.

Scotty had nothing to worry about. Every bond desk in New York ran on people like him. Joanna, however, was a special find. Somehow, she discerned that *we* could *reprogram the simulation* if we wanted to. Maybe that's because women have a fine-tuned, high-fidelity reality-scanning mechanism, Andy thought. An evolutionary side effect of being the weaker sex. Andy knew that her naive objections to the mechanics of business were driven by her youthful maximalism and the finite, uncreative way women saw the function of money—as protection from the elements, sickness, and old age. She needed mentorship. He would teach her how to look at money properly, like a player—as a mere tool, a means to an endless quest. In time and with the right guidance, soaking in the right company, watching the right people, she could be molded into a weapon. Down the line, in crucial moments, people like her could identify and solve the problems that the Scotties of the world couldn't even fathom existed. Then, after fighting a few battles and getting a few scars, she would grow to appreciate the beauty, the poetry of bond finance, the magnitude of its worldly implications, and the power of the levers at her fingertips.

Andy itched to spearhead that transformation, to watch the progress firsthand, to showcase her and to take credit later.

At the end of that summer, Andy made Joanna a generous offer with a five-figure signing bonus, and she accepted. Several months later, however, she got poached by a bigger shop. Andy was enraged when he learned that she was leaving. He made her a counteroffer and almost made a scene trying to convince her to stay. But she left anyway. He had to hide his anger from the other traders, who couldn't understand what the fuss was all about.

That was eleven years ago. Now, in her mid-thirties, Joanna had grown into a well-connected derivatives saleswoman at the credit desk of a large European bank. She entertained clients at all the major business conferences and industry get-togethers. She knew who got poached where and who had what trade on. She knew everyone's risk appetites and axes and book sizes but also the grudges, the rivalries, the silent wars. She had the best intel and the best gossip, and people sought her company.

When Andy and Joanna ran into each other at conferences, she was, as any successful saleswoman should be, cordial and ever ready to do business, probing him for what kind of "paper" and "yield" and "risk" he was looking for, and Andy felt that behind her friendly front there was always a sly dig at his heartfelt attempt to keep her under his wing all those years ago.

"You are 'credit,' and I'm 'investment grade,'" he would usually tell her, and she always laughed at this explanation.

Andy pressed a button on his turret phone that had a pre-programmed direct connection to Joanna's desk.

"Hi, Andy," she said with a welcoming, smiling voice. "Long time no hear. What can I do for you?"

"I need to get a quote on something," he said.

"Okay."

"Where would you guys sell protection on Concordia-Walden?"

"Since when are you trading credit?" Joanna asked and didn't wait for an answer. "What size?"

"Uhm. How about ten?"

He heard her keyboard clicking fast.

"Huh. It's not a name that trades a lot. I have to run it by my guys. Let me get back to you."

"Sure."

"Andy. I'm glad we're doing business again," Joanna chirped. "Give me half an hour or so. Don't call anybody else. I'll show you a good level."

For the last few years, Joanna had been dating Misha Pomerantzev. The two were jet-setters and foodies who could get a reservation at Momofuku Ko with one phone call. They once flew to Copenhagen for one day just to have dinner at Noma, the world's top-rated restaurant. But then Misha quit his job and showed up alone at Andy's birthday party, unkempt and in a sort of searching, unmoored state, and rumors began to swirl.

Joanna's number displayed on Andy's turret five minutes later. He picked up.

"So," she said sounding a bit subdued. "Because it's such a cuspy name, my guys will show you nine points upfront and two hundred running."

"What? Come on, really?"

"They say it's still a pretty good deal."

"Nine points upfront, that's robbery."

"So, a 'no' then?"

"Not at the moment, no. But thanks for the offer," Andy said.

"Always happy to help."

"Let's grab a drink one of these days."

"For sure."

VI: Lauren

Andy had met Lauren at a fundraiser for a women's breast cancer charity, a "great way to pick up chicks," according to Caldera, who chaperoned Andy around town after his separation from Madeline. At the charity venue's welcome stand, they received pink lapel ribbons and, with the comportment of humbled solidarity, waded into the sequined, bare-shouldered, champagne-sipping crowd.

"That?" Caldera said in mock horror when he saw Andy zoom in on a stylish, frizzy-haired young woman. "How are you going to maintain your Woodrow when she quotes bell hooks at you?"

"Who?"

"Come on. You have to get conversant in their lingo," Caldera said. "What about those two?" Caldera pointed with his eyes at two thin, blond, polished women in their thirties.

Caldera introduced himself and Andy to the women as longtime friends of the charity. After the initial chit-chat—"good cause," "thank you for your support"—Caldera pointed at Andy and said that *this* guy plans to start a new fund that invests in socially and environmentally responsible causes.

"We are entering a new enlightened era," Caldera said solemnly. "We need a different way of thinking."

Andy kept mum, playing along, thinking that Caldera would've made a great actor.

Lauren, the younger of the two women, turned to Andy and asked him if this new fund would invest in the arts.

"Of course," Andy said. "We need art now more than ever. Technology explains the hows; art explains the whys. I think that we've been lacking in the 'why' department."

Caldera glanced at Andy with astonished approval. He patted him on the back. "You better stick with this guy," Caldera said. "He will be on a magazine cover one day."

Lauren gave Andy her business card, and Andy gave her his. She told him that she'd be interested in talking more, as she was involved in several art projects.

"Let's have coffee one of these days," Andy said.

"I'd love to," Lauren replied.

"See? That's how it's done," Caldera said when the ladies walked away. "I just sensed some repressed sexual energy there that is looking to drain itself on the right guy. Why can't it be you? Let me see her card."

Under her name, Lauren's card listed several titles: philanthropist, entrepreneur, filmmaker.

"Huh," Caldera said. "Bet you fifty bucks she's a rich divorcee with too much time on her hands. You hit the jackpot, man."

Caldera was right. From a brief scroll through Lauren's Instagram, Andy learned that she was divorced—there were pictures of her and her child, a six-year-old boy, but no signs of a husband. She split her time between a large waterfront mansion in the Hamptons and an apartment in Manhattan, and attended gallery openings, Sunday brunches, and fundraisers.

As he scrolled further through the pictures and the videos, he saw that after her divorce Lauren had gone on a journey of self-discovery. The journey was guided by a fashionable bestseller, a book club favorite, the imperative *Fly, Girl, Fly* that had inspired scores of restless middle-aged white women to "leave everything behind and find one's true self." On the book's cover there was a breezy, soft-focus image of a woman in a diaphanous gown on a wooden jetty about to leap into the water, and he felt that Lauren, in her travels, sought to imitate it. She posted pictures of herself in a kind of caught-in-a-dream ease, looking away from the camera, or in mid-action, browsing through the fish and farmers markets in picturesque town squares of Northern Italy. He wondered who took those pictures.

On their first date, at Babbo, Andy told Lauren that he worked in "finance," and she replied that her ex-husband was a hedge fund manager, and she gave him a name, and, of course, Andy had heard of him and of his book—that is, assets under management—that was much bigger than his own. He mentioned the former but not the latter to her. Lauren then talked a lot about self-actualization and empowerment. Andy listened, keeping keen eye contact, interspersing her talk with nods and words of encouragement.

Now that Lauren was divorced, the philanthropy, at least the part that required large-sum donations, was put on the backburner. She still attended several fundraisers a month, mostly to show her face to friends and—especially—enemies, and to be up-to-date on social currents, but her focus had now switched to filmmaking. With her girlfriends, she made a short documentary about an elderly woman in Queens who couldn't pay her medical bills and faced eviction and was miraculously saved by an anonymous GoFundMe campaign.

"How did you know in advance that she'd get enough money from the campaign to cover her bills?" Andy asked.

"Well," Lauren said and looked at him like he was an idiot. "We set it up."

"Ah. Clever," Andy said. "But then it's not really a documentary. More of a reality TV show."

"It's a heartwarming story. People love those stories," Lauren said.

"If only there was an army of Laurens out there helping desperate old ladies," Andy said warmly and saw that Lauren was pleased with his takeaway.

A young raven-haired waiter came by and in a native Italian accent asked if Lauren wanted a second glass of wine and she coquettishly said, "Oh, yes, please, grazie."

For her next project, Lauren planned to tackle a more serious topic, a refugee crisis in Europe. "A full-length doc, an hour and a half long," she said between sips of Chianti.

"You have a fascinating life," Andy said. "Can a boring guy like me hop along for the ride?"

Lauren laughed.

The Italian waiter brought a dessert menu.

"I know a good dessert place," Lauren said. "We should go there."

Andy was glad that Lauren wasn't bookish. She rushed between causes, unsettled, unsatisfied, but she carried with her the promise of a bohemian adventure, of thoughtless indulgence. She was a timely, congenial prescription to his ennui. In the back seat of the taxi, Andy put a hand on her knee and leaned over to kiss her, and Lauren responded with restless, yearning vibrancy. He tried to remember the last time he'd had a similar night-on-the-town experience—hopping from place to place with an attractive woman at his side, with a prospect of a late-night denouement at his or her apartment—and realized that he'd have to reach as far back as his early twenties.

The dessert place was a cupcake store in Chelsea. They got out of the taxi in front of its pink and purple storefront. The place was closed.

"It's my store," Lauren said. "I own it." She took out the keys from her purse and unlocked the door.

"Wow," Andy said. "I guess this is the 'entrepreneur' part of your resume."

"That's right," Lauren said haughtily.

In the glass vitrine inside the store was an assortment of colorful macaroons. Lauren went behind the counter. Andy followed her.

"I think they sold all the cake inventory for today. But these macaroons are delicious. You want to try one?"

He put his arms around her. "There's a macaroon I want to try," he said and buried his tongue in her mouth. Lauren's fingers slid down his crotch. Breathing heavily, she unlocked his belt. He fished, impatiently, for a condom that had gained a permanent residency in his wallet, among the hundred-dollar bills, and tore its silver wrapping, nervous about whether his "Woodrow" was up to task. But his old friend rose to the occasion.

"Not bad for an old man," Lauren said, diffusing an awkward post-coital lull.

They both giggled.

Lauren's cupcake store was a gift for her thirtieth birthday from her hedge-funder husband. Years ago, she got bored sitting at home with a newborn, and, after she complained that she was getting stale and dumb, the husband asked her what she wanted to do. At that time Lauren was into TED talks and *Forbes* rankings, and the idea of calling herself a businesswoman appealed to her.

"You can play with it now," her husband said after he bought a small commercial space on Ninth Avenue. Lauren hired a crew to renovate and paint the store, a retail business consultant to furnish it with all the right fixtures, and a social media intern to create and maintain the store's website. The website and the social media account profiles featured a photo of Lauren in a sharp-shouldered business jacket, in a power pose, with hands planted on her hips. The opening ceremony was lavish, with gourmet catering and unlimited champagne. All her girlfriends and important friends showed up.

Lauren collected identities as if they were weaponry. All her frantic activities, all her vacillations and fleeting interests, seemed like unacknowledged preparations for entering a space that Madeline had stepped into years earlier, stoically and calmly. To protect herself from the vagaries and betrayals of life that she, no doubt, came across during her divorce, Lauren retreated into a self-created emotional world of enforced positivity. She sought affirmations of her new lifestyle in self-help books, seminars, and inspirational quotes that she posted daily on her Instagram. Whenever she learned about a new business or a social phenomenon or a life hack, she hurried to discuss it with Andy, seeking his opinion, but in her description of the phenomenon, she often was at a loss for words and resorted to the use of extreme facial mimicry and arm gestures.

"Oh," Andy would encourage her when she looked at the ceiling in search of a word. "How interesting."

"It's ... it's ... it's groundbreaking," Lauren would conclude, grasping the air with her hands to emphasize her astonishment.

Andy was forgiving to Lauren for her lack of focus and her superficiality. In fact, he was even entertained by it. There was energy in her pursuits, a misguided, dumb energy, but a refreshing one. She was an antidote to Madeline's sterile dispassion.

In the post-nuptial settlement, Lauren told Andy, she got the Hamptons house and the West Village apartment. Andy soon learned that the apartment was a one-bedroom walk-up in need of a renovation, and just as he was mulling the most benign way to ask Lauren about how a family that is accustomed to living large, with a young child, with household help, and with resources to pay for an appropriate-size dwelling ended up owning such a small unit, she hurried to tell him that the apartment wasn't meant to be lived in. Its function was to secure a spot for Ashton, her son, in a good public school nearby. She was going to sell it and buy a bigger one as soon as she sold the Hamptons house. Smooth tale, Andy allowed, thinking that there was, perhaps, a story behind the Hamptons house as well, that ceding the beachfront property wasn't some grand, benevolent gesture on her ex's part. Indeed, he found out quickly enough that her ex had stuck Lauren with a huge tax bill on the house that she would now have to pay out of her own settlement. Smart motherfucker, Andy thought. "What a douchebag," he said to Lauren, shaking his head in dismay.

There were also, most likely, limited partnerships about the existence of which Lauren couldn't possibly be aware, and if she was, couldn't figure out how to extract that money. There were a lot of ugly discoveries that she must've made in the past few years, a lot of grief, a lot of anger, a lot of things that she couldn't even express properly—because most of those ugly things were not about infidelity but about money, a taboo topic, and because in order to describe how badly she got fucked, she would need familiarity with obscure legal and financial terminology. Andy felt that anger, that bitterness, in her gestures and voice when she mentioned her ex.

Could she have stood her ground? Could she have gotten past the legalese and demanded to be compensated appropriately? Could she have quantified and argued what "appropriately" meant? Could she have foreseen that her innocuous habit of enjoying a joint every now and then, which the husband had never had a problem with before, would suddenly become a pretext for a custody battle and a resulting diminished alimony?

Poor, poor Lauren. She's a nice girl who got squashed by complexity. Women like her, fair and pretty and thin, benefit from all these legal and moral gray zones—the nuances, the clauses, the fine print, the offshore accounts, the unexamined implications—until that complexity runs them over like a steamroller. She must've thought, like many young, beautiful women in love, that there was an understanding that didn't need an elaboration, that certain norms would always be upheld. Especially when there's a child, especially when that child is a boy. Smart, attuned women sense that crucial moment when the silent agreement is nixed, when the unraveling begins, and become—immediately!—upright citizens, caring, selfless mothers and loving, long-suffering wives. Lauren should've trod carefully—no weed, no outbursts, no late-night absences, not even mimosas with girlfriends on weekends. But she missed the signs, and she failed to detect a trap.

Once her husband wanted her out, she was done. He could plan her moves several steps ahead. He knew how to get her riled up and when to call the police. He knew that once it dawned on her that he claimed himself to be the victim, and she the perpetrator, the audacity of it, especially in the presence of law enforcement, would put her in apoplectic fit and seal the case in his favor. Her verbal and communicational skills weren't up to par to counter such gall without getting derailed by emotion. At that moment she needed clarity of thought, a cold mind, precise articulation of grievances, the cataloguing of abuses, a recommendation of appropriate remedy. And she would have none of that. She'd be hysterical and incoherent. She'd have mascara running down her face. The cops would find a joint in her handbag; she'd fail a piss test. By the time she got a good lawyer, it was probably too late. By the time she got to read a carefully crafted statement—"Your Honor, my actions, which I regret, should be put in a broader context. I was not driven by malice. It was the result of accumulated et cetera, et cetera"—the court already had recordings of "What was I supposed to do when he called me a stupid whore?" and "He never had a problem with me smoking weed before" on file.

"Your husband preempted you in court, didn't he?" Andy asked her to see if his hypothesis was correct.

"He's just an asshole," Lauren replied with an eyeroll, unwittingly confirming it.

VII: Between the Primal
and the Cerebral

For Lauren, despite her conspicuous disinterest in the utilitarian, any charitable or artistic engagement had to carry a tangible utility: to show off a new dress, to get a photo of herself in the press, to make a useful acquaintance. When she invited Andy to a Soho gallery opening, he didn't want to sabotage her aspirations and so put on a nice dinner jacket and a pair of super-uncomfortable but slick Ferragamo shoes. He expected that the gallery scene would be young and glamorous, and that if there were older art lovers in attendance, they'd be coiffed Upper East Side widows with pebble-sized stones on their bony fingers. Instead, he found nosy and activist Upper *West* Side old ladies in comfortable shoes and stretchy, formless clothes who liked and overused words such as *caftan* and *Baryshnikov*, and who walked around with canvas bags, and whose raison d'être was to continually search for and adopt whimsical causes with no concrete ends.

As if sensing Andy's disappointment, Lauren whispered that these ladies were going to sponsor her refugees documentary and told him to please be nice.

"I'm always nice," he said and switched his attention from the crowd to the art on the gallery walls.

"Mystic Town" was the theme of the exhibition. The collection featured several depictions of a city at night—blue buildings, yellow lampposts, glistening asphalt. Then there was moody Hopperian geometry, full of melancholy shadows and loneliness. There was also a series of pictures of Manhattan as an anthropomorphic entity, where its skyline rested on a reclining subterranean body of a demimonde creature, a dark-haired, scarlet-lipped siren in a carnal red dress, her head under Battery Park, her curvaceous hips under Harlem.

"Oh, I love that!" Lauren said, posing next to one of those pictures, and then turned back to the group of activist ladies to continue her fundraising spiel.

Andy wandered farther into the gallery. In a corner, neglected by the schmoozing crowd, he saw an underfed, slouching artist who stood next to a canvas with an image of a tiny cabin surrounded by vast dark woods, emitting a faint light. On a closer inspection, the cabin turned out to be a city, with craftily drawn minuscule shapes of buildings.

"Does it sell well?" Andy asked the artist.

"I'm hoping it will," he answered.

"That's not how you should answer that question. You're supposed to say there's a list of people wanting to buy it. Can't paint them fast enough," Andy said.

"Thank you, sir. That's solid advice."

"How did you come across this theme?"

"I always thought that the woods touch us on a deep level. There's something primal there. Whatever it is, it doesn't appeal to reason. Perhaps we feel like that flickering yellow light in the middle of a vast, indifferent nothingness is us, metaphorically speaking. You can live in a dense city, surrounded by people, but still feel like that lonely cabin in the wilderness."

Andy stared at the painting. "Have you heard of Ludwig Wittgenstein?" he asked.

"Of course." The artist sprung from his doleful posture, brimming with cautious hope.

"He lived in a cabin on the mountainside of a fjord in Norway. I saw it when on a boat trip there a few years ago. A little wood hut on a hilly slope, surrounded by pines, almost a fairy-tale image. I remember that I wanted the ship to stop, so that I could come ashore and take some pictures of it."

"There you go," the artist said and smiled feebly.

Lauren, with a champagne glass in hand, who had been migrating from cluster to cluster, posing for pictures, stopped by Andy and the artist. Striking a vixenish pose, she signaled to the party photographer to snap a picture of the three of them.

Andy took the artist's business card and gave him his own and told him to keep in touch.

Lauren wanted to mingle more, but Andy told her that he had to be home around nine to have dinner with Ava. Lauren hugged and air-kissed each of the old ladies, promising to send them "updates on the progress."

"I'd love to meet your daughter one of these days," Lauren said as they stood on the sidewalk, scanning the West Broadway traffic for the light of an in-service taxi. "Perhaps I could mentor her on some things. School. Boys." She sighed. "I wish I had a mentor when I was seventeen. I had to learn everything myself. What does she like?"

"She's into horses," Andy said.

"Me too!" Lauren exclaimed. "I love horses."

"I mean she competes on a regional level. She's a skilled equestrian."

"Good for her," Lauren said. "I used to do gymnastics. But I had a knee injury and had to quit. But I was very good. My coach thought I could make it all the way to the Olympics. Ah, well."

In a taxi on the way to the West Village, Andy took Lauren's hand and put it on his crotch. With a naughty giggle, Lauren gave him a nice quick rub, so nice that he didn't even make it past Seventh Avenue. He told Lauren that he felt "too spent" to go upstairs when the taxi stopped in front of her building.

"There's nothing left down there," he complained, and they both laughed. He smooched her goodbye and told the taxi driver to take him uptown. On the way to his place, he thought of the chances of Ava becoming like Lauren and what needed to be done to prevent it from happening.

Andy's Manhattan apartment was located in Midtown East, a bit of a dead zone culturally and transportationally. Among its redeeming qualities was the proximity to his office; it was in a brand-new building; and it was a condo—a decisive factor. Initially, Andy had scoured the co-op market in much posher areas on the Upper East Side and on Central Park West, but the prospect of going through the trauma of a comprehensive financial disclosure and temperamental assessment by a co-op board soured his plans. He didn't want to subject himself to an intrusive vetting by dissatisfied, headshaking busybodies determined to find faults with every applicant and demand an anal probe, figuratively speaking (though the way things were going, it could become quite literal in the near future).

Andy maintained his apartment in a spartan and uncluttered state, in a bid, perhaps, to neutralize his indulgent suburban lifestyle. During the day, the apartment was filled with light, and its high floor and thick, soundproof windows kept it quiet. Its prevailing palette was gray and silver, although the master bedroom walls were painted in a whimsical deep magenta color and the kitchen counter was made of pink marble. The living room coffee table, in front of a plush couch, was the only object among the bland and inoffensive interior to have had an interesting life. It was made of reclaimed wood that came from, as his interior designer assured, a seventeenth-century pirate shipwreck. On its worn and dented-by-adventure surface were stacked hardcover picture and photography books, all in pristine condition.

Ava was sitting on a high stool at the marble-top kitchen island, with one foot on the seat, the other dangling. She leaned over her laptop and propped her forehead up with her hand. Her long, silky hair kept sliding forward, and she kept sweeping it back and blowing air from the side of her mouth on the unruly strands. Her nails were painted black, and on her thin wrists she wore a collection of handmade bead and thread friendship bracelets.

"Hi, Dad," she said without lifting her eyes.

On Ava's laptop screen was an interactive map of Northern California. Ava had spent last summer in the area, in a riding camp, and now there were reports of local forest fires near the camp's stables. Ava followed the news closely, monitoring the spread and the direction of the fires. Now she had learned from the local news reports that a man had been arrested for arson, and this piece of new information had broken through her normally stoic front.

Andy cooked a bowl of spaghetti and put a plateful of it in front of Ava. He leaned on the kitchen counter and looked at her screen.

"What's the latest?" he asked.

She shut her laptop in exasperation. "This is unfathomable. Why would anyone do such a thing deliberately?"

"Perhaps that man was upset about something," Andy said, knowing that his flippant take would prompt a stimulating discussion.

Ava took his bait, looking at him in rattled disbelief. "Seriously? First, the magnitude of what he's done does not in any way correspond to any grievances he might have. And second, how exactly do innocent creatures dying mitigate his pain?"

Ava spoke quickly and with a high, uneven voice, but her words flowed in an orderly, dynamic fashion. What a pleasure it was to listen to her make her passionate argument. *What a bright, articulate young woman my Ava is*, he thought and smiled.

"Why are you smiling?"

"He's either a dickhead or just a sick man," Andy said. "He wanted to say something important, but, unlike you, he can't structure his thoughts into a coherent sentence, and this is what he decided to do."

"And that is his excuse?" Ava's voice rang with indignation. "Are you suggesting we should take a sick man's opinion into account?"

"Perhaps this one is an extreme case, but generally when someone is in distress, he deserves to be heard."

"Not if he threatens harm! Why should we care about opinions of malicious idiots?"

"Because in a democracy we allow for a full spectrum of opinions."

"What he did is not an opinion. It's an action. One shouldn't be able to just walk into the woods and wantonly set it on fire just because he's upset about something."

"What if he were Black? Protesting injustice?" Andy needled Ava with a tricky hypothetical.

"Now you're just trolling."

"I'm not. I'd love to hear your take."

"I think that you're intentionally diverting this into a dishonest and incurious aside," Ava said, sounding annoyed. "To answer your question—it makes no difference. However, you'd have to agree that given the recent events, a Black man would have more reasons to be upset. Besides, we should be able to distinguish between the whims of callow, attention-seeking punks and the concerns of the genuinely weak."

"And a Black man is weak?"

"A Black man is … is …" Ava bit her lip, searching for a word. "He is a first-loss piece of the society."

His heart melted. It was natural for girls her age to care for the downtrodden, especially now, in times of social unrest. He loved her yet-unspoiled, heartfelt magnanimity and sense of justice, but he especially appreciated her use of finance lingo. He had been exposing Ava to his professional terminology since she was a baby. She grew out of the princess stories pretty fast and demanded that Andy compose his own bedtime stories, featuring animals, and Andy obliged as far as he could.

"And then the hedgehog got a job as an apple-picker and the dragon got a job as a real estate agent."

"And then?"

"And then they saved some money and opened a zoo," he improvised. "With the dragon as the main attraction."

"Was the dragon in a cage?"

"Oh, no, pumpkin. The dragon got a good deal. He lived in a spacious compound. He got a base salary with health benefits and a year-end bonus."

"And then?"

The adamancy. The dissatisfaction.

"And then they went into private equity and made a lot of money," Andy would say, tucking her in and kissing her on the forehead.

"Where?"

"Private equity."

Ava was unimpressed. "And then?"

Andy mulled possible scenarios to top this feat, but his imagination seemed to have hit a wall. "That should be a fitting end, dear, no? Go to sleep. I'll tell you tomorrow."

Years later, already in her teens, Ava asked him to describe his workday, and he got into a long tale of bond finance and discounted cashflows and capital structure and valuations, thinking he bored her. But Ava listened closely and, as it turned out, absorbed most of the information. The capital structure of a bond particularly spiked her interest. It was like a layered cake, Andy explained when she asked him to elaborate. If you spill milk around it, the bottom layer— the first-loss piece—takes most of the damage, and the top layers are spared. That's why the holders of the bottom slice can and should demand to be paid a higher rate for the risk.

"He carries the risk. He should be compensated for that risk," Ava said now, spooling a spaghetti noodle on her fork.

"How? Monetarily?"

"I don't know. But at the very least by being heard."

"Too many people want to be heard these days. Everyone is trying to outshout each other. Being heard is the most valuable currency. All our airwaves are clogged."

"Yes. Therefore, we have to be selective."

"Aha!" Andy raised his finger. "And how would we go about that selection? Will some be heard at the expense of the others?"

"Uh, yeah. An arsonist shouldn't have the right to be heard. He forfeited that right by starting a fire." Ava fiddled languidly with the uncooperating pasta on her plate and put her fork down. "It's all very upsetting. Stupid people are upsetting."

"Sometimes, honey, there's just no way of policing idiots." Andy softened his tone. "A smart person has to anticipate other people's stupidity. Anticipate and plan for it and make provisions to mitigate it. If one knows about the stupidity of others and fails to protect against it, then the blame is on him, not on the stupid one." He sighed.

"What a dreadful conclusion," Ava said.

"That's life. I deal with idiots every day."

"Like Caldera and Scotty?" Ava asked.

"Yeah. Like Caldera and Scotty." He kissed her on the forehead and ruffled her hair. "Now finish your dinner."

After Ava went to bed, he thought that Madeline was right when she banned Ava from all social media. That imposed informational vacuum, enhanced by the debate club demands for discipline and focus, gave Ava's curious mind and teenage restlessness an outlet, and she channeled all that youthful energy into sharp, spitting analysis. There was a seriousness about her; she was spared from dismissive levity that abided in her classmates. No, she won't be an airhead like Lauren, he reassured himself. She will be impervious to bullshit and ruthless to its vendors—a precious quality for a young, beautiful woman.

VIII: A Night on the Town

Andy and Caldera were sitting in a posh Midtown bar a few blocks north of Grand Central Terminal. The happy-hour crowd began to trickle in, and Caldera took off his jacket and put it on an empty seat between them.

"Joanna is joining us," he said.

Andy felt a tingle up his spine. "I heard she and Misha broke up," he said.

"That's why I invited her." Caldera grinned.

"You're not her type," Andy scoffed with a heavy feeling.

"Why not? She laughs at my jokes."

"She laughs at everybody's jokes."

"Are you jealous?"

"Like I said, she's out of your league."

"Remember that time years ago we went to the Modern?" Caldera said. "I knew right then and there she was going to go far, that girl. She's got what it takes."

Oh, Andy remembered it.

That day, years ago, he had taken his summer analysts—Joanna, Scotty, and two other Wharton grads, Brett and Kyle, for dinner to celebrate the completion of a big project. They went to the Modern, a trendy dining spot for the Midtown finance crowd at the Museum of Modern Art. Somehow Caldera was there too; he had an innate ability to sniff out the happenings all over town and show up at the right place at the right time.

Caldera was dressed in a well-tailored striped suit with a pink carnation stuck through the lapel's buttonhole. There was a certain presence about him. As he moved through the dining room, glad-handing patrons and staff, he seemed to generate a power field that bent the space and cleared a path just for him.

Caldera scouted the room. He spotted Andy sitting at the table surrounded by the younglings and invited himself to the feast, sending the waiter to get an extra chair. Andy was in the middle of explaining the inner workings of a swap contract to the four analysts, and they diligently listened with somber expressions, taking careful bites of mushroom risotto, but when Caldera showed up with a theatrical "Hey, look who's here!" yell, their faces lit up.

"What's this?" Caldera asked with a cringe, pointing at a half-full bottle of white wine resting in the nearby silver bucket. He called the waiter and ordered three more bottles without looking at the wine list. "So." He rubbed his palms. "What have you been working on?" Caldera addressed the question to no one in particular, but then stared at Joanna.

"Today we finished a big project on prepayment penalties," Joanna replied with the crispness of an overachiever. "Basically, we consolidated a bunch of various data sheets into one database and then stratified the resulting data—"

"What's your name, young lady?" Caldera interrupted her with a beaming smile.

"Joanna."

"Joanna, dear." He put his hand on her wrist. "And how exactly will this exercise impact your P&L?"

Joanna paused. "I guess it's somewhat removed from the business side of things, but—"

"Stop harassing my team." Andy came to her rescue. "Joanna has a bright future in the industry."

The wine that Caldera ordered had loosened him and the analysts. For the next fifteen minutes, he rambled about how he was once nearly shot by a well-known CEO on a hunting trip and dropped names of celebrities with whom he was doing business.

Pleased with the effect his tales had on the young bankers, who listened to him in awe, Caldera leaned over to Joanna as if to share a secret and then declared loudly enough for others to hear: "I'll let you in on a secret, Joanna. Mr. Sylvain won't tell you this, but if you want to succeed in this business, you have to understand that the things that you do off the trading floor are just as important as the things that you do on the floor."

Andy rolled his eyes, but Joanna listened with interest.

"Are you in consulting?" she asked.

"I wear many hats," Caldera said with a satisfied, enigmatic smile. "But everything I do is rooted in a simple philosophy. It's so simple that I had it tattooed on my back."

Not this again, Andy thought.

"What does it say?" Scotty asked as if on cue.

"Wanna see?"

"You mean right here?"

"Of course not! That would be awfully inappropriate. In the bathroom." He eyed Joanna. "It's coed here. How very convenient!" His eyes expanded with glee. Caldera stood up and signaled to the analysts to follow him. "Your chicklets will be returned to you unmolested," he told Andy.

Scotty and two other analysts, drunk and giggling, their guards down, stood up and followed Caldera to the bathroom. Joanna hesitated and stared at Andy.

"Who is he?" she asked.

"That's Doug Caldera. A man about town. A crazy person. But also someone you should add to your contacts."

An odd thought occurred to him then. Caldera wasn't wrong when he said that off-trading floor experience was important. Joanna, he realized, faced an impossible choice. She could join Scotty and the bros and follow Caldera into the bathroom and be exposed to silliness and locker room horseplay. Or she could stay here and miss out on informal bonding and network-building that was an important part of a successful career.

If she doesn't go there now, she will forever be cast as *the other*, as a prim, stuffy, humorless killjoy. She will not be one of the boys. Tomorrow, and for years ahead, they will be recounting this formative moment with warm nostalgia and knowing laughter, and she will be left out. They will be able to pick up the phone and dial Caldera for some casual insight, and she won't be. She will grow resentful and bitter, and her career will suffer. How stupid it all is. If only this world rewarded one's smarts and propriety, he thought, and not one's juvenile antics. He thought of Ava and hoped that she would never have to make such a choice.

Andy sighed as Joanna fidgeted, puzzled and impatient, waiting for his guidance.

"If you don't want to feel left out, go see it," he said. "But Joanna," he added as she stood up. "There will probably be an illegal substance involved, and he will say you can't see his tattoo unless you snort it, but he's bluffing. You have the option to refuse it. He likes to brag about that stupid tattoo. He thinks it's clever."

"So, you know what it says?"

Andy and Caldera were old college roommates, and Andy had learned a long time ago what Caldera's tattoo, connecting his shoulder blades like a bridge, said: *Who will stop me?*

Joanna stood up and went to the bathroom. Scotty, Kyle, and Brett came back to the table a few minutes later in a sprightly mood, loud and jostling. Scotty sat down next to Andy and wouldn't shut up about some inane investment idea he'd come up with, and Andy couldn't listen to him, his eyes glued on the bathroom door.

Ten long minutes passed before Joanna and Caldera emerged, giddy and wide-eyed, and Andy thought that ten minutes was way too long for a snort and a show-and-tell. He hated Caldera for it, but he never asked what had happened there, and Caldera never told.

"Joanna," Andy said when they all stepped out of the stuffy restaurant into the cool night. "If Caldera was inappropriate in any way, you have to let me know. I'll deal with him."

"Caldera was very funny," she said.

Two months after she started working for him full time, Joanna got poached by a different shop, and, Andy guessed, not without Caldera's help. There were no rules written for that guy.

"If it wasn't for me, she'd probably still be crunching numbers at your desk," Caldera said now at the bar, sipping his martini.

"You give me no credit. I had big plans for her," Andy replied.

"Oh. Excuse me." Caldera picked an olive from the martini skewer and ate it.

The TV above the bar was tuned to CNBC to accommodate the patrons' sensibilities. On the screen, a seventyish guy, in a Joker-like green jacket and a polka-dot bowtie, with thick-framed orange glasses, was suffering what looked like a mental breakdown. The TV was on mute, but he spoke with such animation and a bug-eyed, spitting intensity, that if Andy had to guess the topic of the segment, he'd pick the current U.S. monetary policy, an issue once boring and arcane but now dangerously potent and emotionally charged. Indeed, the chyron at the bottom read: "Could Yellen kill the markets?"

"Can you believe that guy was once the chief economist at Cubbs Harding?" Andy said and shook his head. "He used to be this boring guy. Dressed in sloppy, cheap suits. Wrote about BLS and Fed data releases."

"Yeah. What happened to the guy?"

Andy shrugged. "I guess he wants to be a TV personality now."

"Could you turn it up, please?" Caldera asked the bartender.

The bartender tinkered with the remote.

The former chief economist's voice was over-the-top cranky, as if he was doing a bit. "I say what a bunch of baloney. It is total bullcrap. Nobody talks about moral hazard. Those people should learn the work ethic by working and not by handouts. Back in my day—"

"He was once sharp," Andy said. "Why does he have to do this? He has enough money. He could've just retired and become an elder statesman."

"I mean holy-moly!" the TV economist continued to rant, his voice an octave higher. "And let me tell you, Bernanke, Yellen, all those phonies, they don't know what they're doing."

Caldera caught the bartender's gaze and signaled to him to mute the TV. "Maybe he feels he doesn't have much time left on this earth, and this is his last chance to make a splash. He's like an old male version of Norma Desmond," Caldera said. "Obnoxious behavior is a cry for help, don't remember who said it. Maybe that fate befalls us all."

"We gotta be vigilant not to miss that moment. Retreat from the scene in time. Recede into obscurity."

"We have time." Caldera sniffed and sipped his martini.

"Good evening, gentlemen."

They heard a playful, singsong murmur. Joanna came from behind and put her arms around both of their shoulders. Andy felt her warm breath on his neck.

Joanna looked dapper in a pair of a soft, high-waisted, wide-legged pants that flattered her lean frame, in high-heeled booties and a meticulously tailored, sharp-shouldered Rick Owens leather jacket. Her long, thick brown hair was swept to one side, exposing a dangling diamond-encrusted earring shaped like an ace of spades. Long gone was the yearning, starry-eyed young analyst. There was now a sparkly haughtiness about her. If only she'd stayed at my desk back then, Andy thought.

Joanna ordered a dry martini. "I know that guy," she said pointing at the TV screen. "He was Cubbs Harding's chief economist way back when. Cubbs Harding was always a bunch of clowns. Just plain weirdos. Every time I met someone from Cubbs, they wanted to show me a card trick. A literal card trick. I think every fucking single one of them carried a deck of cards with them at all times. It was some kind of pathology."

"That's how they distinguished themselves. It was their internal culture," Andy said.

"Yeah, tricksters. They always had some faint veneer of sleaze. I mean, I was young then and very impressionable. But the shit they did, man. I think those decks were stacked."

"Hey, hey, easy, that's where Andy learned the ropes," Caldera inserted.

"Oh?" Joanna glanced at Andy. "I didn't know that. You never told me."

"I was only there for a short time," Andy said and paused. "I did not carry a deck, I assure you." He held up his hands in a display of innocence.

"Search 'im, Joanna," Caldera prompted. "I'm sure it's in his pocket somewhere. Tread carefully or he might get excited."

"You're such a slimeball," Andy said.

Caldera giggled. "Let's go for oysters and champagne," he said, sniffing and rubbing his nose.

"Pearl Oyster downtown?" Andy suggested.

"It's good, but it's too proletarian," Caldera said. "You have to wait in line with everybody else. Let's just go to Grand Central. They'll seat us right away."

The three of them walked three blocks down to Grand Central Terminal and then down the ramp to the Oyster Bar—a subterranean gastronomic hotspot for tourists and a waiting area for the northbound suburbanites. The tourists and the commuters were now all gone, and the place was half empty.

Caldera ordered Ipswich clams and, when the dish came, he couldn't resist making a lewd comment about their phallic shape.

Joanna rolled her eyes. "You're so penis-centric. It shows a certain degree of insecurity about your own manhood," she said, and Andy silently applauded her observation.

"Don't be such a prude, dear," Caldera said. "And just so you know, I have no reason whatsoever to be insecure."

Joanna slurped a meaty Bluepoint oyster from a shell and took a sip of the sparkling wine. "You have an unhealthy fixation," she said. "It's a sign of deeper problems. I remember when I was in elementary school, we had a flasher. You know, an exhibitionist. He was a classic case, trench coat and all. I was six or seven. One day we come out of the school and go to a nearby park to wait for our parents. We sit on the bench. And there he is, coming out of the bushes, with all his equipment out in the open. Other girls shrieked and ran, but I stood there and stared at his junk. It was limp and bluish. It looked so improbable—not even the limpness of it, but the entire idea, the questionable functionality of it, the wrinkly accoutrements—it could not possibly be true."

"Whoa, whoa, too much information," Caldera hollered.

"I thought it was some horrible atavism, some abnormality," Joanna continued. "I thought that this person was, rightly, shunned by civilized society for possessing such an ugly appendix and that this was his lot. I laughed with that cruel little girl laughter, and he retreated back into the bushes. I think they caught him later. Of course, mere days later, I learned from my girlfriends that every boy had one of those. Things were never the same."

"You learned that when you were seven? A late bloomer." Caldera chuckled.

"Caldera was showing his dick to the girls while still in his cradle," Andy said. "And, Joanna, I have to commend you for not allowing this horrible experience to keep you from growing into a functioning, mentally sound adult."

She sighed. "You gotta feel sorry for the guy," she said thoughtfully. "He wanted others to see his brilliant mind, but that was impossible, so he showed the world his cock instead."

"I think you're right about that," Caldera said, suddenly placid. "It was an act of desperation."

Andy's phone buzzed with a text message.

"It's Lauren," he said. "She wants to go out."

"Tell her to come here," Caldera said.

"She wants to go to the Boom Boom Room. Why don't we all go?" Andy said and looked at Joanna.

"It's not what it used to be. It's full of degenerates now," Caldera said.

"Humor me, would you?"

They took a taxi downtown. Caldera sat in the front passenger seat, giving instructions to the driver—"take Fifth down to 13th." Andy and Joanna sat in the back. Andy took his phone out and typed:

Stay away from Caldera ☺, he's a lecherous old perv.

Joanna's phone pinged with a message. Andy glanced at her, and she got his prompt, looking at her phone. She smiled and quickly started typing.

Lol, she texted back. *I know, he's fun though.*

Just saying.

We're strictly platonic.

Phew. Andy theatrically mock-wiped his forehead, and Joanna laughed.

The taxi dropped them off on the corner of 13th Street and Washington. They met Lauren, dressed in a metallic-colored tunic that slid off her shoulder, at the Standard Hotel lobby and took the elevator upstairs to the club.

With an oily smile, Caldera exchanged a few words with the club hostess then turned around and gave Andy a thumbs-up. The hostess, a young model in a short white dress, ushered them inside the sparkly, loud, glamorous pandemonium. The low bass waves of a monotonous two-note dance tune with a heavily synthesized female vocal thumped against Andy's skin and ears. As they barged their way through the jungle of warm, gyrating bodies, Lauren was saying something to him, but he couldn't hear it, and he didn't want to ask her to repeat herself. He just nodded along and smiled. He saw that Caldera was shouting something into Joanna's ear, and she listened and smiled in the same aloof manner.

In the center of the room was an oval-shaped bar with a brassy funnel like installation in the middle of it. The funnel's stem served as the 360-degree liquor shelf, around which the bartenders revolved, filling patrons' orders. Its upper end expanded exponentially into the ceiling, like the mouth of a cosmic vortex that, via a wrinkle in space-time, siphoned intelligent lifeforms from faraway corners of the universe and dropped them into this odd Meatpacking District portal. The lifeforms at the bar and on the dance floor, however, looked like they had arrived here in a more mundane manner, via bridge and tunnel. Downstairs, at every parking spot, New Jersey plates dominated.

The hostess led them to the sunken part of the nightclub, toward a semicircle of soft, crème-colored banquettes. She removed the Reserved sign from the glass cocktail table and gave them menus.

They ordered their drinks. Caldera took Joanna's hand and tried to usher her toward the dance floor, but she demurred. He stood up and walked over to Lauren. "Shall we?" He bent himself, like a medieval vassal, in a dramatic bow.

Lauren stood up. "Come on," she said, trying to entice Andy to join her and Caldera.

"I know too much to be dancing," Andy replied.

"What?" Lauren asked, leaning toward him.

"Never mind," Andy said. "Go enjoy yourself." He waved his hand.

Lauren and Caldera walked away. Lauren loved to dance and was good at it. She had a good command of her body and liked to show off. That's why Lauren liked nightclubs, Andy thought. On the one hand she got to act like she was still twenty, like she still possessed a blithe spirit of youth, and on the other hand a discotheque was a perfect communication vehicle for someone who can't and doesn't want to express herself verbally. Here, amidst the strobe lights and deafening beats, she was in her element. She could prove something to the world with her moves and her fashion. Lauren's interest in making movies had to come from the same handicap. Images don't need explaining. Is there a nuance in the plight of refugees? It's people fleeing for their lives. Who could possibly criticize her work? It's so black and white that it's criticism-proof.

Andy and Joanna sat on opposite sides of the low table, in an awkward lull. He gazed outside the window, where, in the distance, Jersey City flickered across the dark ribbon of the Hudson River. The waitress brought their drinks. Andy took his glass and moved to the banquette next to Joanna.

"What happened with you and Misha?" Andy asked, leaning closer to her ear.

"Oh, he told you," she said, stirring the ice cubes in her glass. "He's a bit brooding. He lacks a fun gene. Typical Russian."

"Ha, he is."

"The funny thing is, he wasn't always like this. When he was still running the credit desk, he'd call me up at like 3 p.m. on a Friday and we would decide on a random trip and be on a plane by 6 p.m. Those were the days."

"And then he made thirty million and became a bum," Andy said.

"Yeah," Joanna said. "Ironic, isn't it?"

Lauren and Caldera came back from the dance floor. Caldera's face was flushed. He plopped onto the banquette.

"Oof. Someone should make a movie about us," Caldera shouted, fanning himself with the menu.

Andy looked at Lauren. "Maybe Lauren will. Once she finishes her documentary."

"I'll look into it," Lauren said. "I gotta have a script though."

"We'll help you write it," Caldera said.

"What we do is not cinematic," said Andy.

Caldera sighed. "Yeah. Unfortunately. Not cinematic but still breathtaking. For someone who knows what's going on, it's a thriller, like *The Bourne Identity*. It's art, what we do. And who cares if no one understands it? We can make it just for us. Show it at conferences and at panels. It will be a niche production for a niche audience."

"Are you a filmmaker?" Joanna asked Lauren.

"Yes."

"What kind of movies do you make?"

"I'm working on a documentary now."

"How exciting. What is it about?"

"Syrian refugees."

"Wow," Joanna exclaimed and looked at Andy. "And here we are, jerking off bid lists," she said ruefully.

Andy pressed his lips in silent agreement.

Lauren gave Joanna her business card, and Joanna looked at it with a well-practiced show of fascination.

"Yep," Andy said. "Lauren is a Renaissance woman. She does a lot of things."

Lauren kissed him on the cheek.

"Call me," she said to Joanna. "Let's have lunch."

Rain had washed over the city's streets while they were inside. The asphalt shimmered, steam rose out of the manholes, and the otherwise potent smell of sidewalk trash was temporarily impaired by the metallic freshness of the ozone-rich air.

Lauren exhaled. "What an amazing city! It just fills me with … energy. It's so …" She grasped at air, looking for a word. "It captures you whole. Mind and body. It makes me feel like I'm on the verge of something big."

They hailed a cab. As they made their way up Tenth Avenue, Andy stared at the gleaming, blurry streetlights that reflected on the uneven patchy surface of the pavement and thought that, while naïve and starry-eyed, Lauren's sentiment had some validity. There was a centripetal force in this city. It conscripted everyone into a willing, adoring bondage. He remembered the painting at the gallery that depicted New York City cradled in the bosom of a lustful, Lilith-like spirit. If the city was a woman, then Lauren embodied it. The same sexual energy underpinning every interaction, the same frantic vacillations between fleeting extremes, the same restlessness, the same confusion. The same unending quest for relevance, for a new thrill, new activity, new lover, but never a satisfaction, never a conclusion. The same grandeur of ideas and mediocrity of execution. The same impatience and hostility toward those who question the place's circular algorithm, its purposes and methods, as if those questions would threaten one's own delicate truce with the city. This lack of anchor, this denial of a firm footing, had to be a feature designed by the nameless architects of the megapolis to maintain its pull, to perpetuate its mythology.

"It's our safe space," Andy said, noting that his usual excitement about the city had somehow devolved into a dull resignation. "It keeps us busy."

IX: Misidentification of Evil

When Andy learned that Lauren was a member of Soho House, an exclusive private club for artists, he asked her how much she was paying for the membership. She told him that it was the wrong question to ask, and that it wasn't about the money—although the fee was several thousand dollars a year—but about one's contribution to the New York arts scene.

"You mean I can't just walk in and buy a membership?" Andy asked, incredulous. "You mean to tell me that you can be a member and I can't?"

"Nope," Lauren replied with gleeful satisfaction. "You have to be an artist or a filmmaker. They don't want bankers in there."

"Why not?"

"They don't find you interesting."

"Fuck 'em then," Andy said.

But art was about the money, after all. Lauren was a producer on several brewing projects that needed bankrolling, one of which included a horror movie, and she broached the idea of investing in the movie with Andy and Misha. They both found the idea entertaining and asked to meet with the director first. Lauren scheduled a meeting in Soho House on a Wednesday afternoon to avoid crowds, and Andy had to take half a day off from work to attend.

He met Misha by the Soho House entrance. Lauren wasn't there yet, but their names were on the list, and the smiling concierge let them inside. They took the elevator to the second floor. From the elevator they stepped into a spacious room that was staged like a co-working venue. There were large communal tables and a bar in the middle, and more private nooks with cozy armchairs alongside the perimeter. Most of the tables were occupied by creative types who looked like cultured lumberjacks. They leaned over their open laptops. The room smelled of good, freshly ground coffee.

Misha and Andy got drinks at the bar (Misha a soda, Andy a beer) and searched for a place to sit. In the corner of the main lounge there was a glass-walled room with a foosball table. It was empty.

"That'll do," Andy said.

Inside the room Andy circled the foosball table, testing its handles. "Come, let's play. I used to be pretty good at this."

"Nah," Misha waved him off. He put his can of Coke on the floor and prostrated himself like a Roman emperor on the soft cushions of the low leather sofa. "I've never played it before. It always seemed rather silly."

Andy found a ball and put it in the middle of the playing field. "Come on, I'll give you a handicap."

"Oh, yeah?"

"Yeah, I'll give you three points ahead."

Misha sipped his Coke. "And how did you come up with the three points?"

"I dunno." Andy shrugged. "It seems like a fair head start."

Misha propped his head with his hand and watched Andy spin the foosball skewers. "I used to build models," he said. "I tweak x, I tweak y, and the results fall into some kind of range. You can see it in a nice smooth curve. That curve allows you to put things into perspective, to make some predictions. But what if we introduce a constant into the formula? What if we say y equals x times b plus thirty? That 'plus thirty' is not really a part of the regression. It is not a natural component of the function; it does not contribute anything to the function's curvature. It's introduced on a whim by a human. Like you just did with the three points. You could've made it into a hundred, into a thousand. It is this arbitrariness that bothers me. Because who gets to decide that number? And how does one arrive at it?"

"Yeah," Andy said. "You're thinking too much."

"I was making a million a year. And then I made thirty million. It wasn't two million or three. Those numbers would be more mathematically justifiable. How did it get to be thirty x?"

"I don't understand. Are you complaining?" Andy scored an easy goal with his plastic team outmaneuvering a dead defense.

"No. Just trying to figure out the essence of this. Whether it can be expressed by a formula. Think about it. My effort is x, my hours worked is y, my intellect and accumulated experience is z, and the previous year this combination of variables produced a million-dollar compensation. But there's only that many hours in a day, that many brain cells in my head. How should I have tweaked all of these components a year later to make it into thirty million? Other than simply adding that thirty to the equation? You see what I mean? Formulaically, it doesn't work. It's a completely arbitrary constant. There's a human factor in it."

"It's the percent of profits. That's the formula. Stop dwelling on it," Andy said.

"You're missing my point," Misha said, exasperated. "No." He raised his finger. "I think you do understand what I'm saying. You're not a stupid man, Andy. You're just afraid of the implications."

"Like what?"

"Like where are the constraints? Who sets the constraints?"

"Three-nothing, cocksuckers!" Andy yelled at the nonresponsive rival-team figurines.

"I see you guys are having a good time." They heard Lauren's voice. "Caleb will be here in five minutes. I hope you took the time to acquaint yourselves with his work."

Andy had. Earlier, Lauren had sent him and Misha an email with a list of Caleb's accomplishments as a director. Andy had also looked him up on IMDB database. The auteur's (Lauren insisted on calling him an auteur) website, bio, and deck were impressive. His films screened at festivals, and he won some awards, not that Andy had heard of them, but, hey, those were awards.

Caleb showed up half an hour later. He was young, maybe in his early thirties, bespectacled, with eyebrows slanted in an upward dome that gave his whole persona a look of cherubic innocence. He didn't apologize for keeping them waiting, and Andy thought that whatever this guy's skills were, they didn't extend to being able to read the room, to discern the balance of power. He was there to ask them to fund his next film, but he acted like he was doing them a favor. The auteur's nonchalance grated on Andy, as, in his own overstructured world, being late even five minutes was, at best, a mark of unseriousness.

Caleb plunged into an armchair in the corner and placed his skinny ankle in a beige suede shoe on top of his knee. He pressed his palms against each other, as if in prayer. His pitch was smooth.

"What I'm aiming for is a low-budget, high-impact sleeper hit," he said. "In recent years this has proved to be a winning formula. You might have heard of some indie horror movies made for a million dollars that brought in a hundred million at the box office. It could be a slasher film full of gore and not much plot, or it can be something subtler, with a story, more psychological horror."

"Okay," Andy said. "And what are you more interested in? As a director?"

"Personally, I prefer a psychological tale. It's actually cheaper to make because you won't have to deal with expensive props and CGI. There will be no severed heads." Caleb chuckled. "But it requires a solid script, which I'm already working on."

"What is it about?"

"It's like *One Flew Over the Cuckoo's Nest* but with elements of the surreal. It takes place in an asylum."

"I read parts of it. It's very dark," Lauren said excitedly and looked at Andy. "There are some bone-chilling moments and characters."

"Uh-huh," Andy said. "What's the appeal of horror? I mean, I was never a big fan myself."

"We are drawn to what we don't understand," Caleb replied. "We feel a certain thrill while swinging between the comfortable and the familiar and the unknown and horrifying. That's why horror movies are always a sure bet."

"Huh," Andy said, nodding. "And what do you think is the return potential there? Give or take."

"Like I mentioned earlier, we're talking about a possible home run of a thousand percent return if it ends up being a hit. But even by conservative estimates, I think it can end up being within five-*x*-to-ten-*x* range."

Under his breath, Misha mumbled to his drink: "Ten x and a thousand percent is the same thing."

"Films like these are festival darlings," Lauren said quickly. "And as producers, you'll get the red carpet treatment."

"This is wonderful, Lauren," Andy said and turned back to Caleb. "And how much equity are you trying to raise?"

"One-point-two, one-point-three million. We've already raised about half of that from multiple investors. In fifty to hundred-and-fifty thousand-dollar lots."

"Can we see the names of the investors?" Andy asked.

"If there's serious interest on your part, sure, this can be discussed in more detail," Caleb said carefully.

Misha, who had been quiet up to this point, cleared his throat. "Who is the perpetrator in your movie?"

"A very good question," Caleb said and smiled. "An evil force that operates via a little girl."

"Yeah, about that," Lauren said. "Could it be a boy?"

Caleb pressed his lips. "Lauren, I promise you, I'll find a role for Ashton in another movie. But in horror it has to be a girl," he said. "Look at all the classics. *The Exorcist, The Shining, The Ring.* They all feature little, pre-teenage girls as channels of evil. *Come play with us, Danny, forever and ever.* If those two were boys, no one would be scared. But the girls, they give us shivers."

"And why is that?" Misha said, rubbing his chin. "Why are boys not scary?" He gazed around the room, but everyone was quiet. "I think it's because we generally know how their minds work. The mind of a boy is pedestrian; his evils are boring and predictable: he is mean, greedy, bloodthirsty, and obsessed with hierarchy. We adults do not find any of this scary, because we understand where he's coming from. We are all operating in the same mutually under-stood, dominant social framework. But a little girl? What drives her? Nothing that would make sense in our adult world. She's interested in nature and ponies. The realm of nature and ponies is alien to us. Those residing in that realm are scary because we don't know how their mind works. Nature and ponies are signifiers of things that do not fit into our modern value system of money and profit. Like, do the girls from *The Shining* really care about their future careers or earning potential or meeting a nice guy?"

Lauren giggled, but Caleb and Andy were quiet.

"Because they don't speak the language that we speak, because they don't yet understand and don't really care about"—Misha made air quotes—"'how business is done, how the world works,' we realize that we can't reason with such a person and thus can't cure her pos-session. At least not until she hits thirteen. Then we can all exhale with relief and welcome her to our normal, real world."

Caleb listened to Misha, his ankle fidgeting, his palm on his jaw.

"This is what's scary about little girls," Misha continued. "With their irrational behavior they telegraph the existence of a world that operates with notions that don't produce profit or pleasure. She's a carrier of bad news, of this unprofitable sentiment that, implicitly, is a threat to our normal way of life. We find her more horrifying than a monster because we know what drives a monster—it needs our flesh or brain to survive; its behavior can be rationalized and thus harnessed. But a girl—who the fuck knows what's on her mind? She's on par, in her terror factor, with the goons from *Halloween* and *Friday the 13th*."

"Wow," Caleb said after a long pause. "What a profound analysis."

"That's not all," Misha said. "Notice how the films featuring the possessed girls never venture to explore this very mystical aspect of girlhood. Instead, the plot usually revolves around curing them of the evil ailment or sending them back to hell. We want to save the main protagonist—a rational adult. But there's never a plot where such a girl 'cures' an adult of his, shall we say, misconceptions."

Caleb took off his glasses and rubbed the bridge of his nose in silence.

Misha sighed. "You see, Caleb," he said. "I would give you the money. I'd fund your whole movie. It's not the money. It's that I think we have way too many movies that show us how things are instead of how things should be. We already know how depraved we are. You won't break any new ground with this narrative. We wish to know how we *should* live, and no one shows us that. I think that movies should be kind, even naïve, however preposterous that sounds. The movies of my childhood were like this. If it's a cautionary tale, people will be incapable of processing it as a cautionary tale. People are stupid. They don't have the mental toolkit to discern good from bad. By pinning malicious intent onto a little girl, we contribute to and perpetuate the misidentification of evil."

"A solid point," the young director said. "Except no one will watch a preaching movie. I mean, one can make those kinds of movies, but only after he'd made several hits and doesn't care to turn a profit."

"Yeah. So, I guess we're fucked in perpetuity," Misha said.

They parted ways by exchanging niceties and business cards.

"I guess we can cross Misha off as an investor," Lauren said when she and Andy got into a taxi. "What about you?"

"I don't know. I have to think about that. It's a high-risk project."

"You can put in fifty grand and forget about it and then the next thing you know it made a million dollars," Lauren said breezily.

"First, fifty grand is not peanuts. And second, that kind of return is not guaranteed. And third, your guy didn't seem like he appreciated us being there. He was half an hour late. One who asks for money can't be late."

"Artistic people have a different sense of time," she said.

"Not if they come to talk business. You're really into that guy, huh?" Andy teased her.

"Okay." Lauren took a deep breath. "He's on a festival panel where I submitted my short," she spilled.

"Ah, I see." Andy smiled, marveling at the dynamic at hand. "You're trying to buy his favor with my money. Very nice, Lauren."

"Don't be such a dick. What's a girl to do?"

"Don't you want to win on merit and not through outright bribery?"

"It's not bribery. It's a foothold. And are you trying to tell me that in your business you win on merit?"

"In my business …" He waved his hand. "Lauren, I think that all these titles that you're chasing—entrepreneur, filmmaker … You're spreading yourself too thin trying to impress somebody. Pick one thing and stick with it. Or just relax and enjoy life."

"Don't patronize me. I can do many things," Lauren huffed. "And I'm not doing it to impress anybody."

"But you can't excel at any of them."

"What do you mean by that?"

"You have a business. A pastry shop. It hasn't made a profit."

"Not everything has to be about profit."

"True, but not if it's a business. If it doesn't make a profit, it's not a business. It's a hobby. And you can't call yourself a businesswoman."

"You're just jealous."

"Why would I be jealous?"

"Like, who are you if not a trader?"

Andy almost choked.

"Like, what else can you do if you don't trade your stocks?" Lauren pressed, sensing a weakness.

Stocks, Andy thought in horror. She thinks I'm trading stocks.

"I do one thing, but I'm good at it," he shot back.

They spent the rest of the ride in silence.

Back at his place, Andy felt bad for needling her. He apologized and then verbally committed to giving Lauren the money for her next project. Lauren was lenient that night, and, as he climaxed, Andy thought that he, too, should try to be more tolerant toward her vanity and her illiteracy.

X: Madeline's Fears

Madeline was planning to stop by the Bedford Manor house during the week to pick up the rest of her personal things from the basement, and, when she asked Andy when would be a good time (which he interpreted to mean "when you're not there"), he replied "anytime" and made sure to be in the house for the occasion, taking a sick day from work.

Andy came down to the basement, a sprawling, alcove-shaped vault. When the house was built, the basement was designed to serve as an entertainment complex, with a six-seat movie theater, a pool table, a cigar nook, and a compact but well-stocked bar with a liquor shelf and a sink. He recalled the moment when he finally had enough money to begin having leisure. He was already in his late thirties. He still came to the office by 7:30 a.m.—an ingrained bond trader's habit, but he left work early, around 5 p.m. Even with time and money to spare, the leisure was still hard to come by. His hobby initiations were whimsical and frantic, and his interest in an activity waned quickly.

Today, the basement had become a museum of aborted aspirations. It was a testament to a life lived by spells of enthusiasm and indifference, manifested by the accumulated cache of expensive but now discarded accoutrements: skiing and diving equipment, a mountain bike, a Nordic Track elliptical machine. In the corner, the drum set that Andy had bought to practice for his sketch at the Street Bohemians party (and the only article in the room for which he still felt a gentle affinity) was now collecting dust. Behind the set, on the shelves, photos of Andy at various fundraisers with the New York governor and the Bedford Manor mayor stood next to Madeline's vast collection of equestrian trophies.

Madeline was already there. She had assembled a sheet of cardboard into a box and was picking up and wrapping her trophies one by one.

He sat on the stairs and watched her. How different was Madeline from the wives of his colleagues and friends. With growing awareness of imminent decay and irrelevancy, those women had coated their slow disintegration in desperate, theatrical intensity. They became more restive, pestilent with projects and invitations, loud and deliberate in their friendliness. Maybe it was Madeline's charmed, privileged youth, her sheltered maturity, and her eccentricities that spared her from the trauma of elbowing her way into society and from developing the brutal markers of the hustle. Her wrinkles were graceful, her face serene, her eyes knowing. She had secured a place from which she could display the equanimity that, in others, would be considered an admission of defeat. Her assured moves were the moves of a person who doesn't care about being watched, each action imbued not with coquettish suggestion but a clear, direct purpose—the result, perhaps, of a lifetime of commanding a large animal with a mind of its own.

He watched her for two minutes, hoping for small talk, admiring her ability to be immersed in a simple task. Madeline dusted off an acrylic deal toy—a heavy, glassy tombstone with engravings of the deal's details—and tossed it to Andy. He caught it and looked at the inscription: *$200,000,000. Senior Secured Credit Facility*. And below, in smaller letters: *Andy Sylvain. Senior Vice President.* It was a memento from the fateful transaction he closed eighteen years ago.

"You never got mad at me for leaving you in Montauk that time," he said. "Why?"

Madeline paused. "That time," she chortled. "You mean the wedding?"

"Yeah. Why did you let it simmer for all these years? Maybe if we had resolved it then …"

"And what would you have done?"

"Perhaps then we would have established a precedent."

"You mean you would not have gone on my mere say-so?" Madeline's voice chimed with feigned incredulousness.

"Possibly."

She took a small trophy from the shelf and held it in her hand, contemplating it for a few seconds, then wrapped the trophy in packing paper and put it in the box.

"You *wanted* to do it," she said. "You *wanted* to jump on that boat and have a blast and be the toast of the town. You wanted everyone to talk about you."

She paused and whooshed a strain of hair from her face.

"But I'm not mad at you for that. I'm not mad at you for anything. I'm not mad at all. You were young and ambitious. Young men need that kind of attention. I understand."

"Young men are the engine of progress," Andy said, feeling the urge to defend his younger self and his kin. "Even if they break the rules sometimes."

"And what progress are they the engine of?" Madeline asked with a puckish grin and acerbity in her tone, always an invitation for a verbal jousting.

"The kind that solves problems," he replied.

She looked at the Big Dog robot that was now consigned to a space behind the pool table. Its front and hind legs had been shoed into two pairs of ski boots by some anonymous prankster.

"What problem does this thing solve?" Madeline pointed at the robot.

"It's ... it's a taste of things to come. It shows us what's possible."

"What's possible did not receive proper scrutiny," Madeline said. "I'm suspicious of the young men's initiatives. They drag us along with them into a strange, chaotic world with no rules. I want to live in a world with a set of rules that cannot be broken." There was now apprehension in her voice.

"Ah, Madeline. Even when you were twenty-five you were already a reactionary," Andy said. "And now you're calcified in your backwardness."

"I'm tired of disruption," she said. "I'm tired of getting used to a thing that, just after a few years, is rendered obsolete by men who claim to be clever. They change their mind on a whim and then expect me to change my entire lifestyle according to that whim. They offer solutions to the problems I don't have while insisting that I have a problem."

She sealed the carton box with tape and moved on to the next one.

"They tell me that technology will save us, but they don't explain what it will save us from. Were we oppressed when we had a rotary phone? And how did a cell phone save us from that oppression?"

"Are you serious? It made us instantly connected!" Andy exclaimed.

Madeline rolled her eyes. "Connected so that we can exchange banalities."

"It's not the inventors' fault. They can't be held responsible for content."

"They should be. They failed to consider the risks."

Andy shook his head. "You're asking for the impossible, Madeline."

"I'm asking them to consider the side effects. And about those they have nothing to say. They just shrug it off."

"It's out of their jurisdiction," Andy said. He wondered how he found himself in the position of defending some nameless Silicon

Valley bros. What Madeline was saying wasn't meritless. Was this quibbling a part of his decades-long quest to understand her epistemology, or was he dissenting because an agreement here would create a complication in his conception of himself, his goals, his rationales?

"It's easy to do a thing," Madeline said. "It's much more difficult to not do something. Because no one will know what you didn't do. Action is easy. Restraint is difficult." She glanced at him as if she could read his thoughts.

"A man does what he has to do," he said. "There's a time for action and a time for restraint."

Madeline sealed the last box. Andy helped her carry the boxes up the stairs and to her car.

"I'll be traveling soon and will have some spare time to read," Andy said, not wanting to part on a sour note. "You think you could send a copy of your thesis my way?"

"I could," Madeline said and smiled. "But now that I think of it, perhaps it's better if you don't read it."

"What do you mean?"

Madeline shrugged. "There are things there that will clash with your frame of reference. Things that might scare you."

"Really? Now I want to read it."

She got into her car.

"Anyway, please send me a copy," he said.

Madeline drove away.

Andy went back to the basement. He sat on the stool behind the drum set. He blew the dust off the cymbals and tapped his fingers on the snare drum and looked around for the drumsticks.

He heard a knock on the doorframe above and saw Oleg peeking into the basement. Andy invited him to come in, and Oleg came down the stairs.

"She was mad about the robot?" Oleg asked, pointing with his thumb at the exit.

"She wasn't mad. Madeline is never mad. Just irritated," Andy said.

Oleg gazed around the room with awe. "This is a tremendous instrument," he said, zooming in on the drum set. "Can you play it?"

"I could. I need some practice," Andy said.

Oleg examined the shelves on the wall. "This is cool," he said, taking from a shelf a miniature replica of a Viking ship that Andy had brought back from a European vacation. "That's Viking."

"Yeah. I got it in Scandinavia a few years ago," Andy said.

"You know that the Vikings founded my hometown, Novgorod, back in the tenth century. We called them Varyags."

"How interesting. They were a great culture."

"Yes, great culture. Great warriors too." Oleg put the wooden trinket back on the shelf. "I wanted to talk to you about the paint. I think that your basement needs fresh paint. There are some cracks that need to be waterproofed. If you put the house on the market, it has to be in top shape. But here, look." Oleg scraped at a spot on the wall. "It's peeling off. It feels dated. And you need to change color. It should be mint green."

"You think? Okay. Give me a quote then," Andy said.

Oleg put his hands on his hips and observed the room with a businesslike squint. "It should be not more than two thousand dollars."

"And you'll take all this stuff out too?" Andy asked.

Oleg brightened. "Of course!" he said. "I take it out. Maybe something you don't need?"

Andy chortled at Oleg's suppressed excitement. "I guess I can get rid of a few things," he said.

Oleg sniffed and looked at the robot.

"You want it?" Andy asked.

"Yes," Oleg said. "But I don't have money right now. Maybe I can pay you in parts."

"You don't have to pay me. Just take it. It's yours."

A rapturous wave rolled over Oleg's face. "I pay you. You can't just give it away like this. In six months, I pay you."

"No, no. Just take it. I don't want to hear anything about money. Take it today. I want to clear this space."

Oleg came over to the Big Dog and patted it like it was a pet. "*He* will be in good hands," Oleg said. "I take care of *him*."

"Take the ski boots too. And the bike. In fact, take anything you like," Andy said.

Oleg stared at Andy like a startled child. "Drum too?" he asked.

"No," Andy said. "Leave the drums."

XI: New Mexico

Andy left New York three days before the start of the Las Vegas industry conference and flew to New Mexico to redeem the voucher that he won in the raffle at the Pierre Hotel party. He planned to chill at the meditation resort on the Indian reservation north of Taos, near the Colorado border, and then drive to Vegas via a scenic route.

A twelve-seat Mercedes Sprinter picked up Andy and several other resort attendees at the Albuquerque airport. Andy cautiously assessed the passengers. He saw mostly West Coast techies, creatures of a different world, with different truths stamped on their faces. They were former disruptors who now, in their maturity, sought entry into sainthood. Some had messianic beards, some were clean-shaven, but they all shared the bearing of someone on a spiritual slope from savvy to benevolent, aware of and already bored with their stealthy might, and now searching for peace. There were also, out of nowhere, two grinning Europeans in tight T-shirts with soccer club logos, cross-body man purses, wrinkly capri pants, and funny, thin-soled sneakers that no self-respecting American would be caught dead in. The Europeans were excited, like they were about to board a rollercoaster ride at Disneyland.

In the van, a thirtyish man in a plaid shirt asked Andy if this was his first time. After Andy nodded, the man told him, with the luminosity of a sect member, that this was his third visit and that he was thinking of selling his IT consulting business and making regular pilgrimages here.

"I think it's a great idea," Andy said languidly.

He stared out the window for the rest of the ride. As the van moved north and uphill, the flat vistas gradually transformed into hills, then into mountains, and the scarce desert vegetation turned to lush alpine forests. In two and a half hours, they rolled past the ranch-style gates of the resort at the foot of a green mountain and crawled the final half mile over a winding dirt road toward the main camp. They crossed a narrow bridge over a clean mountain brook that ran through the property, and Andy saw the living quarters—single- and double-occupancy log cabins, scattered among the aspens and spruces.

Andy's attention was briefly caught by a stone cairn on the side of the road that was fashioned into a sort of shrine with deer antlers resting on top of it. In front of the cairn stood a skinny, scruffy man in a Buddha pose, on one bent leg, holding the other in the air, with his arms spread like wings. He moved slowly, in what seemed like a deranged, improvised wushu routine. He bowed to the cryptic installation, then to a nearby tree, and then waved at the passing van.

Andy thought that if he saw this man on a street corner in New York, he'd hold his breath and pass him quickly and at a safe distance.

"He's staff," the plaid-shirted IT consultant whispered into Andy's ear. Seeing Andy's dismay, he added: "If you approach this with reason, you won't see the urgency, the application."

"Okay."

The resort's welcome hall was a spacious, tipi-shaped wooden lodge built on a foundation of rounded cemented boulders. The stone steps led to a wide porch and the main entrance, where an enormous copper gong was suspended from a sturdy crossbeam frame. Wind chimes dangled lazily over several rocking chairs. Inside the lodge, decorated with dream catchers and other Native American handicrafts, a stone wall with a large fireplace separated the lounge area from the reception desk. As Andy walked in, he smelled burning incense and a mix of aromatic oils.

In front of the fireplace, several people sat on the floor in a circle. They came from the same pool of white professionals as the ones who just arrived in the van, but their sandals and dreadlocks spoke of a spiritual journey that was on the brink of full enlightenment. They all listened to a man with a ponytail, who was now pontificating about "softening the ego boundaries that perpetuate the feeling of isolation."

Andy felt an uneasiness that reminded him of his broke years in college. He remembered feeling a similar dread when hanging out in the incense-filled dorm room of a hippie friend. There had been a sickening sense of exposure and instability in that room—not just financial instability, but poisonous mental aimlessness. Everything esoteric—the healing crystals, the soft shuffle of bead curtains, the beanbag chair as shapeless as his stoner friend's brain, had seemed like attributes of sloth and an almost deliberate, performative failure. There had been an absence of rigor, an abandonment of effort in that room. Ever since, every time he smelled the sweet, nauseous aroma of incense, he wondered how one could choose to wallow in such indolence and not want to go out and be a man and make money and have a decent, productive, prosperous life. That was how he ended up sharing a dorm room with Caldera. Caldera had seemed like a reasonable guy, impervious to the arcane.

The clerk behind the check-in counter, a red-haired middle-aged man in a Ralph Lauren polo business shirt who warmly introduced himself as Billy, gave Andy a release form to fill out. There were basic questions on the form about occupation, medical history, and emergency contacts. Andy paused over the Occupation line, then wrote "financial advisor." He checked all the boxes next to the medical conditions as "no." He listed Madeline as the emergency contact and gave the form back to the clerk.

"Oh, a colleague," Billy said after scanning it, delighted. "I was once a financial advisor. More on the accounting side though. They hired me here a few months ago, as no one knew how to manage the books at this place. Filling out forms and filing taxes and all. When I came, all the receipts were lying around the office; no one even bothered to enter them into the system. The accounting software they had was twenty years old."

Andy shook his head. "That's horrible."

"No one around here knows much about business," Billy said quietly, leaning over the counter. "They're all into mindfulness and all. Which is good, don't get me wrong. But someone has to manage it. Someone of sound mind and a good business sense."

"For sure. I hope they pay you well."

"Can't complain. But hey." He winked at Andy. "If you get tired of the food here, I can hook you up with a pretty good steak place."

"That's great to know, thank you," Andy said.

"Wonderful to have you here, Mr. Sylvain. You have any questions or concerns, you come to me," Billy said.

"Will do."

He got the keys to his cabin and walked out, passing by the assembly on the floor of the lodge. The ponytailed lecturer was now musing about "a return to a quantum foam, to a primordial goo, to vibrating muons."

I'll give it one day and then I'm outta here, Andy thought.

As he dragged his suitcase on the dirt path toward his cabin, he saw the cairn worshipper. The bum was now sitting on a large mossy boulder, barefoot, hugging his skinny knees with his arms. He gave Andy a gap-toothed smile.

"I see thee. Each stone is a soul. Each soul is a stone. Hail unto stone," the bum proclaimed.

"What?"

"I walk, I dance, I live magnificence. I speak of the mystical quantum. An innocence comes to me."

"That's great," Andy said. "But I gotta run. Nice meeting you."

"I see thee," the bum said, pointing a finger as Andy sped up toward his quarters.

* * *

The next morning, after breakfast of quinoa, baked yams, hummus, and chai tea, the newcomers lined up to enter a small tent behind the dining hall. Inside the tent on a folding chair sat an old man with the face of a dried prune, wrapped in a speckled wool poncho. On his head he wore an ornamental Native American feathered headdress. The resort staff tiptoed ceremoniously around him, bringing him hot tea and shushing the loud talk among the people outside the tent. Each visitor got summoned by the staff for a one-minute audience with the shaman. The shaman looked at people's faces, sometimes asked to hold their hands, rendered his judgment about their readiness, and sent them on their way.

Everyone in line got the verdict of "ready." When it was Andy's turn, the shaman examined him with a longer look, took his hand, and felt his pulse, gazing directly into his eyes. He shook his head and smacked his lips.

"Not ready," he said and waved him off.

A young female staffer nudged Andy away from the shaman.

"What does he mean?" Andy asked the young woman.

"This way, sir," she said, ushering Andy out of the tent.

"What does he mean I'm not ready?" he raised his voice.

"Don't worry, sir, it's not binding," the staffer told him. "It's merely an opinion."

Andy turned to the shaman and said: "Do you know what I do for a living?" He turned back to the staffer. "What a poseur. I bet he's not even real."

"It's merely ceremonial, sir. You will have the same experience as everybody else, I assure you."

"Not ready," Andy fumed, although his tone got softer. "I'm more ready than anybody here."

The resort's staff directed the guests inside the meditation room, a one-story pagoda-style structure the size of a basketball court, with large windows and parquet floors. A tanned fortyish man in cargo shorts and a beige, multipocketed safari shirt stood by the entrance.

"I'm Josh. I'm your guide for today," he greeted each entering guest with a calm, confident voice.

About two dozen mats were placed in rows on the room's floor. Each mat was accompanied by a plastic bucket and a folded blanket.

"Buckets?" one of the two Europeans lined up behind Andy asked, frowning.

"For contingency," Josh replied.

After all the participants were inside the room, Josh opened with a short introduction.

"Our session today is entry-level," he said. "You will receive a very mild dose of psylocibin tea. It's a natural psychedelic substance derived from a certain type of mushroom. All the doses are standard." He pointed at a row of cups lined up on the table. "For beginners, we usually use two, two and a half grams of the dried product. But it is your individual brain chemistry and your psychological predisposition that will determine your experience, despite all the doses being equal."

"What should we expect?" Andy asked. "On average?"

"A brief peek into what's possible," Josh said, smiling. "A mere cracking of the door. Some of you might experience slight nausea, some will have intense visuals, and some will feel nothing at all."

A bang of the gong outside marked the beginning of the ceremony. Through the window, Andy saw that it was the barefoot cairn bum who had issued the signal with the dramatic strike of a wooden hammer.

The cups on the table were filled with an oily yellowish liquid, like an extremely rich Japanese tea. People came to the table one by one, quickly drank the contents of their cup, and sat down at their designated mats.

"Don't smell it, just drink it in one gulp," Josh told Andy when it was his turn. Andy gulped it down. He lay down on the mat and stared at the ceiling, waiting for the effect. The two dorky Europeans lay beside him, in happy surrender. For a while, nothing happened. He saw the shaman enter the room. The shaman sat on the floor in the corner and began murmuring some simple, repetitive native verse, rocking back and forth.

Andy closed his eyes, and all he saw were floating multicolored circles, imprints of his pupils. He was hoping for a quicker high and was initially disappointed by an uneventful beginning. He thought of a large slate of economic data that was supposed to be released by the Bureau of Labor Statistics today and wondered about how the markets had reacted. In about forty-five minutes, he began to feel a slight tension in his chest, a tension borne more out of worry than out of any physical malfunction. He took short, nervous breaths. The worry grew, and he found himself resisting it.

Feeling nauseous, he gazed around the room. Everyone was lying down, quiet in the grips of a trip, although a lady on the far end was beginning to cry softly. He felt alone and insignificant and scared. There was now the presence of a disturbing force in the room. His self was diminishing, melting, and he was grasping for that self, unable to let go. Something was approaching, some awful inevitability, something breathtaking and revelatory, something that would hold a mirror, wicked in its honesty, up to him at the moment when he was most defenseless and least ready to look at it.

Now more people in the room began to cry. The shaman chanted louder and beat on his handheld tambourine. A wave of inexplicable horror washed over Andy. The sensation wasn't a drunken high. It wasn't a high at all. He was of sound mind, he knew where he was, what he was doing, and his senses weren't blurred or dulled. And it was the very soundness of the experience, its very clarity, that was the source of the horror. He knew the realness of it not with his enhanced imagination but with his whole being.

Andy's stomach contracted, and he reached for the bucket. Yellow bile gushed from his throat. He thought that the bile was sentient, evil. It was somehow connected to him, to his innards, through an invisible umbilical cord that was dragging him to a place where he did not want to be. Tears and mucus and drops of vomit covered his face.

"Enough. That's enough. Make it stop," he wailed.

"Ride it out, brother. Ride it out," came a comforting voice from nearby. Someone kneeled near him and put a warm blanket over him. "There's only one way through it. You're doing good. These are pangs of a new birth."

Two tawny, veiny hands extended him a cup of hot, milky liquid. He looked up and saw the cairn bum.

"It's chai," the bum said, holding the cup to his lips. "You're in for a soft landing. You did good."

"Fuck you," Andy said, wiping the vomit from his chin. "And fuck this place."

The horror subsided. Andy was still in a stupor, sitting on his mat, clinging to the blanket with both hands as if it were a shield. The sun was setting, and the shadows from the windows' grid moved slowly across the floor. Stupefied, Andy tracked that movement, as if those lines were clock hands and he was waiting for his turn to leave. Once one of those lines merged into a larger shadow, he stood up, wobbled toward the exit, and walked to his cabin. He drank two bottles of Fiji water from the mini fridge and went to sleep.

He rose early the next morning, packed, and went to check out. Billy the clerk met him with an understanding nod.

"Not your cup of tea, eh? Pardon the pun," he said.

"No."

"Do you happen to have a business card on you?" Billy asked after

Andy finalized his account and got the receipt. "In case I'm ever in New York. Never been but always meant to visit."

"Sure," Andy said and dug through his backpack's pocket. He found one card, wrinkly and worn out, dwelling there since the times when he still had to let people know who he was.

"Keating Mills. I've heard of them." Billy lifted his eyebrows, impressed. "A managing director. You know," he said, tapping Andy's card on the surface of the counter, "I overheard the staff talking about you. How the shaman dismissed you yesterday. They were laughing, but I said to myself: this is the real guy right there." He chuckled. "This is the guy with his feet firmly on the ground. Not sure how you ended up here, but hey." He shrugged. "Where to next?"

"Vegas," Andy exhaled.

Billy beamed with approval.

"Good for you."

XII: Vegas

Andy originally planned to take the slower scenic route to Las Vegas through the Navajo reservation, but now he wanted to get to civilization as soon as possible. He asked the resort driver to take him to a car rental place, and, as he left the camp, he texted Caldera that he would be in Vegas tonight.

How was psychonautics? Caldera texted back.

Never again, Andy replied. *No more downers.*

Lol.

No. No more downers. No more vibrating muons. No more self-inquiry. From now on, good times only. Sooner or later, every man comes to an understanding that uppers are ultimately a better drug. It's a drug of comfort and optimism. Perhaps Hunter S. Thompson was mistaken about the valence between psychedelics and Vegas, Andy thought. There's a vast disconnect of function. Psychedelics demand an inward gaze, while Vegas is exhibitionist and voyeuristic and *forgiving.*

He was happy to see Taos in the rearview mirror. He drove down to Albuquerque and got on Interstate 40 West for a daylong trip to Las Vegas.

After an hour of driving in silence, he scanned the FM radio. Gospel, Latin hits, insipid teen pop. And then a reprieve, a peppy, vibrating riff of AC/DC's "Thunderstruck"—a perfect song to dissolve the melancholy of a long drive, to forget the last few days. The lead singer's neurotic squeak tore through the humming monotony like a hissing stream of air escaping a compressed space. His tight and potent vocals had the unfocused raw energy of a pubescent boy, and Andy, grimacing and bobbing to the rhythm, began to sing along.

There's something about a good rock song. The lyrics have to be dumb and robust, the riff memorable, simple and bouncy like a trampoline. The delivery has to be visceral and unrehearsed. Yes, those boys scored some chicks and had a good time, and that's all there is to this song. It probably wouldn't fly today. Everything is too airbrushed and anesthetized now. But can anyone doubt the singer's sincerity? That's it. It's the sincerity. A lack of pretense. That's what makes a rock song. The sincerity negates the problematic sentiment. Earnestness, even when mistaken, is true art. It aims at the gut, not at the mind. That's why, decades later, the song still resonates.

Two hours later, near Gallup, New Mexico, he got off the highway and circled around town, searching for a place to eat. He longed for hearty, unpretentious diner fare. He wanted a place full of fifties-era mythology—with nickel fixtures, a jukebox, Elvis on the radio, and an aging showgirl waitress with bright red lipstick and a low, hoarse voice. At the edge of the desert, he saw a gas station, and across the dusty parking lot from it there was a diner—a rectangular box of drywall and chipped sidings. It was perfect.

Inside there were no nickel fixtures and no rockabilly mementos, but the waitress was spot on: hardship-marked late forties, once a beauty, tall and blond, who made a wrong turn at some crucial point in her life and never recovered. She smelled of cigarettes. Her name tag said Krystal. She brought him a giant menu cast in plastic and said, lethargically, that today's special was meatloaf.

"Well, when in Rome," Andy muttered.

"What?" the waitress asked.

"I'll have the meatloaf." Andy smiled at her.

A group of bikers walked in and proceeded to sit at the counter. The waitress seemed to know them. She hurried to pour them coffee into the thick-rimmed mugs. Andy stared at their wide backs. The bikers' leather jackets were engraved with short-fused, ill-tempered sentiments—"Don't tread on me," "I plead the second," "Come and take it"—as if expecting a confrontation, but their demeanor was reserved, and their talk quiet.

He thought of what his life would be like if he wasn't a bond trader. He imagined being in construction or trucking. He'd have a wife with a regular name that she'd spelled creatively—Alisyn or Kyrstyn. He'd treat her to shopping sprees at Kay Jewelers and romantic dinners at Ruth's Chris Steak House. He'd own a boat that he'd haul behind his truck. He'd probably have an opioid addiction, or, at the very least, an alcoholic one. But he would have no shortage of opportunities for adventure. He could just wake up one morning, kiss his wife goodbye, tell her "be back in a week," summon his comrades, and roll across the country.

He looked outside the diner's window at the arid, serene vastness. Sporadic Joshua trees covered the ochre hills under the enchanting pale blue sky. Out in the distance, a long freight train—Andy counted at least a hundred cars—was chugging along the tracks. He wanted to believe that some vagabonds were aboard. No, he would rather depict this kind of life than live it. He could've been a movie director. He would capture the nomadic life and the romanticism of the road. He would find the essence, the nuances, the redeeming qualities under the drifters' menacing front. He would use auteur techniques, like long shots and eerie music, a steel guitar wail that would let a spectator linger on the image, savor it.

He took a picture of the landscape and sent it to Joanna. *On my way to Vegas*, he captioned it. *See you there?*

He tried to eavesdrop on the bikers' conversation. He discerned words like "gold bullion" and "storage." Please be planning a bank robbery, he pleaded silently with them. Then he heard a lament about the "cost of carry," and a counterargument: "You'll thank me when the shit hits the fan."

He asked the waitress for the check and, after leaving a twenty-dollar tip on the table, went to the cashier to pay.

"Excuse me, gentlemen," he said to the bikers after paying his bill. "I couldn't help but overhear your conversation. Gold storage is a logistical nightmare. If this is your axe, you should look into shorting Treasuries through index. There's zero carry. And zero headache."

"Not if the markets cease to exist," the gold bar enthusiast said, turning to Andy.

"There will always be markets."

"Huh. An optimist," the biker said, and his buddies laughed. They returned to their meals.

Andy got back behind the wheel and drove for the rest of the day, stopping only for gas and bathroom breaks.

At sunset, Las Vegas showed on the horizon, its reflective surface popping up from hot, dusty nothingness. In a world that insisted on sliding into entropy, Las Vegas served as a barometer of civilization. The city's redundancies and excesses had a purpose: they provided a buttery layer of protection, a high-caloric buffer that softened the adversarial forces in the capital structure of life. Vegas vaccinated society from chaos by injecting a pre-approved amount of it into each of the visitors. It was a safety valve, a happy receptacle of society's detritus and vice, that halted the disintegration of humankind in the same way it held back the elements—the desert, the heat.

Scratch off all the tinsel and all the buffoonery, and underneath you'll find a soothing promise of stability. A smart portfolio manager would classify Las Vegas as a barbell trade, encompassing the most luxurious with the most plebeian and thus rendering the whole structure indestructible. Vegas tells an anxious tourist that he is safe, that everything will be all right. Before the entropy comes for penny slots and Cracker Barrel, it'd first have to come for East Coast bond traders, and conference crowds, and Cipriani. And that could never happen. For as long as a place like Vegas exists, the world can't possibly be collapsing.

Andy left his rental car with the Wynn Hotel and Casino valet and walked, rolling his suitcase, to the check-in desk. It was nice to hear people talk business again, he thought while standing in the VIP line that swarmed with fellow conference attendees. A group of suits in front of him were discussing credit spreads on CMBS and corporate bonds, and, hearing their chatter, he was overcome by a sense of warm comfort. He was back in his element.

The check-in clerk, a pretty and upbeat blonde, asked him whether he preferred the Strip view or the golf course view, and he said it didn't matter so long as the room was close to the elevator. She tinkered with her computer, leaned over to him, and whispered with a conspiratorial smile: "I think I can give you a free upgrade. Would a suite on a low floor be okay?"

"That would be perfect," Andy said and thought that this place almost exuded a gratitude for his presence. It felt like everybody was happy to see him. He could, of course, get white glove treatment in New York too, but that top-notch care, it seemed to him, always came with a reprobate look, with a gauging of his status, with an expectation of a generous tip. On the East Coast, they made him feel guilty. In Vegas, one could indulge oneself without the gnawing feeling of remorse.

He received his room key, and, as he walked toward the hotel elevators, he stumbled upon Doug Caldera, who was sitting at the blackjack table. Caldera, too, had a suitcase beside him. He had checked in earlier but on the way to his room had "stopped by a few tables," he said. Andy made Caldera take his winnings to the window and cash out. They took the elevator up to their suites.

"You want to party?" Caldera said and dangled a dime bag with a white substance in it.

"You just got here. How the fuck did you even have time to score that?"

"I flew private," Caldera said, shrugging.

Andy wanted to party. He wanted to erase the glimpses of the inexplicable. "Let's meet in your room and take it from there," he said.

"Thatta boy."

Andy took a quick shower, changed into comfortable jeans, a polo shirt, and a club jacket, and went up to Caldera's room. He snorted the cocaine that Caldera had prepared for him from the smooth surface of a glass table in the middle of the room. The icy jolt of the drug up his nostrils cleared his mind and electrified his body. The medicinal bitterness tickled his throat. He rubbed the rest of the powder on his gums and flexed his shoulders.

"Let's go," he said, grinding his teeth.

Downstairs they met Scotty. The three of them took a taxi to the nightclub at Caesar's Palace.

In the taxi, Scotty went into a tirade about his recent date and the pitfalls of dating in Manhattan. "So, I ask her, what does she like? And she's, like, what do you mean? And I'm, like, what do you like to do? And for some reason she got mad," Scotty ranted. "Did I ask something wrong? It's an innocent question."

"This is not a good question," Caldera replied. "This approach is actually quite stupid. She doesn't know what she likes. How old was she?"

"Twenty-one."

"Right. So she felt that this question was an attempt at mockery or a threat. What can she say? She's twenty-one. She doesn't have the money yet or the taste to like certain things. She hasn't lived long enough or seen a lot of things. She can't quite articulate it. People like her wait for you to make an offer. All you had to do is get tickets to whatever and tell her 'Here, darling, we are going.' Make it a statement of fact. And she'll be happy. Because if it's good, it's good; and if it's bad, she'll have someone to blame. You. Which is also good. You can have make-up sex afterwards."

"Huh," Scotty said.

"Believe me, I know what I'm talking about. I hooked Andy up with his current girlfriend. Tell him, Andy."

"He did."

The Strip was clogged with traffic and hordes of drunk, howling bachelors carrying two-foot-long beverages, and Caldera cursed the driver for not taking the faster route via the back road. They ditched the taxi and walked the rest of the way to Caesar's Palace, entering the casino through the Forum shops.

The club buzzed with conference types in casual dress who crowded out the regulars—the LA weekenders, the gym rats with gold neck chains, the tanned cabana boys with bleached hair—and occupied all the best booths around the dance floor. Some of the businessmen, having reached the optimal ratio of courage and carelessness, came down to the floor and bent themselves in angular moves before the flocks of young women in short, tight dresses who spiraled in smooth, sinuous waves.

The front row booths came with a minimum of twenty-five-hundred-dollar bottle service, the hostess with Cleopatra makeup informed them in a soothing, unassuming tone.

Caldera smiled gregariously at her. "We wouldn't have it any other way."

They followed the hostess to their table. Andy and Caldera sat down, but Scotty caught the beat and pranced, flapping his elbows like a chicken, toward the dance floor. He disappeared into the boiling lattice of bodies.

Two girls in their twenties passed by their table, and Caldera signaled to them to join him and Andy. The girls looked at him critically, and he stood up from the table and, overcoming the noise, screamed something emphatically into their ears. They briefly consulted each other, assessing Caldera and Andy, and then slid down into the booth.

Any conversation was impossible. The most that Andy could muster amid the deafening bass beats was to get the girls names—Cindy and Angela—and have them order whatever they liked on the menu. Under the quickly changing colors of the disco lights, the girls appeared to be older, their eyes and faces more mature than their attire and conduct suggested, and, for some reason, Andy found himself feeling sorry for them. If sitting here with two schmucks like him and Caldera was something that these women wanted, or worse, had to do, he'd rather not know about it. Andy's high wore off, and, now overcome by exhaustion, he looked forward to the moment when he could curl up in his bed, alone. By 1:00 a.m. he was nodding off. Caldera stirred him up by dropping an ice cube down his collar, to the delight of the girls.

It was around 1:30 a.m. when they exited the club, and Caldera suggested they all go to get some sushi. Andy excused himself by saying that he had to host a business panel tomorrow morning and wanted to get some sleep. The last thing he wanted to do now was entertain strangers.

"Boo," Caldera said. "You're so boring."

"It was a pleasure meeting you, ladies," Andy said, trying to assuage his departure by turning on his most charming mode. While Angela coquettishly allowed him to kiss her hand, Cindy's carefully curated face betrayed a sudden and unsettling awareness.

"Mr. Caldera here will take good care of you," Andy said and patted Caldera's back, extending his last energy on cheerful pleasantry.

In the taxi heading back to the Wynn he kept thinking about Cindy, hoping that it wasn't today, it wasn't just ten minutes ago that she understood her hustling days were coming to an end. He'd hate to be that guy.

XIII: Zombies, Fat Tails, and Teddy Bears

Andy messaged Caldera the next morning to find out how the rest of the night had gone. Caldera had a "wonderful time" with Angela, he texted back.

There was also a text from Joanna saying that she was flying in today and would be having cocktails at the Wynn lobby bar with some clients at around 5 p.m. She invited him to stop by.

The discussion panel, which Andy hosted that morning, wasn't a demanding affair. It was a routine gig he did every year at the request of conference organizers. The topics of discussion were loosely defined, allowing him an extemporaneous discourse on any dominating subject of the day. He could shift between a ten-thousand-foot macro view of the markets and the granular minutiae of a particular trade, usually a disastrous one. He considered his participation on the panel as dues that he had to pay forward to the new generation of players, and he tailored his analysis to a broad audience—newbies, analysts, middle-office staff looking for insight and a leg up.

Andy walked through the convention site, picking up vendors' swag—pens, keychains, coasters. Inside one bag, from a bond-pricing software company, he found a nice yellow baseball cap and a sports water bottle.

The 8 a.m. panel was sparsely attended. The sleepy attendees, with Styrofoam coffee cups in their hands, filed into the conference room and tiptoed along the rows of chairs, arranging themselves in a considerate checkered pattern. They were mostly industry rookies and back-office staff who sought to move up the ranks, to establish a connection with a well-placed, well-timed comment or question, yet unaware that all the consequential networking happened later in the day, at parties and dinners.

Andy stepped on the stage, where three chairs encircled a low table. Three bottles of Poland Spring water sat on top of the table. A moderator clad in a tweed jacket, editor of the industry's newsletter, shook Andy's hand. The second speaker on the stage, already propped up in the chair, was Zeke Klein, a panel regular and Andy's unreliable partner in performance art. Andy and Klein exchanged smiles and hand waves.

The moderator opened the discussion with a pressing issue. "Large mutual funds have been selling out of their big bond positions and yet didn't cause any major move down. Why do you think this is happening?"

This was the theme on which Andy had engaged various audiences countless times before, and he jumped right in. "Fed balance sheet expansion is driving today's asset valuations," he said. "An individual bond's characteristics really play a secondary role, or no role at all, in the current environment. So, every small fund out there has to see what the macro guys are doing and follow them to this new reality."

"Uh-huh," the moderator said. "And under what circumstances do you think a reversal can happen?"

"Those guys are heavily regulated and overcapitalized by now," Klein cut in before Andy could answer. "It's hard for me to imagine those positions unravelling like they did seven years ago. It's time to admit that we're in a different zeitgeist. We have different problems: yield drought, not across-the-board defaults."

For the next hour they talked more about how the Fed was a seven-hundred-pound gorilla in the room, and how the paradigm had shifted, and how one should not try to be a hero and get squashed like a bug on the windshield of monetary policy.

"Everything is so sterilized and choreographed that the real danger in today's markets is that we will all be bored to death," Andy concluded.

A young man in the front row raised a hand. The man reminded Andy of a young Scotty: the same high-voltage, first-year-analyst energy, the same round face free of doubt. Andy made a quick mental taxonomy: a private-equity bro. He pointed at him.

"Do you have any thoughts on alternative investment strategies?" the young man asked.

"Can you be more specific?" Andy said.

"Like something that deals with low-probability, high-impact events. For example, zombie-apocalypse insurance."

Andy and Zeke Klein looked at each other. Andy thought that the young man was being clever.

"You want to buy zombie insurance or sell it?" Andy indulged him with a chortle. "'Cause if you're a buyer, I'll sell it to you."

"I mean, I can buy it on the cheap, right? And then if it doesn't happen, I lost a minimum, but if it does happen, imagine the payoff."

There was something odd about the young man's tone and delivery. He didn't sound like he was in on the joke. He sounded like he didn't think it was a joke at all.

"Huh." Andy rubbed his chin, pretending to humor the questioner. "Two things. One, you're watching too many zombie movies. And two, describe to me what a credit event would look like in your case."

Andy expected some reaction from the audience, but the room remained eerily quiet.

"The credit event doesn't have to happen," the man said, maintaining his cool. "What matters is how those contracts behave under the broad public perceptions. If the public is scared, the contracts will rise in value, and you can then sell them at a profit."

Andy allowed for that explanation. At least the bro wasn't insane. He simply wanted to create an investment instrument without any sort of underlying fundamentals and engage in the good ol' pump-and-dump. Crude and potentially criminal, but understandable.

"But on the other hand," the man said, "think of all the frozen viruses that could thaw out from the permafrost and infect us. There's a non-zero chance that it could happen."

"There's a non-zero chance that some virus could be thawed out, yeah," Klein injected. "But there's zero chance that that virus will turn people into actual zombies."

"Just because we haven't seen it before doesn't mean it can't happen," the young man countered.

The room was quiet. Andy closed his eyes and rubbed the bridge of his nose. Something was definitely off with this guy. Andy noticed that the guy's biceps and deltoids, bulging from under his shirt, pointed at an inordinate amount of time and effort devoted to appearance—the time that should've been spent reading the tape and massaging spreadsheets and data, and that his wrists were covered in tattoos. No, this was not a private equity bro. And it's not even because PE wouldn't hire the guy. It's that *he* would find any PE firm to be too straitlaced for his style. This man sought a brawl, he soaked in attention, and he welcomed the public scorn.

"What shop are you with?" Andy asked.

"I run my own fund," he said with a challenge in his voice.

"Right."

This was a new strain of hubris—an anarchic, nihilistic, unempirical strain Andy had not seen before. There was time and place for rule-breaking and for bold new ideas, but not like this. This wasn't Scotty's pliable idiocy that could be supervised and guided. This was something deliberately structureless and pugilistic. This one was impervious to mockery and to scientific rigor and took his reflexive contrarianism as a point of pride. Andy though of Madeline and her fear of young men.

"How would you falsify your theory?" Klein asked the young man.

"What do you mean?"

"Think of something that has to happen in order for your theory to *not* be true."

Andy turned to Klein. "He doesn't understand what you are talking about. He doesn't think on that level," he said, and then looked at the bro. "Prove that zombies exist."

"No one can prove that they don't."

The moderator tried to defuse the situation with an awkward hand clap and an "All right, why don't we move on to closing remarks," but Andy felt that this malignant growth had to be nipped in the bud.

Normally, Andy had an all-purpose spiel ready for any sort of closing remarks. For a younger audience, he'd usually segue into advice mode, talking about how one shouldn't expect any handholding and gold stars, how one should focus on the task at hand and do it well and do it quietly. He'd talk about how senior management is not interested in your opinions, because you don't yet know enough to have an opinion. How your boss doesn't care about the peculiar quirks of your personality, or your witty remarks—the kind that you think are witty, or that your favorite book is *The Art of War.* How the only thing that matters is the job that you do and the manner in which you do it.

But these were the words for a different world, a world of rules and merit, not of chaos and bluster.

"What you're saying is idiotic," was all that Andy could muster now.

"I'm simply asking questions to which you have no answers."

"All right," the moderator said loudly. "We have about two minutes left." He looked at his watch. "Maybe one more question from the audience? And then some closing thoughts?"

There were no more questions.

"Are you familiar with the concept of Occam's razor?" Klein said, addressing the audience while Andy was gathering his thoughts. "You walk in the park, and you see a man with a child. What is more likely? That it is a father taking his child for a stroll? Or that the man is a part of a clandestine child-trafficking ring?"

"There's always a possibility for the latter," the bro said.

"This is a classic case," Klein said with a tired voice. "Confusing possibility and probability." He looked at the young man. "You shouldn't be allowed anywhere near the managing of people's money."

The moderator cleared his throat. "Thank you all for coming!" he yelled.

The room began to disperse.

"If this is a sample of what's coming, God help us!" Klein said to Andy, sounding resigned. Andy waited for Klein to say anything about that time at the Bohemians party when Klein had stood him up, so that he could dismiss it with a joke, but Klein seemed to have forgotten all about it.

"The funny thing is," Andy said. "if that guy had ever set his foot onto the real trading floor, if he spent a year or two in the trenches, he would become immune to conspiracies. He'd know what's what. He would learn that what can be done with P&L and leverage is much grander than what any conspiracy can conjure up."

"Yeah," Klein said. "If only we could mandate an investment-banking internship for everyone, college grad or not, the world would be a better place."

Some attendees made a beeline toward the stage with questions and resumes, and Klein lingered. Andy made a quick exit through the side door, checking his phone to avoid eye-contact and solicitations.

* * *

At five o'clock, Andy came down the hotel elevators and walked onto the casino floor. He steered around the rows of slots on the way to the bar. The machines, hosting emotionless, glassy-eyed patrons, jingled intermittently in idle cheer. Old Asian ladies, clutching their expensive purses, and doughy white retirees in Hawaiian shirts were pounding on the slot buttons in a trance. They seemed to be plugged into a blissful, anesthetizing ether, from which they didn't want to emerge. Even a big win wouldn't break their stupor; there was no jumping and screaming for joy, like in the promotional videos. The winner would wait for a floor assistant with a businesslike detachment. These people are not here to win, Andy thought. They're here to deliver themselves from life.

When he entered the lobby bar and proceeded to the counter, he saw Joanna standing next to two suits. She was in the middle of telling a riveting story to the men, who listened and eyed her lasciviously.

"… and he once tried to sell me a residual piece that probably had one or two months of cashflows left on it at, like, twenty handle! What balls on that guy!" Joanna huffed, and the men laughed. "You guys are laughing, but that fuck made a hundred million dollars last year. On that kind of level, up in the stratosphere, one doesn't have to be that smart. Just … shameless." She sipped her wine.

"Andy!" she exclaimed when she saw him. "Good to see you."

Andy was relieved that he was spared from inserting himself unsolicited into their conversation. Joanna introduced Andy to her companions, and Andy remembered one of them, Todd, from a bad trade that had been in the news a few years ago. Todd's claim to a brief infamy was that he had a long position in Icelandic banks back in 2008 and lost tons of money when Iceland let its banks fail and bailed out the people instead, and yet here he was, alive and grinning and still doing business.

"What are you working on these days, Andy?" Todd asked.

"Reading Fed's tea leaves," Andy replied.

Todd grinned. "I think we'll see some moves rather soon," he said.

"I think the current yield environment is unsustainable. We could be in three-four-percent territory within a year."

Andy gave Todd an I-don't-entirely-disagree head wobble.

"Thinking of shorting some debt," Todd continued.

"If this is your axe, you should short the long end of the curve. Long-duration bonds will be hit the hardest," Andy said.

"I had the exact same idea!" Todd said. "Great minds think alike."

Joanna looked away, suppressing a giggle.

Andy asked Joanna, as casually as he could, about her plans for the evening, and she told him that she had to attend a client dinner.

"And after?" Andy asked.

"If there's an afterparty, I'll text you," she said.

After Joanna and her clients left, Andy sat down at a blackjack table. He bought in for a thousand dollars, betting fifty dollars a hand, and spent the next hour winning, then losing, then winning again. He drank scotch and generously tipped the waitress and the dealer. Then he caught a hot streak and increased his bet size to a hundred.

A lanky man of indefinite age sat down next to him at the table. The man wore an embroidered Western-style shirt and a cowboy hat decorated with turquoise stones. His cowboy ankle boots were encrusted with silver tips and rhinestones in the back of the heels. Neither the boots nor the shirt nor the hat appeared to have ever been near any cattle or inside a corral, or to have seen any dust or manure. Andy noticed that the man's hands were delicate and pale, with the long fingers of a pianist.

A pit boss accompanied the stranger, carrying a plastic chip rack with five stacks on it, each stack consisting of twenty white hundred-dollar chips. The pit boss took each stack out of the rack and put it on the table in front of the man.

"Ten thousand dollars," the pit boss announced to the dealer and left.

The stranger flirted with the waitress and ordered two drinks— whiskey sour for himself and "a refill for the gentleman" as he eyed Andy.

He placed a bet, a stack of five white chips.

"Are you here for the investment conference?" the man asked Andy.

"No," Andy lied, looking down at his stack.

Andy hoped that his curt reply would impress on the stranger that he was in no mood to socialize.

"I'm thinking of shorting Treasuries." The man continued with the chitchat, ignoring Andy's antisocial posture. He waited for Andy's answer and, receiving none, continued. "I think that it is a political trade." He shuffled his chips. "But then everything is political these days."

"For that trade to work, you have to have deep pockets and patience, and your timing has to be flawless," Andy finally said.

"I have both," the man replied and exchanged glances with the dealer.

The dealer dealt each of them a hand. Andy got a jack and an eight and glided his hand over his two cards. The stranger tapped on the table with his jack and deuce. The dealer gave him a six, and he stood. The dealer dealt himself a king and a nine and scooped both of their stacks. The stranger placed another five-hundred-dollar bet on the green felt square.

"I'm Zebulon." The man extended his hand to Andy.

Andy didn't shake it, not even out of rudeness, but out of his inability to place this odd man on a social map. But he gave his name in response and then asked, "And what do you do, Zebulon?"

"I, uh, I study fat tails," he said in a soft lilt and stared at Andy with fishy, watery, old man's eyes.

"Yeah, well, you got the wrong guy, Zebulon."

Zebulon looked at the dealer and smiled, unfazed by Andy's hostility. The waitress brought their drinks. Zebulon tossed a hundred-dollar chip to the dealer, asking to break it, and the dealer shipped back two green chips and ten red chips. Zebulon tipped the waitress with two red chips.

"What I mean by fat tails is the state of chaos that permeates every-thing," Zebulon said. He picked the straw out of his drink and stood it vertically on the table, holding it with his thumb and index finger. "If you look at this straw as an axis, everything around it is symmetrical. Each point of the table is at the exact same distance from the straw's spherical perspective." He drew a virtual circle around the straw with his left hand. "But symmetry is a highly unstable state." Zebulon removed his fingers, and the straw fell on its side. "Symmetry always breaks. When symmetry breaks, chaos ensues. Our world," he said, gazing around the casino, "is the result of the quantum symmetry breaking. So, chaos, then, is the natural state of things. Statisticians call it fat tails."

"Yeah," Andy said. "Wow. You should have a TED Talk."

"TED talks are a scam," Zebulon scoffed. "A feel-good crutch for people whose epistemology is broken."

Andy was trying and failing to assign this man into a workable cat-egory. A mad scientist? A rich eccentric? An oddly enlightened tech entrepreneur? "Broken in what way?"

Zebulon took a gulp from his glass. "They fail to see what every business model—and I mean every business model—comes down to: smart people barricading themselves in certainty. And shifting the risk onto the rubes. That's all there's to it." He sighed. "It's obscene what we're allowed to do."

The dealer scooped another stack of white chips from Zebulon. Andy won a hand, and the dealer moved chips his way, matching his stack.

"That's why you're here," Andy said.

"Yes," Zebulon said. "The only place where risk still exists." From his depleted stack, Zebulon tossed a fifty-dollar chip to the dealer, and the dealer caught it.

"Thank you, Zeb," the dealer said, knocking with the chip against the metal edge of the table.

"You're my man." Zebulon stood up. "It was a pleasure talking to you," he said to Andy, picking up his chip rack.

"Likewise," Andy replied.

"Who is that guy?" Andy asked the dealer as Zebulon walked away.

"That's Red Zeb."

"I mean who is he?"

"He founded some tech company. Cybersecurity or something. Then he sold it for a billion dollars."

Andy typed *Zebulon* and *cybersecurity* into a search engine on his phone. Multiple results and headlines displayed: "CopyFace software firm sold for $900 million," "Deep fake software founder Zebulon Redgrave distances himself from his creation," and "Rogue billionaire behind unionization push."

"Huh," Andy said and looked at the dealer. The dealer leaned closer and whispered:

"He had some falling out with the guys who bought it, and—" he stopped midsentence and shifted his mode back to a rote focus at the sight of an approaching floor manager.

"A billionaire commie," Andy marveled.

"Yep," said the dealer's lips.

Around ten o'clock, Andy put his chips into the rack, tipped the dealer twenty-five dollars and took his winnings to the window. He returned to the bar, where the industry meet-and-greet had been churning earlier in the evening but had by now fizzled out. Two drunk commiserating analysts with bad haircuts and in square-toed Kenneth Cole shoes were all that remained of the event. Andy sat on a stool. The surface of the polished wood counter was sticky, but he leaned on it anyway and ordered a scotch. He couldn't get Zebulon out of his mind. He kept thinking of how one had to be either extremely rich or borderline crazy to reach out to another person, a complete stranger, without the prerequisite introduction and niceties, without an interlude, and expect reciprocity. If Andy tried to pull a trick like this with anyone in his orbit, if he tried to strike an extemporaneous, non-obliging conversation, if he'd mentioned philosophy or quantum physics, his motivations would be found suspect, his angles would be scrutinized. "Cut the bullshit, Andy," he would most likely hear from his interlocutor. "What are you trying to say?" How can people even talk to each other anymore?

"I'm attracted to men with low T." He heard a purr behind him.

He turned around and saw Joanna. She was looking at him, smiling. Was she the one who had said it? There was no other woman nearby.

"Oh?" he said after a baffled pause. His heart pounded.

"They're like teddy bears. Cozy and soft. I like that."

He gulped and looked around the room. "I'm not a ... I don't ...," he mewled, wincing.

"Oh, stop it. That's a compliment!" Joanna sat on a stool next to him. Her eyes glistened with mischief. "Low testosterone compels one to be interesting. Interesting is better than muscles."

She leaned forward, put a hand on his knee, and stared directly into his eyes with a brazen smirk. There could be no maneuvering out of this zugzwang.

He thought that he didn't even have the chance to properly object. Her come-on was so direct and left no wiggle room. He had no standing to reject her assessment of him. What was he going to say— I'm a triathlete?—and have her burst out into that haughty, bubbly, head-turning laughter of hers?

Ten minutes later they were in her hotel suite, undressing hastily, and in five more minutes it was over. They lay in bed, staring at the glimmering, pulsating Strip outside the room's glass wall.

"I'm nowhere near as interesting as Misha," Andy said.

Joanna patted his stomach. "You don't brood," she said. "You're just a normal guy."

How much she had changed. She used to be earnest and asked the kind of questions smart people quickly learn not to ask. Now she'd matured enough to concern herself with the way things were, not the way they ought to be. He searched her face for even a hint of discontent, for traces of that youthful clarity.

"I remember when you first came to the desk," he said. "You were so serious and high-strung. Always asking questions that made others uncomfortable. Questions that could undermine our entire business model." He chortled. "You acted like it was some kind of case study in business school, and you were fishing for an A. Raising your hand and all. It was so cute."

"Oh yeah? I didn't have to fish for my As. I earned them." Joanna feigned offense.

"And what's become of you now."

"What's become of me?"

"You're a shark."

"And that's bad?"

"No. I mean it in a good sense."

He yawned and dozed off. Joanna worked on her laptop for another hour, occasionally tugging him to quell his snoring.

In the morning they made love again, this time lazy and slow, and then ordered a decadent breakfast, with champagne and caviar. An hour later, a starched steward rolled the breakfast trolley into the suite, assembled it into a bedside table, and covered it with a crisp white tablecloth and jingling silverware. He lifted the brass coverings from the plates one by one, describing the delicacies. Poached eggs, lox, and bagels. A side of truffle fries. On a round crystal plate, a gastronomic cornerstone—a tablespoon dab of Beluga caviar—was plunked in the center, with the radial sections garnished with finely chopped onions, capers, crème fraiche, and mini-blintzes. Two tiny mother-of-pearl spoons accompanied the lavish spread.

The steward opened the champagne bottle and poured its auspicious contents masterfully into two flute glasses. "Enjoy," he said and, after asking whether they would be needing anything else, retreated from the room.

"Ah, I feel like I could eat a bison," Andy said, constructing himself a New York-style layered pyramid of cream cheese, lox, capers, and onions on top of a sliced bagel. Joanna scooped a dash of caviar, put it on a blintz, and ate it in one bite.

"This is heaven," she said.

"Mm-mm," Andy concurred.

Between bites, Andy told Joanna about his adventures of the last few days, refashioning the most horrific moments into a dark comedy. He told her about the shaman, and about the bad trip, and about the billionaire gay socialist cowboy who tried to hit on him at the blackjack table. Joanna listened and laughed.

"And yesterday during the panel, there was this one guy who wanted to buy zombie-apocalypse insurance. In all seriousness. Reminded me of Scotty, too. Remember Scotty?" Andy said. "We are being replaced by idiots. What's the world coming to?"

"There always were and there always will be stupid people," Joanna said. "We can't do anything about it, only to correctly navigate their stupidity."

"Yeah." Andy sighed.

Joanna poured orange juice into her champagne, and the concoction hissed and bubbled, almost spilling out of the glass. "You still have that CW position that you wanted a quote on?" she asked after sipping her mimosa.

"Yes. Why?"

"From what I can tell—and you didn't hear it from me—there's a bunch of guys trying to buy protection on CW bonds in size. Don't know what their axe is, but that's what I'm hearing. Just some color I have. Hope that helps."

"Huh. What guys?"

"Some activist guys." She stared at him.

"At nine points up front?" Andy scoffed.

Joanna didn't share in his amusement. "Andy," she said. "I just don't want you to get caught with your pants down. That trade sounds like something you can't unwind quickly. If it ever comes to that."

"I appreciate the intel," Andy said. "But frankly, I plan to ride it out to maturity. Concordia Walden has solid credit, solid balance sheet. Those guys have a powerful lobby."

Joanna chewed on a French fry. "What I mean to say is that in this case it's not the market default that you should be worrying about," she said. "It's the manufactured default. I know guys, aggressive guys, out there who are looking to expand into that niche. CW could be a prime candidate for that. It's barely traded, and things could get very opaque. Just saying."

Andy sighed. He stared wistfully at the colorful, solicitous pixels of the digital billboard outside the window that cascaded from an image of a red racing car into the naked arched back of a Bally's showgirl. "There's no room for sportsmanship anymore."

"Sportsmanship!" Joanna exclaimed. "What are you, an aristocrat?"

"I'm old enough to remember the times when skills and craft were important," Andy said. "Now it's just thuggery."

"It's not illegal." Joanna cringed. "People look for yield, they can't find it. And then they get … creative." She pressed her lips in an apologetic frown.

How astute she is, Andy thought.

"Let's stop with the business talk for now. It's too frustrating," he said, stretching on his back, putting his hands under his head.

"Okay, teddy bear," Joanna said and patted him on his belly. "We can talk about something else."

"Who would you be if you weren't in this business?" Andy asked.

"I once wanted to be a journalist," Joanna said.

"I like that. I think you'd make a good journalist. You're impervious to bullshit," he said. "My daughter is like that. She reminds me of you."

Joanna smiled. "How sweet. And you?" she asked. "What would you be?"

"I don't know. Maybe a movie director," Andy said. "But it wasn't an option. I had to make money. Perhaps after I retire."

Joanna refilled her glass with the rest of the champagne. "You know," she said, "I thought about it once. And I concluded that being in this racket for too long alters you in irredeemable ways. You can only make art if you possess a certain naivete. But we know too much. We've seen too many things."

"Yeah." Andy sighed. "It's like we're paralyzed with 'why bother.' There's no getting out of this."

"Let's not be morbid. Many people would like to be us," Joanna said and finished her drink.

They stayed in bed through the entire afternoon, coming down to the convention center at around 6 p.m. for the closing cocktail hour. They flew back to New York that same night on separate flights.

XIV: Summer Doldrums

Lauren was in Istanbul, busy assembling a local film crew for her refugees documentary. Her Instagram was jammed with pictures of herself in a wide-brimmed hat and a silk scarf, strolling through the bazaar, gazing at frescoes at Hagia Sophia, kneeling next to the city's famous stray cats in rustic cobblestone alleys. When, several days later, she traveled to the refugee camps, near Gaziantep—a long, arduous trip that she also documented meticulously—her fashion choices became more muted and the images somber. Her wardrobe featured a military-style jacket, badass leather pants and thick-soled, rugged boots, all bought at Barneys on a pre-trip shopping spree that Andy financed, and now, at the camps, with a dramatic backdrop of tents, dirt, smiling children, and crying women, she posed for pictures wearily, holding her professional full-frame Sony camera as if it were a discharged bazooka. "What a brave woman" was the overwhelming sentiment in the comment section under her posts, with emojis of hearts and fist bumps.

There were problems with the local crew, who asked for more money when they got to the location, and the American staff—the cinematographer and the two production assistants—wanted better security, health insurance, and union wages.

"Everybody is now making movies on Syrian refugees. There are more film crews here than refugees," Lauren complained to Andy on the phone. "There's a deluge of refugee docs on the film-festival circuit right now. It's just not worth it." On her Instagram, she wrote cryptically, "Voices of the dispossessed that needed to be heard got silenced by bureaucracy," and the project was over.

Lauren asked Andy to meet her at JFK Airport, and he told her he'd send a car service to pick her up. Lauren's West Village apartment was now in contract, and she had yet to close on her new one, a two-bedroom on the Upper East Side, so, being between apartments, she asked Andy if she could stay with him, and he said, "Of course, love." She arrived at Andy's apartment with several large suitcases filled with Middle Eastern trophies and mementos—scarves, hats, dresses, a sheepskin jacket, and boxes of film equipment. She said she was too jetlagged and went straight to bed. Andy was relieved to be spared both the conversation and the intimacy. He wanted to get out of the house, and, as he was preparing to go for a jog, he got a text from Caldera, asking him to meet at his tennis club nearby.

When Andy showed up at the club, Caldera was sitting at the empty lobby bar, dressed in a dandy white tennis outfit with a retro elastic headband that slid upward from his forehead and now sat on top of his head like a crown. There was a shot glass in front of him that a bow-tied bartender was filling up with top-shelf tequila. The bartender gave Andy a welcoming and pleading glance.

Andy patted Caldera on the back and sat on the barstool next to him.

"Oh, you made it," Caldera slurred. He downed the shot and motioned to the bartender for another. "You know, Andy, the thing is, guys like us—you and me—we have it," Caldera said.

In Caldera's voice, Andy sensed a hint of the apprehension and urgency of a sober man who had been hit, in a drunken delirium, by a sudden flurry of frightful but as yet unarticulated revelations.

"If I had to do it all over again, I'd go into the Marines. Serve. Show my grit. Get into a fight, like a real fight. Get some scars." Caldera clenched his fist and shook it. "We have what it takes," he bellowed and pounded the bar counter. "But no one summons us. No great force out there calling us for duty. There's no prompt from above. The only scar I have is from a removed appendix. The only people who appreciate what I do are assholes. And you know what?" Caldera wrapped his arm around Andy's shoulder, slumping and breathing into his face with drunken fumes. "We can't handle it. We're rolling like billiard balls, ceded to inertia. Taking comfort in moving forward, away from boredom and irrelevance. Busy with"— Caldera gazed around the empty room—"forestalling the encroaching decay."

Andy looked at the bartender and made a time-out sign with his hands. "We'll call the Peace Corps tomorrow," he said. "What did you want to talk about?"

"I, uh, got some investors that want to meet you," Caldera said. "Some Arabs!" He shouted the last word, either trying to impress this fact on Andy or, more likely, because of a loosened, unsteady command of his vocals.

"Why do they want to meet me?"

Caldera looked at him strangely. He opened his mouth and vomited all over Andy.

Andy called a car service and, holding Caldera by his elbow, shoved him into the limo. He gave the driver a twenty-dollar bill and told him to get Caldera home safely.

"Affirmative, sir," the limo driver replied.

In his soiled clothes, Andy walked back to his apartment, trying and failing to decipher Caldera's behavior. At home, Lauren was deeply asleep, and, not wanting to wake her up, he took a shower and went to sleep in Ava's bedroom.

* * *

Two days later, Caldera called him up at work.

"Sorry about the other day," he said, sounding upbeat.

"You got home okay?" Andy asked.

"Yeah. So, you coming over today?"

"Where?"

"What do you mean where? To meet with the Dubai guys. They're looking to place two billion. Just to start. I thought you might be interested."

"We are not really taking any new clients," Andy said. "I have trouble placing what I have."

"I thought maybe you wanted to branch out." Caldera sounded undeterred.

"Why would I want to branch out?"

"Look. Just come over and meet with them. Do me a favor. They're here in my office. Don't make me look bad."

Andy told Scotty that he was going to a doctor's appointment and would be back in an hour. Caldera's office was located several blocks north from Keating Mills, normally a leisurely eight-minute stroll. But a sudden, frothy New York shower that struck in the middle of the late summer afternoon lunch hour and turned the scorched city into a steam room kept Andy stranded under sidewalk construction scaffolds for about ten minutes, until he, failing to hail a cab, surrendered to the nearby simmering dark mouth of a subway station.

Andy sprinted down the stairs and, after tinkering with the Metrocard vending machine, winged through the turnstiles and onto the train. He exhaled, relieved to have made it, but immediately regretted his haste: the train car was full, and the air-conditioning wasn't working. The smell of fresh and stale sweat permeated the crowded space. Andy squeezed his way to grab a metal pole, grateful that he would be getting off at the next stop.

The train screeched and slowed down, then came to a complete stop in the middle of the tunnel. The vent windows were open, but no air was coming through. Andy huffed in frustration and looked around, searching for solidarity with the passengers, but no one reacted. The commuters sat and stood stoically, playing with their phones or staring mid-distance in resigned stupor. An elderly woman with a fidgety child fanned herself with a children's book. A subdued rhythmic upbeat sound of merengue percussions coming from the headphones of a day laborer, who napped leaning against the train doors, provided the odd soundtrack to an eerily quiet car. A streak of sweat rolled down Andy's back. Fifteen minutes that seemed like eons passed in stifling silence.

"What the hell are they doing out there?" Andy groaned. His complaint landed flat. Some passengers glanced at him but quickly retreated to their subterranean meditations.

"I don't get it. How do you let them get away with this, people? How do you just let it slide? You gotta stop being sheep. Where's your civic spirit?" Andy poured out, unnerved by the passengers' meekness.

"Is this your first time on the train, man?" asked a bearded brother with a hard hat under his elbow.

"Shut the fuck up!" someone shouted in a peeved Long Island accent from the other end of the car. The floodgate had opened. A chorus of pent-up frustration was now coming at Andy from all sides.

"What the fuck do you want us to do?"

"Take a helicopter, white boy."

Andy shut up. He felt nauseous and thought he was going to faint, when the train finally jolted, squeaked, and began its excruciating crawl toward the station. The crowd fell silent again and returned to their somnolent commuting routines.

"You look like you've been through the wringer," Caldera greeted a soaked, disheveled Andy in his office's downstairs lobby ten minutes later.

"Have you been on the subway lately?"

"What am I, a masochist?" Caldera giggled nervously. He flashed his badge to the building's security as they went through the turnstiles to the elevator lobby. "Anyway, long story short, they're from Dubai," Caldera briefed Andy in the elevator on the way up. "Some minor royalty. Young and loaded. Looking to place about two billion in the US. Just to start."

"That's great."

"Are you interested?"

"Like I said, I'm not really looking to expand at the moment."

Caldera rolled his eyes in exasperation. "Everyone is always looking to expand. Just meet with them. Throw some ideas at them."

"What about you? Why don't you take them?"

"I'm giving you a first look, as a personal favor."

The Arabs were young, barely out of puberty. Two of them couldn't even shave properly, while the third one sported a thin, dandy moustache. They wore western suits and kaffiyeh. They sat around a large conference-room table, swiveling in their chairs, drinking Coca-Cola out of vintage glass bottles.

After a brief introduction, the mustached man sized Andy up with a tired look. "What is your investing philosophy?" he asked.

A spoiled, entitled brat, Andy thought. An impatient smile bent his lips. "It depends on many factors," he said. "One being the size of the investment."

"We are looking to invest two billion dollars," the young man said with a satisfied swagger.

"Uh-huh." Andy rubbed his chin. "And what kind of yield are you looking for?"

"High single digits. Ten percent would be ideal."

A clueless one too, Andy thought. He could barely hide his condescension. "In the current environment, there are no instruments that can absorb this amount of capital and yield ten percent," Andy said. "One would have to be leveraged to get even a five-percent return.

Now, two billion dollars is an enormous sum, and the opportunities for its placement are rather limited."

"What about special situations?"

"Special situations are mostly odd lots. They come and go randomly. There's no systemic market there," Andy said.

"Can a special situation be created?" the youngest of the three men asked and looked at Caldera. "You said something about event-driven funds."

Ignorant, obnoxious pups with money, Andy thought. They think they can just swoop in here, with bags of cash, and have us "create" a special situation for them.

"Maybe in the Emirates. But here there are rules," he said and noticed a subtle smirk on one of the princeling's lips. "And even if a special situation comes up, at most you'll be able to place ten-twenty million. At most."

The men were quiet for a few seconds, then exchanged some words in Arabic.

"Are there any opportunities in real estate?" one asked.

"If you're looking to purchase real estate then I'm the wrong guy. I'm not a broker." Andy smiled.

Caldera coughed nervously. "Would you like more refreshments, gentlemen?" he asked and, before getting any answer, rushed out of the room. Seconds later, Andy's phone pinged with a text message: *wtf r u doing?*

"Excuse me," Andy said to the young Emiratis and walked out.

Caldera was right outside. His face was red. He gestured Andy to move away from the conference-room door. "What the fuck are you doing?" he whispered loudly.

"What? I'm not lying to them. I tell it like it is. It's hard to get a yield," Andy said.

"They're practically giving you the money," Caldera squeezed through his teeth. "But not only do you come here looking like a bum, you insult them too. These are delicate men."

"It's just not the kind of money I want to take, and these are not the kind of guys I want to report to, if you know what I mean. They play by different rules. Why the fuck did you bring them to me?"

"You don't understand what I'm trying to do for you here." Caldera chopped air with his hands in an attempt to impress on Andy the importance of his point. "It's a big favor I'm doing for you. I could've brought them to some other guy. Don't you wanna branch out?"

"Why would I want to branch out?"

"You know. From what I can tell, things are kinda slow at Keating Mills."

"What makes you say that?"

"Just a feeling that I get, that's all." Caldera shrugged.

"Yeah. Your feeling is wrong. I don't want to have to answer the phone every time those guys call me for updates and explain my strategies to them. What do they know?"

"You're a fool," Caldera said. He waved his hand in frustration and walked away.

The rain had stopped, and Andy walked back to his office. The crowds of professionals swarmed around him, all on a mission, all operating on the same mental frequency, all marching with the same speed and bee-like agility. Normally, Andy would enter this flow like an old pro, assuming the mutually agreed-upon pace, mindful of thousands of other small pedestrian courtesies, but now, immersed in analyzing Caldera's angle, he slowed down. A young man with a brown paper bag in his hand almost bumped into him, yelling "Watch it!' and, at a pedestrian crossing, a taxi braked before him, giving a long, angry beep. He stopped at a corner and texted *Can I stop by tonight?* to Joanna. He waited for her response for a few seconds and, without getting one, put the phone in his pocket and resumed his stroll.

When Andy shuffled back to his desk, he spotted Sandeep, the IT consultant, chatting with Scotty. Sandeep talked and Scotty imitated busyness, staring at his computer screens. When Scotty saw Andy, he gave him a "Please rid me of this fool" look, but Andy glanced indifferently over both of them and proceeded to his seat.

Sandeep abandoned Scotty and tiptoed toward Andy's desk with a wide smile. "Hi, Andy," Sandeep said. "How are you? I wanted to check if you had a chance to look at my resume."

How situationally unaware this man is, Andy thought, annoyed. Andy remembered how Sandeep once gave him an ugly, unsolicited awareness—that an immigrant, a person of color like him, could be laughing at the expense of *our* Blacks! And who does he think *he* is? White? Where's the solidarity? Does he really think this is the way to build a career in this country?

"I did," Andy said, rubbing his upper lip. "You're a very smart guy, Sandeep."

"Thank you. Do you think there could be a role for me on your desk?"

Andy tapped his fingers on the desk's surface. "You see, the thing is, you have to be a bit dumb to be a trader," Andy said. "Because you're such a smart guy, you will have a tendency to overthink, to consider too many variables, which is not necessarily bad, but you'll make yourself paralyzed at the most pivotal moment, at the moment that requires decisive action. You'll be running all these clever scenarios in your head when all you have to do is pick up the phone and ask for a bid and hit it. It requires a certain mental disposition."

"And you don't think I have it?"

That horrible accent of his, Andy thought. Those blurred, sticky *t*'s and *d*'s like his mouth is full of watery oatmeal. That misplaced sense of superiority. Does he seriously think he'd do well on the trading desk? "No."

"May I ask why?"

The nerve on this guy. "You have to make assessments with incomplete information," Andy said calmly. "Getting the market color right is like reading the room correctly. There are currents and undercurrents that, I don't think, you're capable of detecting."

Sandeep listened with his chin tensing. He had played it all by the book yet was denied the promised outcome. Over and over, he'd been told by business coaches, by self-help books, by career seminars, that ambition is good, that initiative will be rewarded, that one should ask, and one would receive. There were men, powerful men like Andy, who would be well served by his potential but who stubbornly refused to acknowledge it.

"I've read a lot of books on trading and investing," Sandeep said. "Like the *Reminiscences of a Stock Operator*."

Why does he have to humiliate himself like this? "That's great. But you can't read the room," Andy cut him off. "You don't have to try to impress me with the books you read. These are not the books I'm impressed with. Somebody told you that this is what traders read, and you took them at their word. Guess what? They gave you bad advice. Traders don't read shit. They read the tape."

Andy sounded irritated. He knew his tirade was brusque, but he felt like it needed to be said.

Sandeep was quiet.

"Look." Andy softened his tone. "You write brilliant code, you find the bugs, and that's where we need you."

This wasn't something that he wanted to spend an ounce of his mental energy on anymore. He was saved by a blinking light on his turret.

"Excuse me," Andy said and turned away. On the phone was Lauren, asking him what he wanted for dinner. He said he didn't care.

After work, Andy walked home slowly, checking his phone for a message from Joanna. Finally, he got a text: *I'm busy tonight. Can I take a rain check?* He replied *Sure*, and slouched back to his apartment. Lauren was waiting for him. She had ordered pizza and was eating it, sitting in her pajamas at the kitchen island, scrolling through her Instagram.

"I missed a trend," she said when Andy walked in. "I was about six months too late."

"What's trendy now?" Andy asked.

"Appalachia. Poor white trash," Lauren said with the tone that fashion-centric women use to describe the next season's collection. "Look." She showed him pictures of a poorly dressed, overweight white woman with a trailer-park backdrop on her phone. "Think of the kind of stories that could be told. This is happening in our own backyard, and no one talks about it."

Andy carefully suggested that, if she were to dive into a new project focusing on social and political themes, she should change her profile picture, currently a sultry, duck-lipped portrait with an exposed shoulder, into something more professional.

"You're either Dorothea Lange or a sexy vixen, but you can't be both," he said.

Lauren pouted quietly, and he was puzzled by her silence.

"Dorothea Lange was a photographer who took that famous picture of a migrant woman," he explained carefully.

"Yeah, I know. These are different times though. A woman can be many things," she said, annoyed.

"Lauren," he said. "I just don't want you to look ridiculous. You come across as if you're trying too hard. It's not a good look."

"How many followers do you have? Three? I have thirty thousand," she responded. There could be no recourse to that argument.

Neither of them was in the mood that night. Andy went to sleep in Ava's bedroom.

XV: Gradually, Then Suddenly

The next morning, Pinkus summoned Andy to his office for what Andy thought was a weekly debriefing. Andy stopped by the coffee machine and, while staring at the whizzing drip, compiled in his head some bullet points to discuss: spreads, macro trends, monetary outlook.

Pinkus was moody.

"Where do you have CW marked?" he asked Andy with an irritable twitch in his voice.

"Three-fifty over. Why?"

Pinkus poked the finger at his Bloomberg screen. "They're paying points upfront to buy those contracts," he said. "Why would they do that? They're not idiots. Markets cannot be that anomalous without being exploited."

"People overpay for all kinds of things."

"I don't know. It just doesn't feel right. What's our value at risk?"

"The worst-case scenario," Andy said. "Two million."

"On a fifty-million-dollar position?"

"Yes."

"So less than five percent. Those guys can run the same scenario and see that paying nine points upfront doesn't make any sense. And yet that's what they do. Did you run any stress-tests? Jump to default?"

"I did. But what you're talking about would be a six-sigma event."

"Uh-huh," Pinkus said, squeezing his stress ball. "And what's our loss then?"

Andy sighed. "About eighty percent of the orig. But like I said. There's less than a point-zero-zero-zero-one-percent chance of that happening. The bonds are current. They're cashflowing."

"Yeah," Pinkus said. "I hope you realize that if one loses that kind of money, one can lose the platform."

"I understand."

Pinkus bounced in his chair and looked out the window. "Andy. Have you ever wondered why I'm not retired?"

Andy shrugged. "You felt … defenestrated?"

Andy's attempt at humor went unnoticed. Pinkus scratched his chin. "There is emptiness out there. Outside of this"—he spread his arms, gazing around his office—"everything is stale. You buy a race car, travel to every country in the world, you buy pieces of art. You give money to some kids with cancer or whatever. And yet it all tastes like cardboard after a while. The game is the one true thing that keeps a man whole. It is the only thing that matters. I'll be doing this till the day I die."

Andy was silent.

Pinkus shook his head. "Andy." He sighed. "I'm just trying to help both of us. You understand? It is this wholeness that I'm trying to preserve."

Andy went back to his desk. There was a voicemail from Joanna on his desk phone. She asked him if he could stop by her place tonight. She sounded jumpy and worrisome.

At her apartment later that day, Joanna met him dressed in

sweatpants and a stretchy sweater. Without any greetings, she led him to the kitchen and offered him tea.

"Did you talk to Caldera?" she asked.

"Why, yes."

"So what are you going to do?"

"About the Arabs?"

"What? No. About CW."

"What do you mean?"

"Andy." She sighed. "Remember in Vegas I told you about the possibility of a manufactured default? Remember that? I thought you would follow up on that."

"You told me that someone was buying the contracts, yeah."

She closed her eyes and rubbed her temples. "How should I say this?" With her tone veering between apology for being the bearer of bad news and disbelief at Andy's obliviousness, Joanna proceeded to tell him that Caldera's fund had been purchasing credit-default contracts on Concordia-Walden bonds. "They're trying to manufacture default for CW. If they succeed, you're going to lose, like, seventy percent of your principal. If you're lucky. I thought you were able to, you know, put two and two together."

Andy ran his hand over his forehead. "Was he buying it from you?"

"No," she said. "I knew someone was buying it, but that it was Caldera's shop I only learned yesterday."

"That cocksucker. It's criminal what he's trying to do."

"Andy, there's no recourse against it. There are no laws against it. It's been done before. They've done it before."

What Joanna was describing wasn't news to Andy. He'd read about it but dismissed it as an aberration. To acknowledge this creeping new reality would mean to concede that his effort and excellence and the skills that took a lifetime to build and perfect were now useless. The default was not a result of some unfavorable market conditions or of the company's mismanagement—factors that he could have foreseen and mitigated. The default was a result of some blunt, dumb force that deliberately removed all risk element from the game. The bonds defaulted because the party that would benefit from their defaulting could just go and make it happen. He felt like a dinosaur, clinging to the old genteel ways, to the disappearing civility.

"If this is how it's done, then does objective reality even exist?" he asked ruefully.

"No one is talking about objective reality!" Joanna seethed. "We're talking about a brawl!"

Joanna's phone rang. She picked it up. "Yes, he's here," she said grimly and looked at Andy. "Okay." She hung up.

"Caldera is downstairs. He wants to talk to you."

Caldera was sitting on a bench in a park across the street. Without saying anything, Andy sat down on the other end of the bench and stared at the pedestrians.

"Look. It's just business," Caldera said. "What should have I done? Quit in protest?"

"You could've just told me," Andy said through his teeth.

"What good would that do? You wouldn't have had the time to do anything about it anyway. You couldn't unwind in time. Plus, the word would get out. I would become unhireable. Penniless. Who's going to put my kids through college?"

"You don't have any kids."

"That's not the point. The point is, you didn't buy those bonds, and I didn't buy those contracts, and here we are, tasked with cleaning someone else's mess. Life is cruel."

"Whoa. Hold on. You're cutting yourself way too much slack. You are not exactly a detached party here. There's a deliberate plot to make CW fail. It doesn't just happen on its own in a vacuum. And it is your side that's forcing the credit event. And you're smack right in the fucking middle of it."

"Am I supposed to cover for you and risk my whole career? This is what you're essentially asking." Caldera threw his hands in the air. "It's a management decision. I'm a lowly peon. I do what I'm told.

You know how this is. And, unlike you, I don't have eight figures stashed in some Bermuda LLC to say 'fuck it' to it all. I have to hustle till my dying day. You can walk away if you want to. I can't."

Caldera fell quiet, watching a woman with a stroller pass by.

"I tried to help you," he said.

"You did? When?"

"The Arabs! The Arabs were your way out. You were too fucking thick to realize that. You could've started a serious fund with that money. Float them for a couple of years, then close the shop. Say 'Sorry, guys, bad investment climate' and return the damn money. Then start your own fucking shop with, like, fifty million of your own money. Be your own boss. Write your own meal ticket." Caldera scoffed and looked away.

Andy quietly watched an old man walking a small dog. "This isn't about money."

"Yes it is, Andy. Everything is about money."

* * *

The next day, as Andy approached his desk, Scotty and the other traders were unusually quiet, pretending to be hard at work but eyeing him discreetly. There were several messages from financial reporters in his voicemail and in his email. Why the hell do they want a comment from me, Andy thought. Always seeking a comment from someone who got fucked, not from the one doing the fucking.

With an incinerating silent stare from his glass office, Pinkus bade Andy to come by.

"I told you to unwind it, remember?" Pinkus said when Andy walked in and closed the door behind him as softly as he could.

Beneath Pinkus's wary tone Andy sensed a smoldering rage.

"We talked about it. You asked me what the risks were, and we left it at that," Andy said.

"I specifically remember telling you to take it off." Pinkus shook his index finger.

"That's not how I remember it."

"Really? What did you need to hear from me? An official 'go'? A memo?"

Andy closed his eyes for a moment, as there was a pounding in his temples. He felt dizzy but composed himself. "Look. Unwinding it would trigger the exact same result," he said calmly. "That's what happens when a position is illiquid."

"You had months to do it," Pinkus cried. "A million at a time."

"Look." Andy shook his head. "This whole CW situation is a perversion. It's an insult to one's intelligence. What they're doing is not technically legal." He pointed his finger in a random direction. "It's borderline felonious."

"I don't give a shit what you call it," Pinkus hissed. "You had one job."

Andy was stupefied; his temples pulsated.

Pinkus stared out the window. "And that clown Caldera. Some friends you have. If I didn't know you better, I'd suspect some foul play. But I'm not that guy." He turned and looked at Andy with a loaded gaze. With resigned posture, Andy leaned against the glass door.

"All right," Pinkus exhaled. "Get your shit together, think about what you're going to do next."

"Am I fired?"

"Fired? Ha-ha. No. That would be too easy." Pinkus shuffled papers on his desk. "But I do think you should take a couple of weeks off. Or maybe a month. We'll put it down as a leave of absence."

Andy stood for a few more silent seconds, as if waiting for further instructions.

Pinkus stretched an invisible accordion with his irritated hands. "What? Anything else?"

"No," Andy said dismally and walked out.

"What's up?" Scotty whispered, tilting his head toward Pinkus's office.

"He wants me to take some time off," Andy said, plunging to his seat.

"Like, coupla days?"

"More like coupla weeks."

"Okay. So what do we do in the meantime?"

"You report to Pinkus while I'm gone."

"You got it," Scotty said. "And what about CW?"

Andy sniffed. "There will now be a price-discovery process for deliverables. You should make a bid list for the CW inventory and put it out. I think you can get some good levels, especially on the later vintages. We can probably salvage twenty-thirty points, maybe more. And keep me updated."

"Got it," Scotty said.

After cleaning up his desk and sending several administrative emails, Andy stepped outside into the stream of the Midtown lunch hour. As he idled on the sidewalk, human currents swerved around him, issuing annoyed scoffs and headshakes, but he ignored them. He replayed the conversation with Pinkus in his mind. He thought of the rush that had run through his bones when he asked Pinkus if he was fired, and he zeroed in on the nature of that rush. It wasn't one of fear, but of hope, an odd jolt of hope that Pinkus would fire him on the spot. It would be a legitimate, even welcome resolution. It would liberate him. But he was denied that liberation.

He didn't want to go to his apartment, where Lauren would surely meet him with questions to which he had no answers. Aimlessly he shuffled up Fifth Avenue to a public park near 53rd Street, a tiny oasis with a waterfall, surrounded by the concrete towers, and sat on a chair, watching the office workers eat their lunches.

His phone rang. It was Misha.

"What's up," Misha said and, before Andy could reply, bellowed: "Yeah, I know. I called your desk, and Scotty told me you're on vacation."

"Eh."

"You wanna come over?"

"Sure."

* * *

Misha's Tribeca penthouse occupied the entire floor of a red-brick industrial building, with the elevator doors opening right into the sprawling living loft. The loft was sparsely furnished. In the middle of the room stood an extra-long tufted leather sofa and two leather armchairs. On the exposed brick sidewalls hung austere black-and-white photography. At the far end of the loft was a dividing wall, behind which, on the left, was a shiny, brassy kitchen, and, on the right, an entrance to Misha's bedroom. The dividing wall also served as a giant movie screen: a white pull-down projector sheet covered it side to side and top to bottom.

An invisible film projector, hidden skillfully near the ceiling, played nonstop a compilation of grainy art-house reels. There was no sound. The muted images on the screen seemed to serve, like the art on the walls, a decorative purpose.

Along the left side wall a chaotic amateur artist's studio was set up with easels, tubes of paint, and framed canvasses. The paintings were portraits, of unknown men and of one recurring image of a woman, in various stages of completion, but all carrying some significance in the painter's mind. It seemed that the artist, no doubt Misha himself, was in a hurry, starting outlines and loose renderings, then dropping them, moving on to the next, then coming back. There were sketches, hastily put on the canvas with a pencil to be fleshed out later; there were almost finished pieces, and all the faces featured only two expressions: repose and pain. All the men were in pain, their open mouths bent downward, their eyes lifted to the skies in silent pleadings; the woman was depicted in calm contemplation.

"I'm experimenting," Misha said and covered some of the near-completed works with a cloth. "My therapist recommended it."

"Who is the woman?" Andy asked.

"A composite image. Not anyone concrete."

Misha told Andy to make himself at home. Andy sunk into the soft, deep armchair and stared at the screen, where a man and a woman strolled, carefree, along a Parisian boulevard. He found himself enjoying the visuals without caring at all about the plot or the dialogue. There was ease and lightness about that young couple. He didn't know the name of the movie, but he figured it was some 1960s French New Wave.

"Knowing you, I'd expect Tarkovsky," Andy said.

"That would be too on the nose," Misha replied and smiled. "Although it does have Stalker programmed in there. It plays randomly." He rubbed his palms nervously. "I'd offer you a drink, but I got rid of all the alcohol supplies in the house."

"I'll take a soda," Andy said.

Misha brought two Diet Cokes. He sat on the windowsill, slid the window frame open, and lit a cigarette. He opened his can, took a sip, and stared at Andy.

"I don't want to talk about it," Andy said.

"Did Pinkus let you go?"

"He told me to take some time off."

"That's good."

"I'd go to Cancun for a month. But"—Andy sighed—"I'd have to come up with a good-enough excuse for Lauren. So that she doesn't hop along. I don't think I can handle her for that long."

"If you want to disappear for a month, without questions and without consequences, there are ways," Misha said.

"Oh?"

"There's this place upstate. It's pricey though."

"What do you call pricey?"

"A hundred and fifty thousand dollars."

"For one month?"

"Yeah."

"What do they do there? Massage your balls with truffle oil?"

"It's like a special place. They operate by referral only. They call it a wellness center, but really it's just a glorified rehab. They tailor their programs to each individual. Lots of Street people, VCs, hedgies who have a mental breakdown go there. Politicians looking for a clean slate. You pay for discretion."

"I'm not a junkie though."

"You don't have to be. I know people who go there once a year just to chill. Or to network. It's like Mandarin Oriental meets Aspen Institute but in a camplike setting."

"Is this where you went?" Andy asked, remembering that Misha had disappeared from everyone's radar for a time after quitting his job.

"Yeah," Misha said after a brief hesitation.

"And?"

"I quit drinking," Misha said and dragged on the cigarette.

"Let's say I go there. I'd still have to come up with a story for Lauren. And for Madeline, for that matter."

"Tell them the truth. You had a bad trade. You need a break."

Misha brought a laptop from his bedroom and typed a long address in the browser window. The web page that appeared was blank except for a brief statement and two links—to an email address and to an online questionnaire. The statement said:

Inquiries about programs, treatments, and prices should be requested via email only. In your inquiry, please mention the name of the person who referred you.

Andy filled out an online questionnaire and put Misha's name as a reference. "Did you have a personalized treatment?" he asked.

"Yeah," Misha said. "There's a bunch of additional bells and whistles you can choose from once you get there."

"Like what?"

"Like a special diet. For example, medieval peasant: bread and milk, cheese and wine. Also, a vast selection of intellectual pursuits. I picked an immersive course on Romanticism. You know, Goethe and stuff." He paused. "They try to make a better man out of you."

"Ambitious, aren't they?"

XVI: At the Wellness Center

A ndy put a full deposit for the wellness program into an escrow, using his business expense account. After Andy's application got approved, Misha drove him to the retreat, hidden deep in the Catskill Mountains. He dropped him off in front of the wellness center's main building. A bellhop helped Andy with his luggage and explained to him how to get to the administrator's office for registration and other formalities.

"See you in a month," Andy said to Misha.

"Next time I see you, you'll be a different man," Misha replied and drove off.

The center's main building had two sprawling wings: administrative and residential. The cafeteria and the staff offices occupied the administrative wing's first and second floors, respectively. The residential wing consisted of study rooms on the first floor and the patients' quarters—studio apartments—on the second floor. On the way to the administrator's office, Andy passed the entrance to the cafeteria, where, pinned to a corkboard, was a schedule of today's lectures and seminars. He glanced at the topics. They ranged from philosophy to literature to quantum physics. So far so good, he thought.

The door of the administrator's office was open. Andy walked in and saw a woman in her sixties, tall, heavyset, with a grandmotherly stature. Her face was lively, with penetrating eyes behind thick-rimmed glasses. Her gray hair was cropped in a short crew cut, and she wore an impeccably tailored double-breasted pantsuit. On a windowsill behind her desk Andy saw the pictures of her much younger self in a military uniform, with Colin Powell, and, in a business suit, with Paul Volcker. Framed on the wall were the degrees from West Point and the NYU Stern School of Business.

"Welcome, Mr. Sylvain," she said and invited him to sit down. "You can address me as Ms. Cooke." She opened a drawer and pulled out a paper folder. "We're happy to have you here," she said, sifting through the pages in the folder.

"Look, I just need to unwind for a month, that's all," Andy said.

Ms. Cooke looked at him with warm, quiet understanding. "Many of our clients come here with the same sentiment."

"Uh-hum."

"They are the people who make decisions all day. But when it comes to their own well-being, they often don't know what they need."

"And you do?"

"Yes," Ms. Cooke said matter-of-factly. "You've come to the right place. I see that one of our alumni, Mikhail, made a recommendation. Very well. You're lucky to have him as a friend."

"I don't know what you guys did to him, but he can't land a steady a job now," Andy said with a smirk. "And his girlfriend left him."

"We have different metrics of success," Ms. Cooke said.

"Oh."

She slid two pieces of paper across her desk toward Andy. "We require everybody to sign a non-disclosure agreement. The privacy of our clients is our utmost priority. And by signing this contract, you're committing yourself to a monthlong stay. Your presence here is voluntary, and you're free to leave at any moment, but your fee is nonrefundable."

Andy scanned the documents. "I can go to, like, Scottsdale for a fraction of the price," he muttered, signing the papers. "Or I can just go live with tweakers under a bridge. For free."

If Andy had looked up, he would have seen Ms. Cooke regarding him with pity. "No, Mr. Sylvain. You can't."

A staff member, a Hispanic man in his forties with shiny black hair pulled into a bun, clad in a light green uniform that resembled part medical scrubs, part chef's coat, walked in.

"Please show Mr. Sylvain around the campus, Luis. Thank you," Ms. Cooke said.

Luis led Andy to the storage room at the end of the hallway of the administrative wing. The storage-room attendant, a rotund fortyish bespectacled Black lady in a blue uniform, exuding the stern official-dom of a postal worker, took Andy's phone away and put it in a plastic bag. She gave him a form to fill out, and, to Andy's careful inquiry about when could he have the phone back, replied in a practiced monotone: "You'll have the option to use it once a day for fifteen minutes after breakfast."

"What if there's an emergency?"

The woman lifted her eyes and looked at Andy with puzzlement. "Our facilities are well-equipped and well-staffed with specialists to deal with all kinds of emergencies."

"I mean, if there's one on the outside."

She took off her glasses and stared at him. "Mr. Sylvain. If there's an office-related emergency, it will have to be dealt with without you. If there's a family emergency, we will know about it and will inform you. And if you plan to use your phone to seek out emergencies, I'd question the wisdom of it. You'd be sabotaging your own progress."

The presumptuousness, Andy thought.

"Yes, ma'am," he said.

"But if you absolutely must," she said, "we have a phone booth on the premises that can be used for such purposes." From her drawer she pulled out a map of the campus and, with a felt pen, circled a black dot at a remote end, behind the service buildings.

"I'll hold on to this," Andy said, grabbing the map.

"Of course," she said.

From the storage room, Luis escorted Andy to the rehabilitation center's infirmary—a standalone red-brick building. A prim, un-smiling nurse in a starched lab coat measured Andy's height (5'10"), weight (181), and blood pressure (120/82).

"Not bad, huh," Andy said and looked at the nurse to see if she was equally impressed.

The nurse was indifferent. With a quick and painless prick to his arm, she took a blood sample from his vein.

"What's the blood sample for?" Andy asked.

"For diet considerations," the nurse replied. "Among other things."

She put the vial with the collected blood into a tube container on her desk and sat down, writing something on a sheet of paper attached to the clipboard.

"As long as you guys don't lobotomize me." Andy giggled, rolling down his sleeve. "And, just so we're clear, I do not consent to taking any pills."

The nurse gave him a quick, tired look. "A lot of people mistake care for tyranny." She went back to her notes.

"Any more bureaucracy?" Andy asked Luis as they exited the in-firmary.

"No. I will take you to your quarters now," Luis said.

"Great."

Andy's quarters were a motel-type room on the second floor of the residential wing. His luggage was already there. The room combined the elements of both luxury and austerity. On a queen-size bed in the middle of the room lay, neatly folded, several soft Egyptian-cotton towels and a white cotton robe with the rehabilitation center's logo. Above the bedframe hung a painting of a still nighttime landscape, a reproduction of, Andy guessed, Caspar David Friedrich. There was a glass bowl with green apples and oranges, and fresh flowers, daisies, in the vase on the nightstand. But there was no TV, no snack bar, no coffee machine. In the bathroom there was no tub, only a walk-in shower.

On the small desk by the window, Andy noticed a new notepad and a pen.

"For writing down your thoughts," Luis said and smiled. "Our patients usually start having thoughts on the second or third day. No internet service." He pointed his finger at the ceiling.

"Oh," Andy said.

"It's good for therapy." Luis touched his head.

"I'm sure it is."

"And we have a library down the hall," Luis said.

While busy with the formalities, Andy had missed the early dinner that was served daily between 5 and 6 p.m. in the cafeteria. Luis suggested that Andy call room service if he wanted a snack and retreated from the room, passionately refusing the tip. Andy scanned the ascetic, meat-free menu and picked an egg and avocado toast and apple juice. The modest dinner was his first meal in years not aided by technological distractions. He felt handicapped. After he ate, not knowing what else to do, he did some sit-ups and push-ups, took a shower, and called it a day.

He couldn't fall asleep. Moonlight beams streamed across the room's window, coloring the surface of the desk and the clothes piled on the chair in pale yellow hues. The light was so bright that Andy thought it could've come from a lamppost outside. He stood up and walked to the window to make sure. No, it was the moon, round-faced, watchful. An owl hooted from nearby bushes, and its hoots only added to the overall tranquility of the place. Andy noticed a continuous ringing in his left ear that he had not noticed before. He went back to bed and lay still, his eyes open. Maybe he should follow Luis's advice and start writing down his thoughts. Maybe he had a whole novel in him; he just had to sit down and summon his will and put his mind to it. Oh, the stories he could tell. He would be profound and merciless. He would write about the rot that underpins his industry's entire business model, and how universal its implications are. He would write about the intertwined, entrenched interests, about the unaccountable, deliberately formless and faceless entities that back those interests, about the vicious dynamics that had reached an unstoppable velocity, and the underlying complexities that could not be untangled through one's mere good will. He'd let the regular folks know what they're up against. There's a battle going on that they're not and will not be privy to. That every child's future, and even that child's children's and grandchildren's futures had already been forecasted, structured, sliced into tranches, priced, and claimed by those shapeshifting, elusive entities. That would be a great name for a book. *The Shapeshifters.*

He slid into a shallow, sporadic nap and woke up before dawn, trying to remember the richness of ideas and the clever phrases and concepts that kept streaming into his head during the night. He got out of bed and sat at the desk, staring at the clean page of the notepad. He tapped the pen against his nose.

There's a battle going on out there that nobody knows about, he scribbled and paused. *If only people knew about what's going on, there'd be riots,* he added. He doodled at the edges of the page, drawing flat triangles and squares, then giving them dimensions. He wished that someone, anyone, could witness him at this noble, selfless task. It would then be easier to write it all down. He'd get back to it, he thought.

After an uneventful breakfast at the cafeteria—two hardboiled eggs, oatmeal, toast, and hot tea—he hurried to the storage room to check his phone. He gave it a fifty-fifty chance that he wouldn't get to see the device. He conjured up scenarios where he'd be denied access to it under some twisted excuses. But the lady behind the counter produced his phone with a bored look and no questions asked. Andy felt almost disappointed. He dialed his desk's general number.

"Keating Mills," came Scotty's vapid mumble.

"Scotty. It's Andy. Can't talk for long. Just give me the quick skinny. Where's the ten-year right now and how did we close yesterday?"

"Hold on," Scotty said, and Andy heard quick strokes of a keyboard.

"Seriously, you have to look it up?"

"I have, like, ten other things I'm in the middle of. Hold on. Okay. Ten-year is at one point six. We closed up about twelve grand yesterday," Scotty said. "How's the retreat?"

"It's, uh, interesting."

"Good to hear. Anything else? 'Cause I gotta hop."

"Yeah, me too. Gotta run. Thanks."

He hung up and lingered, tapping his fingers on the counter, thinking what else he should know about.

A group of patients, restful men of importance, entered the storage room. They, too, received their phones and hurried to check on the world outside.

"Nonfarm payrolls up by 245,000!" an over-tanned, silver-haired man dressed in shorts and a vest shouted, looking at his phone. There were cheers and boos. Money changed hands. A betting pool, Andy thought. Something to occupy their idle minds.

The old man who announced the payroll numbers came up to Andy. "You're new here?" he asked. "Want to join the pool?"

"What's the wager?"

"The Fed's next move. A quarter-point or a half-point hike."

"Sure," Andy said.

"Twenty dollars," the man said. "I'm Royce. And you are?"

"Andy."

Royce sized him up. "What shop are you with?"

"Keating Mills."

"Aw. You know Dave Pinkus there?"

"He's my boss."

"Small world. Me and Davie go back decades. What are you doing here? Just chilling?"

"Yeah."

Royce patted him on the back. "So, which will it be?" he asked.

"No hike," Andy said.

"Huh, a dove. You're the first so far." Royce pulled out a folded sheet of paper from his vest pocket and wrote down Andy's name and his forecast. "You play tennis?"

"No. Not really."

"Neither do I. But we have a doubles game if you're interested in joining. We're all amateurs here."

"Thank you."

"Maybe see you at the seminar. If that's your thing."

"Maybe. What's today's topic?"

"Who the hell knows? I go randomly, listen to what people have to say. Sometimes they say something interesting."

Andy went back to his room.

Luis met him at the bottom of the stairs, holding a piece of paper in his hand. "Could I interest you in the opportunity to look at to-day's campus activities, Mr. Sylvain?" he asked.

On the list there were three lectures—"German Romanticism," "Introduction to Quantum Mechanics," and one titled "What is Freedom?" Also listed were a tennis game, a fishing trip to a nearby lake, and several spa procedures.

"If something catches your eye, Mr. Sylvain, please let me know. I'll schedule it for you," Luis said. "Everything fills up quickly."

"What's this à-la-carte option?" Andy said, pointing at a bullet point at the bottom of the list.

"That's for more advanced," Luis said.

"Uh-huh," Andy said. "All right, put me down for the 2 p.m. seminar then. And a massage for later maybe?"

"Will do," Luis said. "Also, I thought you'd be interested to know that your blood tests came back. You're in good health, and the only recommendation the doctor made was to reduce your meat and caffeine intake."

"Not hard to do here," Andy said. "You don't seem to have any of those on the menu."

Luis smiled. "Our goal is to facilitate the emergence of a better, healthier in body and spirit, temperate man."

"Quite a goal."

With free time before lunch, Andy wandered around campus. He circled the kitchen, where the workers were already busy chopping salad and peeling potatoes for lunch. He found the gym, the spa, and the tennis courts. He even ventured to find that emergency telephone booth that the storage-room lady had told him about. The booth did, indeed, exist, hidden in the far corner of the perimeter, and there was even a dial tone in the handset. The campus reminded him of a summer camp he used to go to in the Poconos as a child. Here, however, there were more staff and service personnel than there were patients, he noted. If you count all the cooks, nurses, bellboys, trainers, and all kinds of attendants, the ratio could reach three to one, Andy thought. That's why it costs five grand a day.

He returned to the sprawling lawn in front of the main building. There were chairs spread out on the grass—deep, soft recliners set at a perfect angle to provide maximum comfort. Folded plaid blankets had been placed, by attentive staff, onto the chairs' elbow rests. Two of the chairs, about ten feet apart, were occupied by two men, with whom Andy had already exchanged eye contact but not yet a word, earlier at breakfast. He sat down on an empty chair and remained motionless for about fifteen minutes. He made himself focus on the surrounding nature, trying to guess the types of trees marking the edge of the lawn. He was able to identify a pine, a birch, and a maple. After half an hour, the chair became uncomfortable, and he spread the blanket on the grass and stretched out and stared at the brisk, indifferent clouds and the white, disintegrating contrail left by a passing plane. With nothing else to occupy his mind, he again registered the urge to check the quotes on Bloomberg. He wondered why he needed to know, this very second, what the tape said, for he couldn't do anything with that information at this juncture. What bothered him, he concluded, was that everyone, even Scotty, even the clueless interns, knew at this moment more than he did, and what they knew was already old news. They breezily moved on from a possibly consequential piece of information popping up on their news feed that he didn't yet have a chance to put into context and process appropriately. This retardation grated on him. He stared at the other patients. They seemed to have fallen asleep in their chairs. Last night's insomnia caught up with him, and he, too, drifted off.

He dreamt that he was a speaker at an investment-conference panel. For some weird reason, the conference took place at an airport Marriott in Kansas City. The ballroom was stuffy and completely full, with some attendees standing along the walls and between the rows. There were two other traders on the panel with him. They were much younger, in their twenties, and they spoke between themselves, as if Andy wasn't even there. He wanted to insert a comment, but his mouth was dry, and he reached for a glass of water on the table. He drank from it, but it didn't quench his thirst.

"Buy an asset, find a corresponding hedge. Buy the hedge. Book the carry. Rinse. Repeat," one trader said with the creaky voice of an old man.

"Except it's a dying trade," the other trader replied, also sounding like an old-timer. "Everyone got smart. And you can never get a perfect hedge anyway. To hedge a hundred-million position with an index, you gotta have multiples of that amount just laying around. You'd have to short, like, three hundred million."

"We just have to work harder at finding those edges."

"It's all bullshit. It's a game of reductio ad infinitum."

Andy opened his eyes. The traders' voices from the dream continued their conversation.

"And what are we going to be fighting for in the end? For pennies? It's all about who's got sharper elbows, not about who's smarter."

"You're right about that."

The words came from the two men who had now moved their chairs closer together and were having a chat. They saw Andy wake up and waved at him. He stood up and went to introduce himself.

The men, Tim and Stanley, were also newcomers, and the three of them, after a ritualistic, trust-establishing lamentation about the state of the markets, agreed to meet after lunch and go to the 2 p.m. seminar together.

At two o'clock, Andy stuck his head into the study room and was greeted by the instructor, a young woman, who smiled at him and gestured at an empty desk in the back row. The woman must've been an adjunct professor at some nearby college. Faded, worn-out canvas TOMs flats on her feet. A white T-shirt, with a chaste sports bra underneath, a long plaid skirt. Pretty face, with no signs of even minimal beautification but graced by a thoughtful, even sorrowful, furrow between the eyebrows. On the silver cover of her open laptop placed on a small desk were stickers—one of OWS and another of two hands locked in a handshake under a rose.

Tim, Stanley, and Royce were sitting in the room, looking at the young instructor with a skeptical but forgiving slant of their heads. "We get it, a side hustle to pay the bills. Now tell us something we don't know"—their posture seemed to be saying. There was a fourth man, thirtyish, with a narrow forehead and a well-defined hairline, dressed, inexplicably, for a Sunday brunch—in salmon-colored leisure pants, Prada loafers, and a patterned shirt that was unbuttoned, exposing wiry chest hair. A gold bracelet sparkled on his wrist. On his face, Andy detected a mix of contempt and curiosity.

Andy smiled back at the instructor and crouched in his seat. On top of the chair he found a study guide, a two-page printout titled "A Citizen, Not a Customer."

"If we can get anything, we don't know what to want; if we can do anything, we don't know what to do," the woman began. "Is life without constraints a good life?"

"Excuse me, what's your name, young lady?" Royce interrupted her.

"I'm sorry," she said with a nervous grin. "I should've introduced myself. I'm Erin."

"Nice to meet you, Erin. I'm Royce," Royce said. "Would you mind telling us a little bit about your background?"

"Of course," Erin said. "I'm studying for a PhD in sociology at Smith College."

"Oh," Royce said with satisfaction. "My niece goes there. Good school."

Erin took a sip from a water bottle and continued. "Today we're faced with endless choices that, we're told, make us free. These choices are usually encouraged and endorsed by a multitude of self-interested parties, the vendors. But is that a true freedom?" Erin paused, pressed her palms together as if in prayer. "If consumption were freedom, then Upper East Side socialites would be the freest people on earth." She smiled.

With this last phrase, Erin got the men's attention. They chuckled with approval.

"Who are we, then, if not customers?" Erin asked.

"Just so we're clear, none of us here are customers, if you know what I mean," interjected the man in the salmon pants. He had a South Jersey accent.

"Come on, let the lady speak." Royce shushed him and turned to Erin. "Please proceed, dear."

"If we defined ourselves not by what we consume, who would we be?" Erin said.

"We're defined by what we do," Andy said.

"Right," Erin said, extending her hand toward Andy. "We find our identity in what we do, in our craft that we perfect over the years. And would you say that while learning your craft, you bumped into all sorts of limits, constraints?"

"Sure," Andy said.

"And those constraints, however counterintuitive, did they make you better at your craft?"

"I guess you can say that," Andy responded slowly.

Stanley raised his hand. "I agree with this," he said in a rusty voice. "Constraints can be good. But only if they're tested regularly."

Erin paused, tapping her fingers. "Would you care to elaborate?"

"What's there to elaborate?" Stanley shrugged. "The regulators aren't doing their job. It's like, because they're so bad at what they do, they're practically begging you to do what you gotta do. First, they don't know what the fuck is going on. And then they get your ass for violations. You see what I mean?" He threw his hands in the air in exasperation. "It falls on somebody like us to regulate the system. What we're doing is a public service, if you think about it. They should say thank-you to us. We're showing where the system's weak points are. Without us they would never know what's wrong with the system. Frankly, I'd give myself a medal."

Erin nodded cautiously, with the welcoming sympathy of a psychotherapist. "I think that Stanley here—Stanley, right?—perhaps unwittingly, touched on a very important theme. Who can tell me what it is?" She scanned the room.

"Why 'unwittingly'? You give me no credit," Stanley said and frowned.

"What did they get you for?" the South Jersey guy cut in.

"Nothing really. Some off-balance-sheet accounting. My lawyers were good. Cost me a fortune though. And this, the rehab"—Stanley looked around—"was part of the deal. It's actually not bad. I think I can hang around here for a month. Have you guys tried the spa yet?"

"They have a spa?"

"A first-class one, I heard. We gotta get rewarded at the end of the day for being good boys." Stanley giggled. "Right? Otherwise what's the point?" He looked at Erin for affirmation.

She smiled tensely and, for some reason, locked eyes with Andy as if searching for someone to share her suppressed bewilderment.

Yep, that's us, was Andy's silent reply. Aloud, he said: "I think what Erin is trying to say is that we have to seek to constrain ourselves without expecting others to do it for us."

"Thank you," Erin said. "This is really not my conclusion. Many philosophers spent their whole lives pondering on this matter and arrived at the same end, independently. Like Immanuel Kant, for example."

The South Jersey guy chortled.

Royce made a screeching sound, the kind that men over sixty use to communicate doubt, and wobbled his head left to right. "Erin, I think you're a smart girl, and this is a noble sentiment, but you just don't know how things are in the real world. You haven't seen life. Look, you can come and work for my firm, if you'd like. We'll compensate you well. You'll pay off your student loans. Do you know Excel? It doesn't matter, you'll learn it. You'll see how everything works."

"Thank you, Royce," Erin said.

"Seriously, you're wasting your smarts on a bunch of degenerates and drug addicts. No offence." Royce glanced at the men in the room.

"Don't do it, Erin," Andy said. "They'll eat you alive there."

"Hey. I'm trying to help out a girl here," Royce exclaimed. "She'll have a better life."

"I wasn't going to," Erin said to Andy then turned to Royce. "But thank you again. I appreciate the offer."

Andy lingered after the class had ended and all the men had left the room. He asked Erin how often she came here (once or twice a week), whether her pay was good (can't complain), and when her next lecture would be. He was sad to hear that she had accepted a teaching position in California and that this was her last lecture.

"Let's stay in touch," he said, reaching into his pocket for a nonexistent phone. "Oh. I'm communicationally crippled. Could I at least get your email?"

Erin dictated her email address, and he wrote it down in his notebook.

"I'm thinking of moving to the West Coast too," he said with excitement. "The East Coast is just too"—he looked up and rubbed his fingers together—"stagnating."

XVII: Can't Identify the Disease

That night Andy dreamed of Erin. He pursued her in confusion, thinking that Erin was Lauren, for she was dressed provocatively in expensive lingerie, and at the moment he realized the mix-up, he awakened, disgusted with himself for having such a dream. There were supposed to be boundaries. Erin was supposed to entice his intellect, not his flesh.

In the morning, after breakfast, he again hurried to the phone depository and checked his phone. There were several texts from Lauren to which he didn't respond. He scrolled through the headlines and looked up his usual quotes on Bloomberg—no big news, no big moves, nothing. He gave the phone back to the administrator.

Luis had scheduled a spa appointment for him later in the day. Andy spent the rest of the morning in the gym, doing an hour-long cardio, then lifting weights, then stretching. After the workout, he went to hang on the lawn, spreading out on the blanket on the grass like the day before. His muscles tingled pleasantly. He lay with his eyes closed, enjoying the sun and a cool breeze.

An odd grinding sound disturbed his peace. He opened his eyes. A middle-aged man dressed only in old stretched-at-the-knee sweatpants walked barefoot on the gravel pathway that ran across the lawn. Two male nurses walked by his sides. The man's ripped naked torso was bent under the weight of a crudely made giant wooden cross, whose long end was ploughing a deep track in the dirt behind him. The man's jaw was clenched, and his lean muscles flexed, but he seemed to relish the challenge. He huffed and groaned, but there was a quiet determination in him to haul the cross to whatever its final destination was.

"What is this? Like an art performance?" Andy asked no one in particular.

The strange procession slowly disappeared behind the corner of the building. Andy made a mental note to ask Luis about it. This must've been the à-la-carte option from the resort's list of activities.

At lunch Andy glanced at the cafeteria corkboard. A lecture titled "A Diamond and A Cross," by some Mr. Dietch, was scheduled for 2 p.m. in the big study room, and Andy decided to give it a listen.

The lecturer, Mr. Dietch, had the robust comportment of a retired military man. He had short, brushlike salt-and-pepper hair and a walrus moustache. He wore a short-sleeved polo shirt and khakis, and his muscular arms and neck were tanned.

"You've probably heard about Plato's duality—the world of things on one hand and the world of ideas, eternal forms, on the other," Mr. Dietch began his lecture. He spoke quickly, with the trained pace and a vocal authority of someone accustomed to giving instructions on how to use a gas mask. "Similarly, Descartes, too, divided the world into two categories: the objective world and a thinking subject. You're with me so far? Good."

Mr. Dietch took a thick felt pen and drew three points on a whiteboard.

"Both Plato and Descartes have one overlapping point—a world of things"—he circled one point on the board with a green pen—"but their worlds of ideas are different. Plato's world is one of abstractions, of constants that exist independent of a human thought; Descartes's world of ideas, on the other hand, is man-generated." He circled the two other points, one with a blue pen and the other with a red.

"So here we have a triad: a material world; a world of ideas that are independent of a thinker, such as mathematical formulas; and a world of a subjective human thought." He connected the three dots into an inverted triangle.

Andy dutifully copied the scheme into his notebook.

"But there's also a fourth dimension, something that is borne out of the three existing realms." Mr. Dietch drew a fourth point on the whiteboard above the triangle. "Karl Popper, an Austrian-British philosopher, called that fourth point a world of historical transformations. That dimension, which we will call a *transform*, includes things like myths, legends, languages, scientific theories, poetry, songs and symphonies, engineering, and architectural achievements." He connected the triangle to the fourth point with two lines, transforming the shape into a diamond.

In his notebook, Andy wrote down "Karl Popper." He'd heard the name many times before. Smart portfolio managers often referenced it while giving talks at conferences, and, judging by the other people's reaction to those mentions, Andy had inferred that this man's ideas carried some significance and that he'd be wise to educate himself on the matter. But he'd never had the time to follow through.

"What we have here now is a tetrad. The outside of this tetrad looks like a diamond," Mr. Dietch said, sliding the pen around the drawing's sides, "but the inside presents itself as a cross." He drew a vertical and a horizontal line within the diamond. "Culturally, a symbol of suffering and perseverance. And, in our scheme, a point of connection between the disconnected dimensions. And what force in the universe has the ability to connect all four points, to serve as a conduit between them? It is, of course, a mortal, imperfect man. Like da Vinci's *Vitruvian Man*."

Mr. Dietch spanned his arms and spread his legs to help the audience recall the famous image.

"A man occupies this spot, this midpoint. His task becomes obvious from his location. Despite—not because of—but despite his folly, his incompleteness, his weaknesses, he is asked to fine-tune the imperfections, to reconcile somehow the incongruities between the three worlds through his creations, his endeavors. In a cosmic sense, this is our task."

He sat behind the desk and tapped his pen against the table.

"Not every man can do it, but every man is born with the tools to do it: a thinking mind and a physical ability."

"Wow," someone exhaled from the back.

"Is banking a transform?" a thin, pale-faced man with dark circles under his eyes asked cautiously. Andy almost sensed the searching for affirmation in the man's voice.

"Does it draw from all three realms?" Mr. Dietch replied.

The pale banker paused in thought.

"Take sculpture," Mr. Dietch said. "A sculpture is a transform. It encompasses in itself all three other spheres. The physical form—marble; the subjective form—the master's work, his vision; and, finally, the world of ideas, an element of eternal forms, a set of prior cultural forms that affected the master's vision. Like Greek or Roman or Renaissance culture. The subconscious archetype that informs the master's style. What part of banking would you define as an eternal form?"

Some men chuckled, and the pale banker seemed to have sunk deeper into his seat, beads of sweat appearing on his high, sloped forehead.

"Not sure about banking, but certain trades are definitely art," Andy said. "When you know when to go in and when to get out, that's art. When you see something that no one else can see. When you have developed a certain radar. It's like a sixth sense. It can't be explained and can't be put into formula. It's almost divine."

"Yeah, but where is the physical matter in trading?" someone said, and the room broke out in a crossfire of chatter.

"In commodities."

"Commodities traders are the dumbest people on earth. I know some guys there who didn't even finish college."

"It's an abstraction. No need to take it literally."

"But he said that poetry is a transform. Poetry doesn't have the use of any matter. So trading is equivalent to poetry then."

"Cash in fist is poetry."

"It's our own mythology. Like *The Iliad*."

Mr. Dietch sat quietly, writing something down into his notebook. "Gentlemen," he finally interjected. "No one here questions your achievements. No need to get defensive. You are all very accomplished."

The praise worked. The noise dissolved.

"Men like you are not moved by religion, by the supernatural. You are too smart for that. What I described is a theory that can help a man—a sophisticated man—find an anchor in life. It is a set of guidelines for how to perceive the world and your place in it."

The pale banker slouched in his seat and then slid to the floor. Mr. Dietch rushed toward him, checked his pulse. He pressed a speed-dial button on his phone, and, minutes later, two male nurses walked in with a stretcher.

"A withdrawal," someone whispered when the nurses carried the banker away.

Andy hoped it was a withdrawal. A withdrawal could be cured.

Mr. Dietch's ideas still preoccupied Andy when, later that day, he walked into the spa waiting room for his scheduled appointment. The serene room smelled of eucalyptus and citrus. Meditative string music was playing softly, accompanied by a soothing trickle from a mini-fountain hidden between the potted plants. A selection of fruit and refreshments was spread out on a long and narrow service table by the wall. Andy came up to a large glass drink dispenser with chilled lemon water and poured a few ounces into a paper cup. He plunged into a soft, low armchair.

Opposite him, almost entirely enveloped by the armchair's cushions and pillows, sat a scruffy, emaciated man. The man gazed mid-distance and seemed not to notice or care about Andy's presence. In his hands he held a peeled orange. His fingers moved slowly, in a kind of automated, mindless rut, separating the orange slices. Once a slice was removed, the man lifted it slowly toward his mouth and ate it in small bites, the juice running down his hands and chin.

Andy recognized the man. He was the cross-bearer.

"How long have you been here?" Andy broke the silence. "I just got here two days ago. You think it's worth a stay?"

The cross-bearer didn't respond.

Andy edged forward in his chair and whispered: "Are you connecting the dots? Like the Vitruvian Man?"

No response.

Andy took a sip of water. "Anyway, I hope you're getting your money's worth here." He leaned back.

The cross-bearer blinked. He wiped his chin with a dirty sweatshirt sleeve and observed Andy.

"I'm Andy … Andy Sylvain with Keating Mills."

The cross-bearer took a long pause, then coughed and smiled at Andy. "You can't identify the disease," he finally said with a tired voice. "Thus, you can't cure it." He sent another orange slice into his mouth and chewed it, barely moving his jaws.

"And you? You know what the disease is?" Andy asked and held his breath for an answer.

A tall young woman in light green cotton scrubs walked into the waiting room. She had a bulky wrestler's complexion, and her arms were covered in tattoos. Without calling his name, she bobbed her head at the cross-bearer and said, "This way, sir." She held his elbow as he slogged away.

"No happy endings here," Andy whispered giddily to the man as he passed, eliciting zero reaction.

Another masseur, a young man, came to collect Andy a minute later.

"Any special requests?" the masseur asked Andy as they walked toward the massage room.

"No, just massage please," Andy replied, and again his witty crack failed to generate any campy reciprocity.

* * *

After massage, in the late afternoon, Andy told Luis that he was going on a short hike, and Luis suggested a few easy trails. The hiking path began at the camp's back gate. A sign made of carved wooden planks outside the gate showed several snakelike trails and their stated lengths—from one mile to four and a half miles. Andy breathed in the tarry air and exhaled with a satisfied wheeze. He walked, enjoying the sound of dry pine needles rustling under his feet. The trees' thick crowns, hanging over the trail like a pergola, converted the sunlight into a lacey embroidery of light and shade on the ground.

After about a mile, the path led uphill at a steep incline, the trees became sparse, and Andy began sweating and panting. He stopped to catch his breath, propping his hands against his knees. He took off his yellow baseball cap, fanned himself, and drank a gulp of water from his stainless-steel hiking bottle. He poured some water on his palm and wiped his neck. He thought that he heard a rhythmic sound, that of human steps perhaps, but as he held his breath to listen more closely, the sound stopped. He slammed a buzzing mosquito as it landed on his arm.

He resumed the hike. Soon the trail would go downhill, he thought, and back under the canopy of trees. Indeed, the pathway snaked between the Precambrian basement rock formations and began a gradual decline, giving Andy's gait an extra boost. The gravel crackled under his sneakers and again he thought that he heard a similar crackling coming from afar, from, perhaps, a hiker behind him. He waded into the nearby bushes and decided to wait out the disturber of his peace. Five and then ten minutes passed, and the woods were quiet, with not a soul in the vicinity. A bird twittered, and crickets chirped in the grass. The road ahead made a sharp, almost nine-ty-degree bend to the right, and, rather than getting back on the trail, Andy decided to take a shortcut through the thicket. The off-road slope, covered in nettles and thistles, was steep, and Andy lost his balance and slid a few yards on his butt until the ground flattened.

He found himself in a dark pine grove. Its floor was soft, covered with layers of rotten leaves, mossy tree trunks, and robust ferns that looked prehistoric. Andy took a piss, aiming his stream for an unfor-tunate bug, and then proceeded in the direction where he thought he'd intercept the trail. He walked for about fifteen minutes, but the path that he counted on appearing wasn't there.

Okay, he thought, this is strange. He ran a quick calculation in his head. After making that ninety-degree turn, the path must've made another sharp turn in the other direction—totally possible, given the map's description of it—and Andy must've missed it tangentially by a few feet. He could continue in his current direction and intercept it at a different point, or he could retrace his move back to the pine grove and then climb back up that steep hill, the point of his original divergence. He decided to continue forward but enhance his strategy by walking in a wide circle instead of a straight line: this way he'd have more chances to cut into the trail as it curled around the woods.

To maintain the circular nature of his movement, Andy used the sun as his reference point, having it to his left, then behind him, then to his right. He hurried, because the sun was moving, and he didn't want its rotation to corrupt his basic calculation. The circle therefore had to be small, maybe a quarter mile in diameter, established by a feel, rather than by any other measurement.

He sped up. Dry fir branches, sticking out like the arms of a scarecrow from the tree trunks, tugged at his sweatshirt sleeves. Thorny weeds scraped at his calves. He didn't notice how he lost his baseball cap.

The sun was now setting, and Andy began to run, as if speed was the solution. He knew, from his teenage camping days, that he needed to sit down, to catch his breath and reassess the situation, but his feverish mind demanded that he keep running, that he find some sort of a familiar sign and an immediate resolution to such an embarrassment.

Half an hour later, exhausted, he was mentally preparing to spend the night in the woods. He decided to give it one final push, toward the setting sun, and in about a quarter mile he stumbled into a clearing. In the dying daylight, he saw a hunched human silhouette sitting on a tree stump.

"Sir!" Andy cried with relief, rushing forward.

The person turned around, and Andy recognized Ms. Cooke. She was sitting with her legs stretched, leaning on a walking stick with one hand, holding a phone in the other.

Andy took a deep breath. "Right on, Ms. Cooke!" he said, trying to sound casual.

"Oh, Mr. Sylvain," she said. "Hope you had a pleasant hike."

"A bit longer than I planned for. But it's good exercise." Andy's sweatshirt was soaked, and he breathed heavily. His sweatpants were covered with prickly thistle seeds.

"You seem spent," she said. "Sit down and catch your breath."

He sat down on the grass. She offered him her flask, but even though he was thirsty, he waved it off.

"No hat?" Ms. Cooke said. "Not smart. There are ticks out here." She took out a handkerchief from her pocket, tied its four ends into knots, and handed it to Andy. He put the makeshift hat on his head.

He stared at the titanium rod fitted into a running shoe that stuck out from under the hemline of her left trouser leg. Ms. Cooke noted his interest.

"Beirut. 1983," she said, knocking on the metal with her walking stick.

"Wait. That was the, uh …"

"When they blew up the American barracks." Her phone buzzed, and she picked it up. "He's here," she said into her phone after listening, "He seems fine." She hung up and looked at Andy with a sad smile. "The further one ventures to go, the more circuitous the journey becomes," she said. "Perhaps we should head back to the camp."

Leaning on her cane and limping on her left leg, Ms. Cooke led Andy through the thicket. In less than two hundred yards, they were at the camp's back gate.

"You missed dinner, but I can make you a sandwich in my office," Ms. Cooke said.

"I'd love that," Andy said. "I'm starving."

Once they were in Ms. Cooke's office, she speed-dialed the kitchen and asked them to bring a chicken sandwich and something to drink.

"Apple juice or water?" she asked Andy.

"Water is fine," he said.

"Bring both," she said into the phone and hung up.

She extended Andy a warm, motherly glance.

"The woods have a way of claiming even the most obstinate men," she said. "*Especially* the most obstinate."

"Wait," Andy said as if something had dawned on him. "So the steps that I heard behind me ..."

"That was Luis. We try to keep an eye on all our guests. We don't want you to get hurt. But you seem to have some skill at escaping."

Luis walked in with a tray minutes later. He put the tray with a chicken sandwich, pickles, potato chips, a pack of apple juice, and a bottle of water before Andy. Andy bit into the sandwich before Luis even left the room. Ms. Cooke watched as Andy wolfed down the food.

"How did you end up running this place?" Andy asked between bites.

"I was once a bond trader like you," she said. "It was back in the eighties, a time when bond traders could do no wrong. When the world was still rational."

"Yeah. A time of innocence."

"In a way." She smiled. "Then in the nineties all these quant funds started to pop up everywhere. QCM, Quantum Capital Management, remember them? It must've been in your time already."

"Yes. I remember," Andy said. "We had them as a counterparty."

"They were all PhDs and luminaries. They built their models and sat back." She scoffed. "That linear thinking exposed their mediocrity. They were not prepared for chaos."

Andy shook his head in agreement, sipping apple juice.

"That's where their models failed. You can't put chaos on a bell curve. You have to imagine the possibility, like a fiction writer. Or like a mother with a small child. If QCM had one woman on the team, they'd still be alive."

"Agreed." Andy nodded with his mouth full.

"Anyway, after QCM collapsed, many guys just moved on as if nothing had happened. Others, very few, more conscientious, had a breakdown. They wanted to correct their course, to get to the bottom of where they went wrong, but they couldn't find the right tools or the community to do it. Some quit; some took a break and returned to the grind. There was never a reckoning. I had already left the bond desk by then and ran a small rehab facility in Vermont. A couple of bond traders came to treat their cocaine habit. They were very smart, and we talked about business a lot, and I could tell they needed more than mere treatment. They needed to know their purpose. And I thought that this was an untapped niche—brilliant men who have everything but who are lost. I invited some philosophy adjuncts from a nearby college to give a couple of lectures. Enrollment grew quickly." She looked at Andy. "After a while, it occurred to me that it wasn't the philosophy they were after. They sought something that is not organically available anywhere. Certainly not in Manhattan."

"Everything is available in Manhattan." Andy huffed.

Ms. Cooke stood up and limped toward the window. She opened the blinds. Outside, on a darkened, empty lawn, under a lamppost,

Andy's old acquaintance, the cross-bearer, was doing push-ups. A man in military fatigues was squatting next to him, looking at a stopwatch, counting.

"See that man? You saw him earlier. He was dragging a cross." Ms. Cooke closed the blinds and walked back to her desk. She sat down and put her hand over her mouth in brief contemplation. "He wanted to use real nails." She poked the middle of her palm with a finger. "I had to talk him out of it."

Andy suppressed a gasp. "Why is he doing this?"

She locked her hands in front of her, slightly twitching her fingers. "Suffering—the curated amount that we facilitate—allows him to lift a certain mental burden. When he completes his program, he will go back to his daily conquests, to his P&L. But in his mind, he will have atoned. You can't put a price on that."

"What is he atoning for?"

"Only he knows. We don't ask questions."

"Couldn't he just go serve in the Peace Corps? Go, uh, work on a … on a farm?"

Ms. Cooke shook her head. She drilled him with a heavy gaze. "He can't. None of them can. It is an impossibility, Mr. Sylvain. You know that."

Andy *suspected* that. But it's one thing to suspect the existence of a troubling phenomenon and carry that suspicion inside, hoping to be wrong. And it's another thing to have that pointed out to you by another party, proven, like a theorem, and bookended by a Q.E.D. Andy felt seen, naked. Worse than naked. It was as if Ms. Cooke had opened his skull and, with tweezers and with the emotional detachment of a surgeon, picked his most intimate fears and follies, like wriggling caterpillars, and showed them to him. And worse still, she then withheld her judgment.

"What about the rest? They seem to be having a good time," Andy asked.

She smiled. "Good times are our most profitable product. They're cheaper to produce."

"Ah. So it's like cross-collateralization," Andy probed.

That's right, her eyes said.

Andy finished his meal. "Thank you for the sandwich," he said. "So, uh, what's the cancellation policy here?"

"You are free to leave at any time. But your fee is nonrefundable. Of course, we'd be sorry to see you go."

XVIII: We're Special,
But Nobody Knows That

"How was it?" Misha asked when Andy got into his car the next day.

"Still trying to figure that out."

"Ms. Cooke, though, huh." Misha glanced at Andy, arching his eyebrows to communicate a furtive admiration.

"A serious lady," Andy concurred.

"She's found a good niche."

"She has. Everybody is trying to cure the sick and the delinquents. She's trying to cure the masters of the universe. A lot of money in that."

"I don't think she's doing it for the money though. That woman is on a mission."

"Yeah. After you meet someone like her, everything you do seems trivial," Andy said and sighed. "I felt like I wasn't even qualified to be there."

Misha's driving-music selection was eccentric: 1970s and 80s progressive European rock, mostly unknown to the average American ear, familiar only to the connoisseurs. As they drove, Andy found himself subjected to complex, era-defining deep tracks with shifting key signatures, carried by rock opera, balls-in-the-vise male vocals.

"What are you listening to?" Andy asked.

"Something I used to learn English by. Back in the day. On smuggled LPs." Misha fiddled with the car stereo and turned it off. "I think that place is an outlet for the bright men who feel betrayed," he said. "They once had aspirations and sensitivities but were made into blunt instruments. They resent it, of course, but suppress their resentment. They once soothed themselves with the idea that when they make MD, when they have a few million in the bank, they will have the chance to use all of their faculties, even creative ones. But then they become MDs, and nothing happens. That outlet just doesn't appear. So all of those talents remain untapped. Such a disconnect, it could destroy a man. People are willing to pay a lot of money to be rid of it."

"Yeah," Andy bleated. "There's definitely something to it."

"I was there during winter," Misha continued. "They had one guy who insisted on living in a tent outside. He seemed to relish the physical strain. He got frostbite, but he was happy. I remember his blissful face when they loaded him into an ambulance."

Andy then told Misha about the cross-bearer.

"Yep," was Misha's curt response to Andy's harrowing tale.

They were soon on the Bruckner Expressway, heading toward the Triboro Bridge. Manhattan residential splinters appeared like white bars on a black chart against the night sky.

"It's good to be back," Andy said, happy to see the emerging skyline.

Misha took the ramp off FDR Drive at 72nd Street. The city welcomed them with sounds of horns and sirens and perpetual motion.

"Uh," Andy said, when Misha drove down Second Avenue toward Andy's condo. "Why don't you take me to, like, the Soho Grand."

Misha looked at Andy in puzzlement.

"Lauren has the keys to my place," Andy said. "I don't want her to know I'm back."

Misha laughed. "Why Soho Grand? You can crash at my pad," he said.

"I'd have to crash for three weeks."

"That's great. You can be a free man for three more weeks."

Andy exhaled. "What do you say we get some Chinese?" he said. "I'm dying for some chow mein. The greasier the better."

Misha took him to a Chinese restaurant, a two-table hole-in-the-wall south of Canal Street. Inside, Andy ordered crunchy spring rolls and chicken lo mein. Misha got a cup of green tea and drank it in silence, watching Andy eat.

Food-delivery men—faceless, hooded, protective of their time—shuffled in and out of the restaurant. They picked up the prepared orders in plastic bags and hurried back on their thankless rounds.

Misha took a toothpick from a glass jar on the table, unwrapped it, and stuck it, ponderously, between his teeth. "I remember, when I just moved here and saw New York in all its colors, in all its glory and ugliness, how disdainful I was toward what I considered 'rabble'—you know, the bums, the retards, the weirdos. The minorities," Misha said as another grim messenger came and went. A spasm gripped his face as if he had recoiled from an embarrassing thought. "Every Russian carries a seed of chauvinism in him. It may or may not break out, but it is always present."

"What? You're being way too hard on yourself," Andy said between bites.

Misha was silent, staring out the window as if deep in thought. "Anyway," he continued at last, "my mother once came to visit. She was an important woman back in the Soviet days. High up in the Ministry of Foreign Affairs. I had a charmed childhood. I grew up a snob, and I was a snob when I came here. I mean, my snobbishness wasn't totally unjustified. I won a couple of math Olympiads back home. Anyway, my mother came here. Stayed at the Plaza. She could've stayed at the St. Regis, but she chose the Plaza because she had seen it in the movies. She refused to go on the subway. She kept asking me how can I live in this pigsty. That's what she called New York. A pigsty. And then after she said that, all of a sudden, I felt like I had to defend this town and its people. And while making that argument, I came to understand that my short tolerance for the riffraff emerged out of my own misplaced sense of specialness. I considered myself special because of the shit I had to deal with before I got to the trading desk and then on the trading desk, the kind of shit the unwashed couldn't even come close to comprehending. You know, the sixteen-hour days, the pitch books, the piece of code that needs to be working by 7 a.m., all of that. The amount of money on the line. The implied, hidden power of what we do. I looked at them on the subway and thought, *If only you knew what I do; if only you knew what I know.* But there was no way for them to know. And I resented them for it."

"If they knew what we do, they'd drop everything and retreat in despair," Andy said as the door chimed and another delivery man came in.

Misha lifted his eyes and stared at Andy. "But we want them to know! We want them to see how special we are. But nobody knows that."

"Yeah," Andy said with his mouth full.

Misha slumped and hunched over his tea. "That's how hate starts," he mumbled.

Andy picked up a spring roll from his plate but then put it down. He felt suddenly sated. He took a gulp of water. "But you're not like that anymore," he said, wiping his mouth. "You're a reformed man now."

"I guess I am." Misha took a sip of tea. "Still, I see no clarity here, no resolution. On the one hand, I despise people who are weak and incompetent. On the other hand, I am angry at the circumstances under which they're asked to perform. No matter how much they're cheered on and prodded and motivated, they just won't do it. And not even because they can't, but because there's very limited space for them on top. I know some smart people, smarter than me, who ended up doing service jobs, by-the-hour temp jobs, because they just couldn't survive in the corporate structure. There's no middle ground." He wiggled the toothpick with his teeth, looking out the restaurant's window. "New York is a construct that sustains itself on the extremes. If you want to be a better man, you have to leave New York."

"Like, where? To New Jersey?" Andy asked with a limp giggle, and Misha scoffed, giving no answer.

After Andy finished his dinner, they walked two blocks to Misha's loft.

"Do you happen to have a copy of Madeline's thesis?" Andy asked. "She promised to send me a copy but never did."

"You mean you never read it?" Misha said, surprised.

"I never had the time."

"I have it somewhere. I'll send it," Misha said. "I mean she spent, like, six years writing it. You could've at least shown some interest."

"Yeah, well, you know how it is."

"Do you at least know what it is about?"

"Nineteenth-century Russia? For some reason she told me I'd be scared to read it."

"She did?" Misha grinned. "Maybe you will." There was some breathless loftiness in his voice, as if he was entertained by the notion of Andy reading the thesis for the first time.

Upstairs, Misha brought Andy fresh sheets and a blanket and arranged the couch into a bed.

"You can stay for as long as you like," he said. "And, please, don't ask my permission if you need anything. Just help yourself." Misha waved in the direction of the kitchen.

When in bed, Andy spent half an hour typing messages to Joanna and erasing them without sending.

XIX: Presence at Dusk

After two days of staying in Misha's loft, thinking that he had burdened his generous host with his presence long enough, Andy decamped to Bedford Manor. He hadn't seen his house in about a month, leaving it in the hands of his real-estate agent. When he walked inside the house, he saw that most of the first-floor furniture had been removed and replaced with rented staged sets of inoffensive Crate and Barrel aesthetic. Good, Andy thought. That means the showings are happening.

He went upstairs to his bedroom, took a shower, and changed into shorts and a sweatshirt from the old dresser that had somehow survived the real-estate lady's heavy hand. While looking for a pair of socks in the top drawer, he found a plastic bag with an old dry joint and a lighter inside, and wondered how it got there. Must be Lauren's old stash. He put it in his shorts' pocket and went downstairs.

His steps echoed as he came down the stairs, crossed the empty marbled-floor foyer, passed the kitchen area, opened the sliding door, and stepped onto the deck. The sun was setting behind the treetops, and the tall pines cast long spikey shadows over the deck. A half-acre manicured semicircle of the lawn adjoined a foot-high ridge of mossy stones that marked the edge between civilization and wilderness. Beyond the ridge, on an upward-sloped grassy hillside, a grand white oak, like a lonely Cerberus, held back with its sprawling branches the gaping blackness of a dense New England forest.

A faint humming sound of unknown origin filled the evening air. It ebbed and flowed in intensity but stayed on the same low note. Andy leaned on the deck rails, held his breath, and listened, wondering about its source. No animal could make a sound like that. With its smooth continuity, the sound had to be nonorganic in nature. He discarded the supernatural, although the eeriness of it gave him the creeps. The hum was stuck on one ominous, monotonous, low-pitched note, like a Gregorian chant performed by an invisible choir of medieval monks inside the darkening dominion.

He lit up the joint and took a few puffs. The harrowing sound could not have come from the woods, he thought with mounting alarm. The forest was motionless in the placid, windless evening, and its tranquility seemed unnatural and almost deliberate, suggesting a forbidding sentience. He thought he saw a dark silhouette wobbling between the trees.

Andy went inside the house, grabbed a heavy brass poker from the living room's fireplace set, and stepped back on the deck. He listened to the sound again, then slinked down the stairs that led from the deck onto the lawn. He gripped the poker, held his breath, and looked around.

The hum was the product of human folly. Under the deck, an industrial-size steel fan that Oleg must've installed to dry the fresh paint on the exterior wall of the basement and forgotten to turn off was conspiring with the forest in sinister synergy. The discovery, beguiling in its simplicity, angered Andy. He swung and smashed the fan with the poker. The fan's protective metal cage bent under the blow, but the fan continued spinning its fins in chocking, irregular intervals. Andy stomped on the dying device then yanked the plug out of the wall. The fan made a few more spins and died down, and so did the sound.

His unease remained. He felt like the forest was now aware of his transience and inadequacy. He turned around and looked at the surrounding darkness.

"What do you say now, huh?" Andy screamed into the murk. His cry went unanswered. The inscrutable forest, now a pitch-black mass against a waning orange sliver of sunset, was unperturbed by a petty human outburst, but its immutable presence was overwhelming, its quiet sentience stupefying.

Andy heard a shuffle nearby and froze, paralyzed by a twitch of adrenaline piercing through his body. He turned around and saw a dumbfounded Oleg, with his jaw ajar and a wicker basket full of mushrooms in his hand.

"Andy," Oleg said, as the basket slid from his fingers to the ground. "Are you okay? I thought you were still at the sanatorium."

"Yeah, well. I'm home early."

"Good. I'm glad you feel better."

"What are you doing here? Where's your van?"

"My friend dropped me off earlier. I needed to touch up a few things." Oleg glanced at the poker in Andy's hand, then at the broken fan. "Aw. What happened to my ventilator?" He squatted over the mutilated device.

"I, uh, I had a moment of … We'll get you a new one. Come. Let's get inside," Andy said.

Oleg picked up his basket, and they went inside the house.

"I just don't want anyone to know I'm here," Andy said, sliding the glass deck door shut. "Everybody still thinks I'm at the, um, sanatorium. You understand?"

"Hiding from girlfriend?" Oleg grinned. "I understand."

Andy pointed at Oleg's haul. "What is it with you Russians and the mushrooms? It's some kind of national obsession."

"I can cook these for you," Oleg said excitedly. "With potatoes. It's very tasty. You'll see."

"Sure. That sounds intriguing."

Oleg sprang into action. He moved around Andy's kitchen with the eagerness of a subordinate trying to please a boss, and with the ease and confidence of a resident chef. Andy noticed that Oleg knew the location of herbs and spices, of pans and utensils, and when he opened the fridge to get himself a soda, he saw a few odd food staples inside that were never a part of his diet, like a jar of pickles and boiled beets.

"It's better if you don't go in the basement," Oleg said, looking over his shoulder while peeling potatoes in the sink. "There's wet paint everywhere."

"Ah, okay," Andy said.

Oleg chopped the onions and dispensed them into the hot frying pan with an ample amount of olive oil. "Olive oil is good, but for better taste it should really be sunflower-seed oil. You don't have it here. I looked everywhere," Oleg said, stirring the onions in the pan with a wooden spoon.

He cut the mushrooms and the peeled potatoes into thin rectangles, and, after making sure that the sizzling onions had reached a near-golden color, poured the fungi and the vegetables from the cutting board into the frying pan.

"You know what I think about you, Andy?" Oleg said. "I think that you're a smart man. An adequate man. And cultured, too."

"Thank you, Oleg. That's nice to hear."

"But the problem is that no one sees that. People are stupid."

Oleg took two dinner plates from the cupboard and put them on the kitchen counter. He brought the napkins, silverware, and glasses and set them up next to the plates.

"But I see it. Maybe you need to meet new people, who can appreciate you."

Oleg lifted the lid of the frying pan and checked the contents with satisfaction. He took it off the stove and put the steaming, ragout-like concoction into a ceramic bowl. He opened the fridge and picked out a container of sour cream and a jar of pickles and brought them to the table.

"The feast is served," he announced pompously.

"Let's hope these are not poisonous," Andy said, picking a slice of mushroom from his plate.

"Poisonous?" Oleg exclaimed. "No! I used to pick and eat this kind from when I was six. Poisonous have a special look that is easy to tell. They have all these … decorations."

"Ornaments," Andy said.

"Yeah, they dress like prostitutes." Oleg chuckled. "The good ones, they look like old grandmas, and they're always hiding in the grass and under leaves."

Andy laughed. The meal was, indeed, tasty, and when Oleg offered to refill his plate, Andy nodded.

"You should come to our barbeque next week," Oleg said with a mouthful. "If you have nothing to do. It's a special party. You'll like it."

"As long as there are no bankers there."

"No. No bankers. Normal people."

"Good. I want normal people."

Oleg texted, then dialed someone on his phone. He spoke in animated Russian, walking back and forth, sounding both pleading and threatening to Andy's ear.

"My friend is coming to pick me up," he said when he hung up.

"What, you woke him up?" Andy asked.

"No. He, uh, accepted a couple of glasses," Oleg said, tipping an invisible cup into his mouth, and Andy understood that it was some kind of drinking-related Russian idiom, translated word-for-word by Oleg.

"You can go rest. I clean up," Oleg said. "And I'll send you a text about the party."

"Please do," Andy said and went upstairs.

XX: Oleg's Barbeque

Andy wasn't sure what kind of party to expect, but just in case, he stopped by the local deli and grabbed a six-pack of Corona beer and a party-size bag of chips. He hadn't done anything this working-class since college, and he felt good about himself. He crossed the Tappan Zee Bridge and then drove south to New Jersey, to a small town off Route 78.

The party wasn't set in the garden, like Oleg had promised, but outside a hangar-sized barn surrounded by compressed bales of hay and farm equipment. Red, white, and blue banners and buntings decorated the barn's outside walls. On the dirt lot around the barn, cars and trucks were parked sporadically. Andy circled around the structure several times and parked on a grassy spot, squeezing between two giant F-150 trucks.

A row of vendors with folding tables under large garden umbrellas welcomed the visitors. Valhalla Construction, Oleg's employer and the event's sponsor, had set up the biggest stand, with volunteers handing out complimentary beer and brochures touting the company's "community leadership." Andy received a can of Bud Light and a brochure, and strolled by the vendors, examining the merchandise. There were statement T-shirts, Punisher decals, yellow Gadsden flags and bumper stickers, and other varieties of swag with Neo-Confederate sentiment.

Andy paused beside a table covered with stacks of apparel—T-shirts, sweatshirts, and baseball hats, manned by a stout, over-tanned blonde with a plastic Viking hat with horns and fake braids on her head. The blonde's large breasts, barely covered by a thin black tank top, rested almost horizontally on her belly. She had a thick gel manicure with glittery nail art, clearly a splurge and a point of pride, as her arms domineered in her salesmanship. She glided her palms over her wares like a good QVC salesperson, and, when a customer got interested in a product and asked for a price, she fiddled with the price tag so carefully, with the pads of her fingers, that her nails never came in contact with it.

She gave Andy an obeisant smile.

"Brunhilde," Andy said and smiled back at her.

"What?"

"You know," he said, pointing at her hat, "the Valkyrie, the warrior lady."

"Oh, yeah, that's me," she said, pleased, in a spiky high voice and then cackled with her mouth wide open.

Brunhilde's attention shifted to a heavy-set old man dressed in a leather biker vest that was covered, like a cosmopolitan traveler's fridge, with stickers and patches and insignia. Andy came closer to gauge this man's worldview and saw a map of Vietnam that was made to look like a monkey, stitched onto the back of the vest, and an American eagle, its wings spread, talons out, swerving above it. Around this artwork was an amalgamation of skulls and bones and Celtic crosses, and a button on the man's left chest that stated "Gun control means using both hands." Next to the biker was his squeeze, a fiftyish lady with a yellow visor on her head. She, too, wore a leather vest, but a pristine one, with no identifiers, and nothing underneath.

"Nah, she don't need a T-shirt," the biker said, peeking at his girl-friend's cleavage as she and Brunhilde giggled like schoolgirls.

Such gaiety permeated the party site. There was a strange affect among these people. Their laughs were loud, their friendliness was solicitous, and their displays of camaraderie overt, as if they had arrived here starved for companionship and now hurried, with showy spontaneity, to fill that emotional void.

A tall, skinny man dressed as Uncle Sam, in a top hat, stripey pants, and a blue frock coat, strode around the venue. He held a stack of pamphlets that he handed out to the amused guests, who took them readily and, after scanning the contents, yelled with approval and pumped their fists.

Andy received a copy. The pamphlet was printed on letterhead featuring the back-slanted, pseudo-Gothic *We the People* font of the preamble to the US Constitution.

We the People demanded:

1. The designation of the United States of America as a stronghold of Western civilization with state policies prioritizing European-heritage population and its cultural and social values.

2. Adjustments to the immigration laws to ensure a permanent European-ancestry majority.

3. The expansion of the Civil Rights Act of 1964 to include equal protections and privileges to the "White" majority.

4. The nationalization of socially important institutions such as banks, mass media, and corporate monopolies.

5. A two-percent ceiling on Jewish employment in vital institutions in order to align such representation with the ethnic composition of the country's population.

Andy folded the pamphlet and put it in his pocket. Squealing microphone static punctured through the buzz of the crowd, and then there was a tap-tap-tap followed by a female-voiced "one, two, three." Against the backdrop of two huge hay slabs, behind a lectern, stood a middle-aged woman in a tight red dress and an ill-fitting suit jacket. She gave the people in the audience two thumbs up and accosted them with a smile that outside a political rally would be considered deranged. With a sharp, bouncy voice she began rambling about the Soros Foundation and the liberal media. While incoherent and self-contradicting at times, she was never at a loss for words, firing non sequiturs and one-liners with the speed and confidence of a sports announcer. She punctuated her delivery either with a pointed index finger or with a quick lunge forward—like that of a striking cobra—of her right hand, extending fingers while at the apex, collecting them back into a fist at the pullback.

At first Andy thought that the speaker was on some kind of uppers, meth most likely, but after listening to her, he concluded that the affect came from the power of her conviction. Her deep-seated, wide-open eyes beamed with apocalyptic urgency. She had found the truth and hurried to deliver it to others. But her listeners didn't need convincing. These people looked happy, even exhilarated in their certitude, like congregants at a religious revival. "You got that right," "Right on," could be heard from the crowd.

"Who is she?" Andy asked a man with a ZZ Top beard standing next to him.

"She's our next state senator," he replied with a grin.

Oleg swooned in and patted Andy on the back. "I'm glad you could make it," he said.

Oleg carried a paper plate with potato salad, coleslaw, and a rack of ribs. He gave the plate to Andy.

"Nice party," Andy said to Oleg.

"You like it? Good. I want you to meet someone."

Oleg ushered Andy toward a wooden garden table with two benches attached to its sides. Straddling one bench was a sixtyish man in a mustard-colored Carhartt hunting jacket over a gray sweatshirt, in golf shorts, and old cherry-colored leather loafers on his bare feet. The man's ankles were swollen, reddish, and flakey, bulging over his shoes. He was gnawing on a rib, and when he saw Oleg approach, he smiled and waved.

"This is the man I was telling you about," Oleg said to the man. "Andy, meet Lloyd. Lloyd, meet Andy."

Lloyd held up his hand to show that it was smeared in sticky barbeque sauce and then extended his elbow for a greeting. He and Andy bumped elbows.

"Lloyd is the owner of Valhalla Construction," Oleg said.

"Please join me," Lloyd said to Andy, gesturing at an empty bench. Andy sat down. Oleg lingered, kneading dirt under his feet, and Lloyd sent him on an errand.

"The sun shines brighter, the food tastes better, when you have a cause. Isn't that so?" Lloyd said, licking his fingers.

"I wouldn't know," Andy replied. "I don't have a cause."

There was a beatific air about Lloyd. He must've been a handsome man in his youth. He was of blue-veined Scottish-Irish heritage, with translucent skin, pale in the shade of green hills, instantly red under the sun. His 1980s-style sybaritic blond bangs, meant to be held together by hair gel and some time in front of the mirror, were in a state of disarray, hanging over his wide forehead like a crashing wave. He maintained those thinning locks by intermittent brush-ups of his fingers and a slight head twitch. The day-old stubble on his once plump but now sagging face looked as if he had dipped his jaw in white sand. His comportment had the gentlemanly calmness of a man with a privileged past, accustomed to having an interlocutor's full attention, but from beneath that surface equanimity emerged the irritable effect of someone who was owed but denied a proper recognition, whose promising future had never materialized. His self-neglect, it seemed, came from a place of spite, and he embraced and brandished his physical dereliction as a lifestyle statement.

"Oleg told me you're a businessman," Lloyd said, taking a bite of potato salad. His voice was soft and his delivery slow, but his eye contact was intense, probing.

Andy shuddered at the "businessman" designation but nodded and said: "In a way."

"And what is your business exactly?"

Andy mulled several options, among them "I run a prop desk" and "I'm a fixed income trader," but questioned the prudence of any of these answers given the circumstances and simply said: "I'm a mortgage broker."

"Ah." Lloyd threw his head backward. "I thought all the mortgage brokers went extinct. You know, after the real-estate bubble."

"I'm a different kind of mortgage broker. On the commercial side."

"Ah, I see." Lloyd wiped the barbeque sauce off his fingers. "Believe it or not, I myself started out as a commercial-real-estate guy. At Cubbs Harding, right out of business school."

Andy's stomach tightened at the mention of Cubbs Harding. "Oh, wow," he said, keeping a poker face.

"Lasted about two years there. They were a guerilla outlet, run by a bunch of Jews. I figured I had the wrong last name to make it there." Lloyd chuckled. His mouth was so small that it didn't stretch at all but only semi-opened in a narrow mail-slot ellipsis. Andy managed to muster a tense smile in response.

"And then, of course, they collapsed. Under their own greed. I guess there's justice in this world."

Lloyd waved and smiled at someone in the crowd. He then turned to Andy and squinted at him, and Andy felt transparent, as if under X-rays.

"Come on, Mr. Sylvain. You know how it is." Lloyd sighed, shifting his gaze over Andy's head into the distance. "Trading credit at Keating Mills makes you privy to a million things that are invisible to everyone else. You can see the entire rotten mechanism."

Andy stopped chewing and froze over his plate. He struggled to swallow the food in his mouth. "I'm not who you think I am," he said.

"And yet you're here."

Andy lifted his eyes and met Lloyd's empty stare. "Oleg invited me."

"Oleg is a good boy."

"My interest here is purely anthropological," Andy said, taking a sip of his beer. "To see the world west of the Hudson."

"Ah," Lloyd said. There were vibes of derangement in his pupils and in his tone. "So? What do you see?"

"I see people who are lost."

"Are they, though?"

Several yards away from the table, a young man of dark complexion hovered, waiting to get hold of Lloyd's attention. He was holding a stack of papers under his elbow. With a languid, welcoming wave of the hand, Lloyd signaled for him to come by. The man was well-dressed, in a Brooks Brothers suit and polished leather shoes. His longish black hair was styled in a wavy sweep from front to back, with its ends converging in the back of his head like the tail of a mallard duck. He smiled at Andy with a crooked smile. He handed the papers to Lloyd, and the two of them huddled over the graphs and numbers for about a minute.

"Good," Lloyd said, holding his finger over a set of data on the page. "We're within striking distance here. And this district will flip a hundred percent. You have an email blast all ready to go?"

"Yes," the man replied.

"Good. Don't mention these numbers."

"Of course not." He clicked his tongue and winked at Andy. "Doom and gloom as usual."

A discernible pleasure unfurled over Lloyd's face when the young man walked away. "Oh, that," he said nonchalantly, reveling in Andy's befuddlement. "He's our pollster. You see, we are not racists here. Everyone is welcome. Like I said, it's all about the cause, not identity. You, too, can be a part of it." Lloyd took a sip from his beer and stared at Andy. "I vetted you. There's a house seat open in Westchester. In your district. A man with your background can win it. And we can help you."

"I think you got the wrong guy, Lloyd." Andy shook his head.

"If you think that these people are lost, don't you want to be the one to give them guidance? A community? Hope?"

"Not like that," Andy said.

Lloyd scoffed. "What I'm doing is a public service. I'm a student of men, you see. There are weak, scared people around us everywhere. They say they want freedom, but what they really want is a safe harbor. What they want is an abdication of responsibility. They want to be told that whatever they do, whatever they believe, is good and right. The task of making that assurance falls to the strong among us, to those who recognize that such weakness is a permanent feature of society, to those who have reconciled with it and availed themselves to do the dirty, ungrateful job of being a guide to the depraved, to the scared, to the misfits. In that cozy, welcoming space, I give them permission to be what they always wanted to be. And they gladly take it and think they're free. Is it not good?"

"It's make-believe," Andy said, shaking his head. "You're selling them a bill of goods."

"I'm a scholar," Lloyd said. His oily, twine-like hair quavered in the soft wind. "I know that an idea is more powerful than bread. There's power in belief. It doesn't matter whether what they believe is true or not. Their fervor, their intensity, can make it true." He sniffed and stared at Andy. "Concordia Walden defaulted simply because someone willed it. That's power."

Andy stopped breathing. He felt the food rising from his stomach back to his throat and gulped loudly.

"You are a smart man. You should understand it." Lloyd wiped his mouth. "And I can see you're searchin', Andy. You searchin'," he added in the porous, crumbly voice of a frail old woman.

Andy was quiet, staring at his plate. A gust of wind shuffled the stack of pamphlets on the table and lifted them in the air like dry autumn leaves.

"My dear Andy," Lloyd said, his tone changing to the saccharine pitch of a salesman. "You know I'm right. Admit it and accept it and you will find peace. And think about what I said. Sleep on it. You can be a congressman." He stood up. "Now if you'll excuse me. I have to attend to my flock."

Lloyd stumbled away, chasing after the flying pamphlets.

Andy couldn't finish his food. He picked up his paper plate and tossed it into a large trash bin. Uncle Sam passed him by. Behind him was Oleg.

"Look at this guy," Oleg said joyously. "How patriotic it is. That's what I like about America. You're big patriots."

"Yeah." Andy took a sip of beer. "They're not exactly friendly to immigrants though," he said carefully.

"Only for a special kind of immigrant. From third-world countries. Me? I feel welcome. There's a *brotherhood* here." Oleg gazed at Andy with his wide blue eyes, unclouded by doubt.

Andy wanted to tell Oleg a few things about American history and the Civil War and Reconstruction and the 1960s, but he didn't know where to begin and how to deliver it all in a concise and compelling way to someone who had a poor command of English, someone enthralled by displays of American insignia, in a holiday atmosphere not conducive to nuanced conversation. Whatever words he could muster could not compete with the primacy of feeling accepted and appreciated, of being a part of something grand.

"So, what did Lloyd say?"

"He, uh, he wanted me to run for office."

"I told him you are adequate man. Solid man." A sly smile touched Oleg's face. "And what did you say?"

Andy looked at Oleg. "I said that I'm too busy."

"Really?" Oleg seemed disappointed.

"Oleg, these are not nice people," Andy said quietly.

"You just have to listen more to what they're saying. They make a lot of sense."

"Yeah," Andy said. The corner of his mouth bent with skepticism, and Oleg must've noticed it.

"They give me work." Oleg shrugged. "They pay cash."

Andy walked back to his car. He saw Brunhilde alone in the parking lot. She wobbled on her short stumpy legs, slouching under a heavy backpack. Her breasts jiggled. In one hand she was carrying a folded table; with the other she was scrolling through her phone. Andy watched her for several seconds, marveling at her ugliness, conjuring up tragic scenarios about her life trajectory and castigating himself for having such thoughts. As she approached an ancient rusty Ford van with curtains inside the windows, his disgust turned to pity and the urge to help, the kind one feels toward a homeless pet. He hurried after her and cleared his throat.

"Excuse me, ma'am," he said.

"What?" She lifted her eyes from the phone. The spiky cheer was gone from her face, and only tiredness and inertia remained.

"Could I ask you a quick question?"

"Sure," she said, composing herself, eyeing Andy with interest.

"Do you really believe in what they were saying?"

"Who?"

"The people at the party."

"What do you mean?"

"I mean, don't you feel like these people are lying to you?"

"Lying about what?" she said.

"You know, about all this Soros stuff."

"Huh. Like, what are you saying?"

"I'm saying that it's all a con, and you're a mark."

"And who are you to tell me this?"

"I, uh, it doesn't matter. I've lived a long life, and I've seen a lot of things. I think that you could be in a tough spot right now. Maybe you need help getting out of this." Andy pointed at her van. "If you need money to stay in a hotel for a few days, or something, to carry you over, I can help."

She stared at him. "Are you hitting on me?" she said coyly. "I have a boyfriend, just so you know."

Andy paused, processing her line of thought.

"But he's away," she added with a wily, stretchy tease.

"Christ! No," Andy said. "That's not what this is about."

"What, I'm not good enough for you?"

"It's not that."

"Well, fuck you then." She climbed into the van and shut the door.

* * *

Can I pls crash at your place? Andy texted Misha. *I'm half hour away in NJ.*

Lol, sure, Misha replied.

When Andy arrived, Misha was in his bedroom. Andy helped himself to a bottle of Perrier from the fridge and sat on the window-sill, staring at the traffic below. From his bedroom, Misha shouted that he would be right out.

A beautiful melody enveloped the loft, a classical concerto or a symphony. Andy wasn't sure who the composer was, but judging by the style and instruments—violins and brass—he wagered that it was Beethoven or Mozart. He searched his phone for a music-detection app and held it up to see if it recognized the piece. The app was buffering, struggling to capture the title or to find it in the database. He came closer to the speakers hidden in the ceiling and stood on his toes, hoisting the phone above his head.

The melody struck him to the point where he strained to breathe. There was a story there. There was struggle and failure and struggle again, as if the forces of light, weak and outnumbered, wrestled inch-es and moments of dignity from the vast, continuous darkness, only to slide back, losing the slim winnings, and then trying again and again, hopeless but undeterred. Then, in a brief respite—clarinets, or was it oboe?—a glimmer of hope. It was a fleeting, false hope, but one that compelled men to continue nonetheless, sustained not by knowledge and not by the savvy, but by blindness and faith alone. Because if they knew, if only they knew, if they opened their eyes …

An unwelcome wave of emotion rolled up from his gut to his throat. This can't be the takeaway, he thought. This piece of music must be about something else. Maybe the composer was writing it for a dead friend or a woman who left him. Who would create such beautiful art so full of despair?

He heard Misha's footsteps and lowered the phone, pretending to scroll through messages.

"Ah," Misha said. He was wrapped in a robe and drying his hair with a towel. "Beethoven's Seventh. Second movement. By Karajan."

Andy's face was flushed, and he stood with his back to the window, hoping that his moment of weakness would go undetected in a semi-dark room. He cleared his throat. "Nice," he squeezed out with a forced nonchalance. His voice sounded like the croaking of an old lady. The pressure in his neck was giving him a headache.

"It's a transcendent piece of music. Written in a time of great upheaval. A lot of people are haunted by it." Misha paused and stared at Andy. "Not all is lost with you," he added.

Andy tried to shake off his melancholy. "Why is it haunting?" he asked.

Misha plunged onto the couch, hanging a towel over his shoulders. "This piece of music hints at the existence of epic battles that happen on a meta level. I think that it makes you realize that the triumph of good, if it ever happens, a big if, will not be brought about by people like us. Because we would conduct calculations, and we would see the futility and would do nothing. But the fools—they will continue. In some twisted way, they are our only hope."

Below, Broadway twinkled and blasted with horns, a sound of New York that always lifted Andy's spirits, but now he sensed some hollowness in it. "We are too late," he said. "The fools got harvested by the crooks."

Andy proceeded to tell Misha about the party in New Jersey and about Oleg, and Misha listened, without being surprised, nodding softly, and staring into space.

"One is either a conman or a victim. Both are respectable American occupations," Misha said quietly when Andy finished his tale.

"Who are we then?"

"We're somewhere in-between."

* * *

Andy stayed at Misha's loft overnight, sleeping on the couch. In the morning, he texted Joanna to see if she wanted to go for brunch. She replied that she had a yoga class and then a cosmetologist appointment.

So high maintenance, he wrote back.

Lol, she replied.

He ventured outside and brought back fresh orange juice, bagels, lox, and cream cheese. He made coffee and woke Misha up, and they had breakfast. Andy cleaned up Misha's kitchen, thanked him for the hospitality, and drove to Westchester.

Andy had about a week left before he was supposed to be back from rehab, and he wanted to get the most out of the remaining free time. He spent the next several days going for jogs, binging on Netflix, and mulling on how to break up with Lauren in the most benign way.

Lauren superseded him. She called him on his official release day, asked him how he felt, and said that she wanted to take a break from the relationship. "I think that you, too, need some time on your own," she said, "to get back on your feet."

"You're right," he said. "This year has been very stressful for me. I've been neglectful, and you deserve better than that."

"I'll leave the key with the doorman," Lauren said. "There's still some of my stuff inside, and I'll send someone to pick it up later."

"No worries. And no rush."

XXI: The Ends

The Street Bohemians had moved their annual gathering to the Berkshires that fall. After word got around about last year's debauchery, the ballrooms around town spiked the prices, and the Bohemians' planning committee sent an official memo to the club members stating that they wanted to test a new format for the festival. The committee presented two options—a *Starship Troopers*-inspired paintball game, and a medieval revival—and put it up for a vote. The majority voted for a revival. The planners rented a ten-acre farm upstate for a two-day retreat and hired a team of carpenters to build a medieval compound to accommodate a hundred spoiled urbanites. For the sleeping accommodations, they brought in trailers and booked rooms in nearby motels.

Andy was on the fence about going until the day of the event. In the morning, after a light jog around the house, he found a package with his costume that he had ordered online two weeks ago and almost forgotten about waiting on the porch. After trying the costume on, he decided in favor of going. He texted Misha to see if he was coming too, and Misha replied, *Will make a late cameo.* Andy drove to the site of the festival, near Binghamton.

Two chartered buses brought in the city folk. Hired actors in period garb greeted each guest with made-for-the-occasion individually monogrammed leather wine sacks filled with red wine. Blue Hill at Stone Barns delivered five roasted piglets, dozens of free-range turkeys, and trays of grilled vegetables for a sunset feast. Local stables brought in horses for a mock jousting tournament. Confused horses stalled and bucked under the cocksure traders, hurling the drunken "knights" into the mud to the crowd's cheers and jeers.

On a small wooden stage, a chamber-music quartet of awkward Julliard students entertained the guests with soothing medieval tunes. Two men dressed in red-and-gold, puffy-sleeved doublets and white tights that bulged rather unnaturally in the groin area were sitting on the edge of the stage, holding silver goblets in their hands. Under the men's guises, Andy recognized Caldera and Hoffman. Friends now those two, he thought. Huh.

Caldera and Hoffman were busy pestering the young musicians with demands to play Jethro Tull. They held invisible flutes to their lips, issuing half-spitting, half-farting sounds, laughed, and sipped their wine. The kids did their best to comply.

Caldera squinted in Andy's direction, and Andy pretended to look away, grateful to be shielded from recognition by his glued-on fake white beard. Andy had come dressed as a wizard, in a long white robe, with a pointy hat, a staff in one hand and an Ikea lantern with a candle inside in another. Soon, as night fell, he took it upon himself to stand guard at a narrow path leading to a row of Porta-Potties hidden in the fir grove, lighting the way for stumbling, drunken partygoers, scaring the women and amusing the men.

Misha arrived late and without a costume. In lieu of a costume he brought along a DJ, a young Israeli, and both ventured about a hundred yards from the main camp, into a beechwood grove at the edge of a lake, where they set up a secluded rave scene with folding beach chairs and acid-colored canvas stretched between the tree trunks. After the chamber music died down, the DJ began playing EDM beats. Some of the guests migrated to the grove out of curiosity, drawn by the throbbing bass and the synthetic, hissing progressions with a rollercoaster of gradual buildups and tension-releasing plunges.

Misha was dancing, spinning the glowsticks, stomping the ground like a rowdy stallion. The Julliard students, two girls and two boys, put down their instruments and joined him for a mini rave. After an hour, with his energy diminished, Misha stood with both feet planted firmly on the ground and swayed his torso monotonously left and right like a zombie. Under the knowing hands of the DJ, the merciless techno sound had softened into a chilling drum and bass, enabling a gentle exit for the exhausted, but incapable of stopping on their own, dancers.

Andy went to the camp's kitchen and brought Misha a cup of hot chocolate. Misha interrupted his pagan sacrament, baffled, as if plucked from another dimension, but drank the chocolate eagerly.

"Come," Andy said. "Let's go rest a little."

They dragged the folding chairs toward the lakeshore and sat down. The woods were now quiet. The lazy drum and bass had finally dissolved, and everyone had gone back to their trailers. Andy took off his sneakers and dug his feet into the soft sand.

"Maybe now we should get back in the game. We've had enough time off." Andy's words sounded flat. "There are scalps out there to be claimed."

"You think?" Misha scoffed. "A man realizes that idleness is torture, that it will kill him and that he must, at once, make his way back to the city and plunge into its forgiving churn," he said in a mocking tone.

"But what else can we do?" Andy sighed. "I sometimes think about if the world could be organized any differently. If, for example, other civilizations exist, one has to wonder how they are organized economically. No matter the planet, no matter the structure of their society, they all have to deal with limited resources that have to be somehow distributed. And pretty soon, one arrives at a situation where, even in those other alien worlds, no matter how advanced, a living soul, just like us, has to earn his keep. He, too, has to get up in the morning and slug through, maybe, morning traffic and get to his desk or whatever and do his job. Of course, he can have tentacles and have, like, three eyes and shit, but I can't imagine his life working any other way. One can't get something out of nothing. Maybe that creature gets paid in some kind of credits, and his pleasures are different from ours, but the concept is still the same. He's born, he works, and he dies."

Misha listened, drawing shapes in the sand with a dry branch. "I once read a sci-fi book where there was a thinking ocean," Misha said.

At the water's edge, by a thick bush with its branches dangling over the shallow water, a small rowboat was roped to a wooden pole, bobbing like a buoy on the lake's gentle ripples.

"You wanna go out on that boat?" Misha asked.

They stepped, barefoot, into the swiveling vessel. Misha sat on the floor, leaning on the boat's stern and Andy took command of the paddles. He rowed to the middle of the lake, scooping the water with deep, wide strokes, happy to give his underworked muscles a pleasant workout. The night fog enveloped the lake like a milky steam.

"Pure bliss," Andy said and put the paddles down. They sat in silence, listening to the soft sounds of the night forest.

"I don't know," Misha said. "I'd be lying if I said I didn't want to dive back into the game. I think it's a welcome distraction. But there's some switch in my head that got triggered, and it prevents me from claiming my old self."

"Come on." Andy's voice firmed. "We'll rent a floor in Midtown, hire some analysts. It will snap you out of your gloom."

"Midtown." Misha scoffed. "Midtown now gives me both panic attacks and nostalgia. But it's a weird nostalgia. It's like a boxer missing the ring, missing being hit on the head and hitting others. Whenever

I happen to be in Midtown and I see a group of bros walking with their lunches back to their offices, their motions and their preoccupations seem to me both meaningful and meaningless. I sway between wanting to go back and be like them again, and to stand on the sidelines and mourn them."

"Mourn them? Why?"

Misha thought for a moment, scratching his upper lip. "Because they don't want to know."

"Know what?"

Misha took a pack of cigarettes from his pocket. "The ends."

"What ends?"

Misha pulled a cigarette out of the pack and lit it. Andy waited as Misha took his first long drag, closing his eyes from the high. "Did you ever notice how most women are not impressed by innovations? They'll use them, but they are not as excited as us to learn about some new technology. That's because on some level they are not interested in means; they are interested in the ends, and some of those are murky for us. We don't have the time to define the ends, because we're busy with innovations. A structured bond is an innovation. A delivery app is an innovation." He tapped his finger on the cigarette to shake the ash off into the lake. "But at the end of the day, it's still us shuffling risk like chairs on the *Titanic*. It's still a guy on a bike bringing you food. On a gut level, women know that something doesn't add up. We present it as if we have solved a problem, but it wasn't the problem that needed to be solved."

"You sound just like Madeline."

"Oh, Madeline knows it. And Ava knows it. Even Lauren knows it; she just struggles to express it adequately. Was Madeline ever impressed by what you do?"

Andy looked down, then away toward the shore. "I always wanted her to be."

"Women nod when we tell them about the cool stuff that we do, like, 'Cool story bro,' but they are not impressed by any of it the way we want them to be. They know what the ends are but are confounded by millions of little barriers—by survival, by procreational distractions, by inadequate vocabulary, by fear of collective mockery from declaring them. By recognizing the hopelessness of trying to argue the point. Those ends are so serious that they're afraid we're going to laugh at them. And they're right. We will laugh *because* it's so serious. *Because* we understand the relevance of their questions. We are horrified by that seriousness." He paused and inhaled and let the smoke out through his nostrils. "So we all just paddle directionless, while constantly improving the quality of the paddle. We can paddle very efficiently now. Our paddle is the best in the world."

He fell quiet. The predawn grayness creeped over the tops of the pines surrounding the lake. A spooked bird darted out from the bracken ferns by the lakeside and flittered over the water.

"And what about Joanna?" Andy asked.

Misha sniffed. "Joanna once knew it too."

"Once?"

"She became a man. Figuratively speaking. Her job turned her into a man. That's why she jokes and laughs all the time. It's her shield. She knows that if she were earnest, she'd lose clients and accounts. Her colleagues would avoid her. Earnestness scares men. They, women, are too close to finding something out, too close to the truth, to something important that threatens the order. I think that, perhaps, Joanna once knew that, because she's not stupid, but had to discard this knowledge to continue. Now she doesn't want to find out." Misha squinted at Andy. "You knew her when she was still green."

"I did," Andy said.

"So you can see the trajectory." He flung the cigarette butt into the water with a snap of his fingers.

They rowed back to the shore.

The camp was now asleep. The guests had retreated to their heated trailers. The Julliard students were sleeping on chairs and on blankets spread out on the ground. They had neither a ride back nor quarters for the night. Andy nudged them gently and told them to relocate to his trailer. He stayed outside, stretching out on the wooden bench under the dining hall canopy, happy to be an incidental purveyor of lovemaking. He felt the chills of the night and breathed in the frosty autumn air and found a strange pleasure in the hardship. An hour later, the camp came to life, clattering with breakfast preparations as the catering personnel unloaded their supplies and heated up the portable stoves.

Andy waited for the Julliard kids to wake up, made sure they ate breakfast, and drove them back to the city.

XXII: A Good American

A "collect" number had been haunting Andy's phone for days, and, after declining it a dozen times, he finally picked it up just to unload a beautiful and caustic tirade that had formed in his mind on the pestering caller. On the other line was Oleg, at once grateful and distraught and stuttering through emotions. Through the barrage of words and exclamations, Andy was able to detect that Oleg was being kept in an immigration detention center and that Andy was the only person he could turn to for help.

"Calm down," Andy said. "Where are you geographically?"

"In New Jersey," Oleg said. "They put me in a cell with all kinds of Mexicans. You gotta help me, Andy."

"How did you get caught?"

"I, uh, they stopped me for speeding."

"Okay. Just hang in there. I have to make a few phone calls."

"Thank you, thank you, Andy. You're my best friend," Oleg whimpered. "If you come, bring cigarettes if you can, please."

Andy called his divorce attorney, who recommended a good immigration lawyer. He called the lawyer, a woman named Betsy, and they agreed to meet two days later and drive to the detention center. He gave her as many details as he could, and she told him that she had handled hundreds of cases like Oleg's, and that they should be able to get him out.

Betsy was a middle-aged Black woman. She waited for him in her car by the court building downtown. In the car on the way to New Jersey, she briefed him on the case. In her assessment, she was cautious and chose her words carefully, and Andy thought that it was just the usual lawyerly prudence.

"He wasn't stopped for speeding," Betsy said when they arrived. "I don't know if you know that. He assaulted a cop during a protest rally."

Andy inhaled through his teeth and rubbed his forehead. "Jesus. Protest rally? What was he protesting?"

"I guess you can ask him that."

"What does that mean? I mean, for his chances."

"It doesn't look good. He had an unlicensed gun. The cop was Black. It's a big mess."

The guard brought Oleg into the meeting room, where, on the table, Andy unloaded several packs of cigarettes, soap, toiletries, and socks. Oleg's face lit up with gratitude, but, when Andy introduced Betsy, he slumped with confusion and disbelief. Betsy calmly explained to Oleg that he could be facing a felony charge and that this was more than just an immigration matter at this point. As she was talking, Oleg shifted his eyes, in growing panic, between her and Andy.

"You punched a cop? A Black cop? What did you think was gonna happen? What the hell were you thinking?" Andy chided him when Betsy was finished.

Oleg sniffed. "I was there with my guys. I, I thought it was the beginning."

"The beginning of what?"

Oleg looked down, silent.

"If you simply overstayed your visa, maybe we could've done something, like try to go the asylum route, but now we can't," Betsy said.

"What does that mean?" Oleg asked and looked at Andy. There was fear in his eyes.

"That means they're probably going to deport you," Andy said, avoiding eye contact with Oleg.

"No, no! There's gotta be something you could do. You gotta help me. You must help me," Oleg pleaded, trying to catch Andy's gaze. His mouth stretched into the quivering frown of a despondent child. He sniffled and wiped his nose with the back of his hand. Andy watched him quietly. "I could have been good American. Model American," Oleg wailed. He buried his face in his palms, and his shoulders shook.

"That's not what America is about, buddy," Andy said softly.

"What is it about?"

Andy didn't answer.

"You're a fool. A fucking fool," Oleg cried when the guards took him away. "To be like you. White and rich. To be respected man. What more can you want? Do you understand how lucky you are? You can just go live your life any way you want. All your problems not real. They are only problems because you make them your problems."

"What happens to him now?" Andy asked Betsy on the drive back to the city.

"Nothing. He'll just get deported." She looked at Andy. "Don't beat yourself up over it. You did all you could. I can't even begin to tell you how many more deserving, hardworking, decent people get caught and sent back to countries they've never even been to. I had one client whose parents brought him here when he was two years old. He grew up here thinking he was an American. He got stopped for some minor violation, one thing led to the next, and he's deported to Somalia. *That's* tragic. Oleg will just be sent back to his home country. He speaks the language. There's no war there. No one will persecute him."

Andy listened to her, staring out the window at the dull industrial New Jersey landscape.

Betsy's car radio hummed with the hypnotizing murmur of a female NPR host. The sleepy monotone of the host was then hijacked by the coarse barking of a presidential candidate. Betsy turned the volume down.

"He's a clown," Andy said, pointing at the radio. "He won't make it past the primaries." Andy looked at her. "He's the last gasp of white supremacy."

Betsy shrugged and didn't say anything.

"I want to ask your opinion about something," Andy said. "About some interesting phenomenon that I observed. Oleg invited me to this party once. I didn't know what it was, so I went. Turned out it was like a modern-day Klan revival. Everybody was white, and many of the attendees looked like they suffered from some kind of mental illness. But there was one Black guy there, doing some work for the main organizer. He must've noticed my confusion, and he gave me this look, like, Hey, man, it's all a game. I'm just a player." Andy sighed. "Anyway, I don't mean to tokenize you, but what do you think of this as a, uh, Black person? What do you think motivates guys like him?"

"I think it's more about power structure than race," Betsy said.

"Still, such a fundamental betrayal of his kin. And for what? Money?"

"He could be a ghetto kid. Ghetto kids have good radars for opportunities. He sensed some kind of opportunity there. A vehicle for advancement, so to speak."

"It's a circus wagon. A dead end. He tied his fortunes to a losing trade. He might think he's savvy, and he might even make a few bucks, but two years down the road, no one will shake his hand. He won't wash off that stain." Andy looked at Betsy, seeking either a confirmation or a counterpoint.

Betsy was mum, doggedly focused on the road. There was skepticism, even resignation, in her silence.

"You disagree?" he pressed.

"That last gasp, when it comes, it will be fast and loose and violent. And he thinks he will be spared," she said.

"I don't think it'll come to that, Betsy," Andy said. "We expunged those demons in the sixties. We elected Obama twice. And Oleg—he's just a confused man. A kind but confused man. He has fundamentally misread the situation. He's been led astray by charlatans. He only joined them because they were the only ones who wanted anything to do with him. They took him in. They gave him a job. And he trusted them."

"If that makes you feel better," Betsy said.

She dropped him off near Federal Plaza in lower Manhattan.

"I bet you fifty bucks that buffoon will lose," Andy said before getting out of the car.

"I like your certainty, but I'll pass," Betsy replied with a smile.

He bid farewell to Betsy by saying "Let's stay in touch" and tapping his knuckles on the roof of her car.

Andy texted Misha, saying that he was downtown and was going to stop by. He didn't get a response. He picked up a pizza at a corner pizzeria. The doorman greeted Andy and gave him several days' worth of mail, bounded with a rubber band, to take upstairs. Andy took the elevator to the upper floor.

Perky music videos from the peak MTV era, with the sound on, played on the screen when he entered the living room. Misha was sitting on the couch, dressed for a night out—in a dark blue velvet jacket. He sported a fresh haircut.

"You finally cut your hair," Andy said, coming from behind. Misha didn't turn and didn't respond. Andy went around the couch and saw a dried puddle of vomit on and under the coffee table. On the glass tabletop were several dime bags with a white substance. Misha's eyes were open, but when Andy rushed to check his pulse, his hand was cold and stiff. He must've been dead for hours, if not days.

Andy called 911. As he waited for the police to arrive, he checked Misha's phone. There were his own messages; then there were messages from a woman, probably a date, first annoyed at Misha's unresponsiveness, then informing him that she was ordering the drinks now, and then a final message, like an epitaph: 'Douchebag.'

A cheerful Duran Duran video came on, and Andy searched for the remote, finding it between the coach pillows. He could only silence the volume. The sunny images remained.

The police came promptly. There was not much they could do other than call the coroner.

"It's most likely fentanyl," the police officer said to Andy, picking up the dime bags from the coffee table and transferring them into a red-sealed evidence bag. "A lot of that going around these days. The dealers just mix it into anything."

The coroner's team wheeled Misha's body away. Andy stayed behind and filled out a police report, stating who he was and how and when he discovered the body.

"Any close relatives that we can call?" the officer asked Andy.

Andy shook his head. "If there are, they're all in Russia," he said. He asked the officer if he could get the results of the autopsy, and the officer gave him a number to call.

When everyone was gone Andy plunged into a chair and sat, staring at the now-muted videos still rolling off the projector. How innocent were the eighties, a decade of greed and excess, in hindsight, he thought. He sat motionless for a while.

Misha died, he texted Caldera.

His phone rang a second later.

"What?" Caldera shouted. "How?"

"They think it's a fentanyl overdose," Andy said.

"How's that possible? He got clean. I can't believe it."

"It was laced into cocaine. He was getting ready to go on a date. If I were you, I'd be careful, if you know what I mean."

"My dealer is solid," Caldera said and paused. "But maybe it's providence trying to tell me something."

"Make of it what you will," Andy said. "Don't tell Joanna. I'll tell her myself. I gotta go." He hung up. He didn't respond to Caldera's attempts to call him back and let it all go to voicemail.

Joanna took the news of Misha's death stoically. On the phone, she gasped and then stayed silent while he described the events of the last hour. She asked him if he wanted to come over, and he said yes.

He picked out two of Misha's paintings and took a taxi uptown. Joanna listened as he told her, over and over, in a cracking voice, that Misha had died while preparing to go on a date, and that it was this fact that upset him the most. "He was ready to dive back into life," he kept repeating, distraught.

He stayed at Joanna's overnight. They cuddled in bed, and that embrace—wordless, unobliging, justified by shared grief—calmed him into a strange, new state of bliss, a previously unknown category of connection. He could sob and sniffle and be weak—and be forgiven.

* * *

The next morning, as he was crossing Grand Central Station's main hall on his way to catch an early train to Westchester, someone called his name: "Andy! Mr. Sylvain!"

He strained not to look around and continued walking.

"Mr. Sylvain!" the voice persisted.

Andy stopped. A red-haired man in a cheap suit, holding a worn-out leather briefcase, rushed toward him. With dismay, he recognized the accountant from the New Mexico resort, but he squinted, pretending not to.

"I'm Billy. From New Mexico, remember?" the accountant shouted. "What a pleasant coincidence. I called your office, but they told me you weren't there."

"Ah, that's right. I remember you," Andy said and forced a smile. "How's it going? What are you doing in New York?"

Billy exuded the twitchy impatience of a busy person who shuffled between appointments and presentations and was talking a lot. "I'm here on business," he said. "I work for an accounting-software firm now. Went back to my roots."

"That sounds great," Andy said. "Good for you."

"This is an amazing town." Billy gazed in awe around the majestic terminal. "Out here, one's gotta spin. That's what I do." He looked at Andy with the mercurial, probing eyes of a salesman. "Hey, what do you say if I stop by your office one of these days and put up a little presentation. You might need a software upgrade, you never know. I can get you a friendship discount." He winked.

"I'm actually between jobs at the moment," Andy said.

Billy's face brightened.

"Well, guess what," he bawled. "You are in luck. We're actually hiring. It's commission-based for the first six months, then you can negotiate a base salary based on your sales volume. Great benefits and health insurance too. And with a resume like yours …"

"I'm not really an accountant, Billy," Andy said.

"Who are you then?"

"I'm … I'm someone who is tired," Andy replied, shaking his head. "I'm just tired."

"I hear ya," Billy said, stepping back. "Well. Let me give you my card at least. What if you change your mind? You never know."

Andy took Billy's card and, before Billy could squeeze in any more pecuniary overtures, said that he had a train to catch and quickly walked away.

XXIII: A Man in Flux

In his final will, Misha Pomerantzev—science-contest winner, atheist, trader, cynic, and humanist—wished to be buried according to the Russian Orthodox tradition. This fact weighed heavily on Andy as he drove for an hour and a half to a Russian Orthodox monastery in upstate New York, where Misha's estate lawyer had arranged for the funeral ceremony.

Andy parked at the monastery's cast-iron gates. In front of the gates, a group of shawled, slouching old women peddled thin, sticky church candles, plastic wreaths, and red and white carnations that they sold in even numbers, as the custom required for the mourning rituals. Behind the gates, on the sprawling monastery grounds, lay a large Orthodox cemetery, with all the graves marked with three-barred, seven-point crosses. Monks clad in black robes shuffled back and forth, on indecipherable errands, between the compound buildings. Too much commotion for a monastery, Andy thought and stepped through the church's massive metal-patterned doors. The air inside the church smelled of candlewax and sourdough bread. Instead of the holy solemnity that Andy had expected to find in the cathedral, the chamber swirled with structureless human motion. There were no pews, only a few chairs along the edges for the elderly and the incapacitated, but they were unoccupied. It seemed that there was a silent agreement between the faithful that sitting down in a house of God was a sign of disrespect. People moved sporadically, came up to the icons that covered the church's walls, crossed themselves before a chosen saint, bowed, turned to the altar, crossed themselves again, bowed again. Who are all these people, all these grim Russians? Andy wondered. Hired pallbearers? Spectators? Misha didn't have any family here in New York, and as far as Andy was concerned, he was Misha's only real friend.

He got a text from Joanna. She was on her way but running late.

"Andy."

Someone called his name. He turned and saw a thirtyish man in a nice suit flanked by two young ladies with an airbrushed Instagram look, Hermes scarves covering their hair, Louis Vuitton purses on their wrists. The man, with whom Andy had spoken earlier on the phone, was Taylor, Misha's estate lawyer, and the ladies were Misha's nieces from Moscow.

Andy expressed his condolences to the nieces, who looked at him with glassy stares and didn't respond. Language barrier, Andy thought.

"They're devastated," Taylor said.

"We all are," Andy replied.

Misha's open casket stood at the transept, in front of the sparkling iconostasis, facing the altar behind it. Andy looked for a dais or any sort of podium. "Is anybody going to say anything?" he mumbled, looking around the lively but indifferent room.

"Maybe they don't eulogize here?" Taylor said and shrugged.

The nieces were glued to their phones.

Andy walked toward the middle of the room and stopped before the casket. He pulled a folded piece of paper from his pocket and cleared his throat.

"A man is tasked …" He began reading from his notes, lifting his head to see if anyone was listening. His gaze was met with a steely stare coming from an imposing figure who stood in the center of the room, leaning on a cane. It was Ms. Cooke, hunched and wobbling and looking more frail than the last time Andy had seen her. He felt an incriminating tilt in her expression, as if she blamed him for Misha's death. He acknowledged her with a tight bend of his lips, caught his breath, and cleared his throat again. His larynx produced an embarrassing high-pitch sound.

"A man is tasked with," he squeezed out before a deacon in a black floor-length cassock came running toward him.

"Not here, not here," the deacon whispered loudly, taking Andy by the elbow. "At the grave site. Everything at the grave site. No speeches in the church."

"Apologies, it's his first time," came Madeline's voice from behind him, saving him from embarrassment.

"Good to see you," Andy said, relieved.

Madeline looked perfect in a black and gold brocade suit—the grand old dame that she was always destined to be. Her face looked a bit hollowed out in the low light of the cathedral, but the underlying boniness was noble. It occurred to him that that's what she always was—a mourner, an old soul, like Misha. A mourner for the center that, as both of them had discerned, could not hold.

Ms. Cooke slowly approached Andy and Madeline, the metal tip of her cane knocking on the stone floor, echoing through the chamber. Andy introduced Ms. Cooke to Madeline as "a warrior, a thinker, and an all-around scholar of man's follies."

"And this is Madeline, my ex-wife and Misha's good friend," he added. The two women shook hands. A sudden realization brightened Ms. Cooke's face.

"Aren't you *the* Madeline who wrote a thesis on Russian monks? I happen to have read it. Misha gave me a copy."

"Yes, that's me," Madeline said.

"I must say it's a superb and thought-provoking work. With your permission, I'd like to include it in the curriculum at our rehabilitation program."

"That's where I went," Andy inserted nervously. "It's like Davos meets the Aspen Institute. Very upscale."

"Oh?" Madeline replied and smiled. "By all means. If you think those Davos men can handle the implications."

Madeline and Ms. Cooke shared a loaded, understanding glance that left Andy feeling like a child among adults.

"And if you have the time and the inclination, perhaps, we could have you come in and give a lecture? For a fee, of course," Ms. Cooke said.

"I would love to," Madeline said. "Let me give you my contact information." ·

"Ah, I have it," Ms. Cooke said. "I believe Andy used you as an emergency contact." She smiled and looked at Andy.

There's some kind of conspiracy between all these women, Andy thought. They always know something that I don't; they always find a common touchstone inaccessible to a regular guy.

A priest, in a burgundy and gold vestment with a high stiffened collar that touched the back of his neck, appeared from a discreet door behind the iconostasis. On his head he wore an imposing brocade headpiece in the shape of a bulbous imperial crown decorated with gemstones. Beside him walked a deacon, carrying a thurible, an engraved copper chalice suspended on three chains that emitted clouds of incense. In a businesslike manner, the priest advanced to the casket, opened his prayer book, and began the liturgy for the departed.

The service was in Russian. The priest had a deep, operatic voice. Andy closed his eyes and imagined that he was at the Metropolitan Opera, listening to *Eugene Onegin*.

The priest chanted and sang for about an hour, and every time he took a pause, Andy thought that this was it; it must be the end. But no, the priest turned the pages in his book, the deacon swung the thurible over the casket, and the service continued in what seemed like a deliberate plot to test the faithful's endurance. Everyone—even, to Andy's surprise and confusion, the frail, hunchbacked crones—stood during the service, showing no signs of exhaustion, crossing themselves fervently, continuously, and, as far as he could tell, randomly.

Getting stiff and tired, Andy shifted his weight from one leg to the other, then rocked from his heels to the balls of his feet and back.

"This is almost the end," Madeline whispered in Andy's ear.

The priest sang for another twenty minutes.

After the service ended, the mourners formed a line around the coffin to say their final goodbyes. Misha's body rested on the white pillowy lining, in a dreadful black suit, his hands folded on his chest. The nieces leaned over Misha's face and touched his forehead with their lips.

Andy sighed and looked down at his friend.

"You look good in a suit," he said and leaned over Misha's overpowdered, waxy face. "They did a hatchet job on your face though."

* * *

"The Misha I knew would be appalled by all of this," Andy said to Madeline as they exited the church and followed the pallbearers toward the grave. "All these Orthodox theatrics."

"He always struck me as a man in flux," Madeline said after a long pause. "Grasping for some anchor. And failing to find it."

They walked in silence. The pathway gravel crackled under their feet.

"I found him," Andy said quietly. "I found him when he died."

Madeline slowed down and looked at him.

"He was ready to go on a date. All dressed up and with a fresh haircut. He looked like he wanted to dive back into a normal life."

"Or to settle for a close approximation," she responded, resuming her pace.

They arrived at the grave site. Andy spotted Joanna, in tight black pants and in a loose camel wool coat, hurrying along the graveyard path toward the burial site. She waved at him and stopped a few feet away, behind the mourners.

The priest asked if anybody had any last words for "God's servant Mikhail." There were no takers. Misha's lawyer, Madeline, and Ms. Cooke glanced at Andy, but his prepared speech was now hidden deep in his pocket, and he demurred, lowering his head and staring at the pile of fresh soil surrounding the hole in the ground. Anything he could say now seemed lame and superfluous, especially after such an exhaustive ceremony, and he didn't want to hold anybody up.

The burial workers lowered Misha's sealed casket into the ground. Sporadic handfuls of dirt tapped on the casket's lid.

Wait for me, Andy texted Joanna.

"How's Ava?" he asked Madeline as they walked toward the parking lot.

"She's good. You should call her."

"I will. And you? How are you, now that you're finally alone?"

Madeline lifted a tissue to dab under her sunglasses. Then she straightened her back and lifted her chin. "I welcome the solitude," she said. "I want to be that old lady that sits on a porch, looking at the world, marveling at its ineptitude and its rudderless zeal."

Andy watched Madeline drive away and walked to his car, where Joanna waited for him. They embraced, and he asked her if she wanted to join him for a drink. She followed him in her car to a dive bar in a nearby town. The place was empty, and they proceeded to the most secluded table in the back. A waitress brought the snacks menu—Buffalo wings and mozzarella sticks—but they both waved it off, signaling that they were there just for drinks. Andy got a beer and Joanna a glass of house wine.

"I have a ringing in my ears," Andy said. "I only discovered it recently, but it could have been there for years. In the city it is masked by the noise. So you don't even know that there's some kind of malfunction."

"I can try and get you a good audiologist," Joanna said.

"I think I need to get out of the city for a while."

"Like where?"

He took a deep breath and burrowed his fingers into his hair. "A quiet place. A farm. A cabin. In, like, Wyoming," he said and looked at Joanna with a probing smile. "But seriously. Think about how gorgeous that place is. The expanse. The tranquility. The nature. No one around for hundreds of miles."

"Yeah," Joanna said and gazed at him with concern.

"Would you be up for something like that?" He looked down and fiddled with the soaked napkin that he pulled out from under his beer glass.

"What are you saying?"

"I'm saying leave New York. Come with me."

Joanna stared at her wine, tapping her thumbs against each other.

"It doesn't have to be a cabin. We can get a nice modern chalet," he hurried to clarify. "With a view."

"And what are we going to do there?"

"We'll buy horses. Go for rides. Or for hikes. Live a good, quiet life."

Andy held his breath. He was expecting Joanna to take a dig at him, at his pathetic, unguarded exposure, and he hid his earnestness under a slightly blithe tone, leaving himself room to retreat into a joke. But Joanna was quiet, as if she was giving his proposal real consideration. He hadn't seen her this thoughtful since she was an intern.

"I cannot do that," she said after a long pause. "I understand where you're coming from, and I appreciate what you're proposing, and I think you're sincere, but it is not something that I could do."

"Why not?"

She propped her forehead with her hands. "It's hard to say. I guess I'm too much of a city person."

"The city is a show, a masquerade. It's not real."

"Whatever it is, it's part of me. It's in my veins. The city, what I do—it defines me now as a person. I will be a nobody if I abandon it."

"No, you won't be a nobody. I saw you. When we first met, I saw who you were. There's a real person there. Remember that day when I threw a *Star Trek* reference at you, and you returned it without missing a beat? Kobayashi Maru? Remember?"

She shook her head. "No, I don't remember that."

"You're the only person who saw me for who I really am. People always mistake me for someone I am not. And then I find myself trying to show them who I am, and I stumble. Except with you. You told me that I was a teddy bear. No one had ever called me a teddy bear. I want to be somebody's teddy bear." His voice shivered.

Joanna sniffled and mustered a smile. "I told you, you have low T." She composed herself, and her voice firmed. "There will be a lot of confusion if I do that. Just imagine what would happen, the kind of gossip that would go around."

"Who gives a shit about that!"

"I can't do that. I worked too hard to get where I am. They're going to give me an MD next year. I'm in a comfortable spot."

"You pretend it's comfortable."

He must've touched a raw nerve.

"You seem to know a whole lot about pretending," she scoffed.

"I do. I hate to admit it, but I did a fair share of pretending myself. I want to live a real life now."

"There's no real life. This is what we have. A framework. We can live within it and be okay—if we don't ask too many questions. Nothing wrong with that."

Joanna was getting a bit agitated, and he blamed himself for allowing the conversation to derail to the point where she felt threatened by his reasoning and sought to defend herself.

"It's unserious," she said with her eyes closed, rubbing her temples. "And childish."

She sat resting her head in her manicured hands.

The waitress came by to check on them, but, sensing a charge in the air, retreated.

"I want to be like a rhino," Joanna said slowly, looking at her wine. "Dumb and blind and impenetrable. Because it's too painful to feel every little bump. It does not benefit a person to be a hi-fidelity record player, to be too attuned. I want to erase the melody from the disc's surface with my sheer weight. Because listening to it too closely could drive a person mad."

Misha was right. Joanna had absorbed a man's hardened mindset.

"I'm sorry, Joanna," Andy said. "I'm sorry that you feel that way."

In the parking lot, before they parted ways, Joanna hugged him and pressed her head against his shoulder. They stood in a wordless embrace for a few seconds.

"If you end up buying a ranch, let me know. I'll come visit," she said cheerfully, getting into her car. Andy thought that with these glib words, with this callous farewell, she somehow sought to placate herself, not him.

"For sure," he replied.

XXIV: Ava's Disappointment

Andy was on the Taconic Parkway heading south. After driving for twenty minutes, he looked at his GPS, changed lanes, and exited the freeway. He crossed an overpass and, in a reversal, took the northbound route. In an hour and a half, at around midnight, he took an exit near Poughkeepsie. He saw a Holiday Inn and pulled into the hotel's parking lot. He rented a room and fell asleep without taking off his clothes.

He woke up around 7 a.m., took a shower, and texted Ava: 'I'm nearby. Lunch today?'

His phone rang. It was Ava.

"What are you doing here?" she asked, sounding both surprised and concerned.

"I happened to be nearby. Mom and I were at Misha's funeral upstate yesterday. So I thought I'd make a detour to see you."

Ava had classes all day followed by the editorial meeting of her college newspaper. She told Andy that she could meet him at around 6 p.m. Andy had breakfast at the hotel and then went to downtown

Poughkeepsie. At Dick's Sporting Goods he bought a fresh T-shirt, a sweatshirt and sweatpants, and a pair of sneakers, and changed into the new clothes in a public restroom. He rented a bike and rode around town and on the Hudson walkway.

Ava texted him to meet her at a vegan place near the campus. Andy got there early. He ordered a make-it-yourself bowl, choosing chickpeas, peppers, lentils, green beans, and peas to go over romaine lettuce. He thought that it would probably be a good idea to eat like this going forward. He asked for an extra chop of the lettuce and watched the young woman behind the counter mince the springy leaves into submission with a saberlike mezzaluna knife. He waited for Ava while observing the chattering students, thinking that in two or three years these kids would become players, like he had once done, but at a different game, the rules to which he was too old to learn, let alone play by.

At a quarter past six, Ava walked in with a friend, a pudgy, dour-faced girl with dramatic eyeliner and indigo hair, whom she introduced as Daria. Daria carried a stack of folded print papers, copies of the student newsletter, the *St. Cleve Chronicle*. She placed the whole stack on the windowsill, and some students came over and picked up a copy. Andy invited Daria to join them, but she thanked him and said that she had homework to do. Ava and Daria went to the counter, and Andy saw that Ava paid for both of their orders.

"No boyfriends yet?" Andy asked Ava with a silly grin when she sat down with a tray.

Ava sighed and rolled her eyes and swept her silky hair toward the top in a nervous gesture. The hair slid back down in a messy cascade. "No," she said, sounding peeved.

"A girlfriend then?"

Ava played with a rubber hair band that she took off her bony wrist. "Daria and I are working on a writing project together. And you're thinking in primitive terms, Dad," she said. "I have not had sex, if that's what you're asking."

"That's good." Andy tapped the tips of his fingers against each other. "I mean, it's not like I'm encouraging you. As your dad, I'd rather see you do things that you want to do, not what others expect of you. After all, you're only eighteen. You have your whole life ahead of you. You'll meet somebody nice, eventually."

"It's not like I didn't think about it," Ava said. "I think that romance, at least the way we understand it today, is an insidious diversion. I don't appreciate the commodification of it and the asymmetry of possible outcomes. And then the physicality ..." She cringed. "I just don't see the appeal. A true romance should be platonic. It should be a friendship, a fellowship."

Andy's throat tightened. He sniffed and took a sip of ice water from his glass. "Well, college is the right place and time to find it. You'll only have four years, so make the most of it. After college, there will be no friendships. Only business."

"Something to look forward to," Ava scoffed.

Andy smiled. "I remember when you were four or five," he said wistfully. "I was reading you bedtime stories. You always wanted to know what happened next. You were pestering me with 'And then? And then?' Remember?"

Ava furrowed her forehead as if straining to remember.

"I had to improvise a lot. Came up with some fantastical scenarios, like a hedgehog working for a hedge fund." He giggled. "And yet you could never be satisfied with it. You always wanted a continuation. You were implacable."

Ava nervously ran her finger over the condensation on her glass. "I don't think it was a continuation that I wanted," she said. She stirred the straw, and the ice cubes inside the glass jingled. "When I first became sentient of myself, in my very deep childhood, I remember having this unexplained sense of dread, a knot in my stomach. I felt that something was very, very wrong, and that not only the adults couldn't fix that wrong, they don't even know that something needed to be fixed. I hoped that, surely, all of their vain movements, the

purpose of which I couldn't grasp, had to be in service of some benevolent end. I guess when I asked you those questions, I just wanted
some assurance that there exists a situation that does not need any
more advancement. Humanity's final destination of sorts. Of course,
I couldn't express it in those terms, so to you it looked like I was being
capricious. And soon I forgot about it myself. Mom got me a pony."
She rolled the wet straw paper with her fingers into a spitball.

It suddenly hit Andy: Ava's childhood anxiety had been of a different nature than he had realized. It's not that she had wanted him to
come home from work, as every working dad imagines his daughter
does, and as every family-movie trope has it. It was that she had as-
signed to him the task of the ultimate arbiter of truth. She searched
him for signs of a benevolent omnipotence, for a clear, tangible takeaway, a happily-ever-after like the ones she found in her fairy tales.
She probed him for substance but found a mushy, slippery relativ-
ism. Her incessant questions had been desperate attempts to arrest
her slipping confidence that there were such arbiters and guardians
among the adults. Her distress had come from the realization that
her father didn't possess the qualities she had awarded him. In her
eyes, he saw that she understood he still, even now, didn't know what
was required of him.

"There has to be an end to an action," Ava said. "A resolution. A
closing mechanism. Where we say: this is good, and now I will stop."

"What is this? Philosophy 101?" Andy chortled. "I don't understand why an eighteen-year-old would be interested in something like
this. Don't you have other, more pressing topics to concern yourself
with? Women's rights? Gun control?"

Ava sighed and closed her eyes. "You met Misha when you were
an adult," she said, ignoring his attempt at levity. "That means a
friendship is possible even in adulthood."

"Misha ... Misha was one in a million."

Ava propped up her face in her palms, her fingers framing her
eyes. "Misha and I had a, uh, recurring correspondence, I don't
know if he told you."

"What? What do you mean 'a recurring correspondence'? Like texting?"

"No. Like emails. He found texting vulgar. After your birthday party, he sent me a link to an article, and a conversation ensued."

"Why didn't you tell me about this?"

"I thought Mom did. Or Misha."

"That guy." Andy shook his head. "First Madeline, now you. He invades my women's heads. And what were you guys talking about?"

"About different things. Philosophy, history. His emails were always several pages long." Ava sniffled and took a sip of soda through the straw. "Remember when you told me about the fools? How we should navigate the world being mindful of their presence?"

"Yeah," Andy replied with caution.

"Misha had a better idea about this."

"Of course he did."

"He thought that fools should not be required to hustle. That none of us should, really. But stupid people especially. They have to be able to live normal, blissful lives without having to know what's going on. That was his ideal world—where one doesn't have to be shrewd. Because once the stupid become shrewd, it'll kill us all."

Andy was quiet. "It's utopia," he finally said.

"You never felt that your shrewdness was sort of a trap?" Ava asked carefully.

"A trap? No. I could walk away whenever I wanted."

"You could?"

There was skepticism in Ava's tone. It's like she sensed the fraud, just like young Joanna had once sensed it. Ava had identified the underlying provenance that feeds all our peeves and conflicts and hostilities, Andy thought. And now she sought to strike at that primal, foundational discordance, at its very core, and not at its surface manifestations. He wanted to tell her to maintain that inquiry, to keep her radar sharp, but there was a danger there. The inquiry could come with costs. It could lead her, like it had Joanna, to hopelessness, to cynicism, to epicurean resignation.

"Did you join any new debate group?" Andy asked. "You can probably put this newfound insight to good use in future competitions."

"No," Ava said, looking down. "I don't want to participate in debates anymore."

"Why not?" Andy leaned back in slight amazement.

"Live debates are all performance. It's all brash, unthinking rhetoric. They suppress the truth rather than uncover it." She looked at Andy, then outside the window. "Truth is found in solitary thought."

Andy drove Ava back to her campus apartment in silence.

"I once knew a young woman," he said when he parked near Ava's building. "She was sharp and inquisitive, like you."

"What happened?"

"She, uh, she became a man. I mean, not in a transgender way. She's just—"

"Joanna? Misha told me about her. He actually used the same exact words." Ava paused and stared at him. "You like her, huh?"

"Yeah ... Yes ..." He looked away. "But she's gone. Too far gone."

XXV: The Hermit

On the way back to the highway, Andy took what he thought was a shortcut through a winding local route. He weaved and veered through the farms and silos and wooded hills for about three miles, until he came to a stop at a traffic light on an empty T-intersection that merged with a bigger road. On the right was a gas station and a small convenience store. On the left he spotted a police cruiser hiding in the roadside bushes, waiting on its heedless prey. The red light was unusually long, and, while he was counting long seconds, waiting, a wild thought struck him. He pressed on the gas pedal and, wheels screeching, bashed through the red light. As if on cue, the cop blared behind him and pulled him over to the curb.

The officer exited the cruiser and walked toward Andy's car. Andy took his wallet and pulled out his driver's license. He also took a hundred-dollar bill and folded it in half. He lowered the car window and put his hands on the wheel.

The officer, a stout fiftyish man with a white goatee, was a deputy sheriff, as the silver star on his chest stated. "Did you see the red light there?" the deputy asked.

"I did."

"License and registration, please."

Andy handed the deputy his license, on top of which his thumb was pressing the folded hundred-dollar bill.

"What's that?"

"You tell me, Officer."

"Excuse me?"

Andy gave the officer a loaded stare.

"Step out of the vehicle, sir."

Andy stepped out of his Escalade and, without any prompt from the deputy and with cartoonish deference, put his hands on the roof of the car.

"Are you okay, sir?"

"Yes. No. Look, I'm not … What I'm saying is … I might have had a few drinks."

"I see," the deputy said, unlatching a pair of handcuffs from his belt.

With eager compliance, Andy placed his arms behind his back.

The deputy stared at Andy with a long appraising look. "Turn around," he said.

Andy obliged. The deputy observed Andy with a weary expression, sighed, put away the metal handcuffs, produced a pair of Plasti-Cuffs, bound Andy's wrists upfront, and led him to the police cruiser with the sheriff insignia on its side. Protecting Andy's head, he gently guided him into the back seat.

On his mobile computer, he ran a quick background check on Andy: a clean slate.

"You have a clean record, sir, and if I were you, I'd try to keep it that way. You having a rough day? Happens to the best of us." The deputy sounded tired and conciliatory. He scribbled something down in his clipboard notes.

"What does a man have to do to get arrested around here?" Andy cried.

The deputy lifted his head. "Are you upset about something, sir?"

Andy sniffed and wiped his runny nose with the back of his hand-cuffed hand.

"All right." The deputy put down the clipboard. He took a breath-alyzer and held it to Andy's mouth through the protective wire partition. "Are you on any cold medication or pep pills?"

Andy shook his head.

The device reported back a crystal-clear sobriety.

"So," the deputy said, writing down the result in his notes. "Why do you want to get arrested?"

"I, uh, I lost a bet."

"Ah."

The deputy put down his pen. "Perhaps," he said, "I'm not the right department to help you out there. But if you really are seeking some kind of attrition, I can give you a citation. I just don't know what to do with you beyond that."

The deputy wrote Andy a ticket. He exited the cruiser, opened the back-passenger door, pulled Andy out, cut his plastic cuffs, and went back to his seat.

"Actually, I didn't lose a bet," Andy said hurriedly. "I want to see if another life is possible. If this is not a simulation."

The deputy smiled at him. "It's above my pay grade. Drive safely, sir." He saluted and drove away.

Andy went back to his Escalade and sat, staring at the dark woods behind the convenience store. There was gravity in that black mass. It absorbed the flickering parking lot lights with ease and without a trace. The forest silhouette, against a dying sky, resembled a soaring rampart, and Andy imagined that this dark wall was actually a giant tidal wave, cresting, seconds away from consuming everything in its path. It would have been a good resolution.

Andy sighed, stepped out of the car, and entered the murk behind the store.

The night was warm and the sky clear. The half-moon was shining through the arcade of branches, but fog was beginning to form
on the ground. Andy walked in the moonlight for about thirty minutes, treading through the thick brush as the fog thickened around
him, until the forest abruptly ended and he came upon a white farm
fence. He climbed the fence and paused, looking at the heavy white
mist blanketing the ground below. He inhaled, jumped down into the
milky mush, and ran.

After a while, he stopped to catch his breath and assess the surroundings. The mist was so thick around him that he felt as if he were
wrapped in cotton. His heart pounded. He felt a big presence nearby
and heard a loud snort, and then a horse's head emerged from the
mist.

"Oh, horsie. Hi, horsie. Easy, easy. Okay. Okay," Andy squeaked
as the horse butted him gently against the shoulder with its velvety
muzzle.

He took a few steps forward and saw the contours of a small wood-
en shed and, behind it, another white fence. He raced toward it as
the horse trotted behind him. As Andy climbed over the fence, he
noticed that the horse's feed, a large plastic box attached to the shed,
was empty. The horse stood near the feed and looked at Andy with
large, sad, plum-like eyes.

"You hungry, big guy?" Andy asked. He jumped back into the corral and walked toward the shed. The door wasn't locked. Inside, he
found neatly stacked bales of hay. They were tightly bound with crisscrossed nylon strings, making it impossible to peel off even a handful.
He tried to tear the strings with his hands, straining and cutting his
palm. He looked around, found a pair of dull, rusty scissors hanging
on a nail in the wall, and managed to cut a few strings. Released
flakes of hay cascaded onto the shed's wooden floor. He picked up a
few pressed squares and carried them to the feed box outside.

"You like hay? Mmm. Tasty hay. Yeah. Tasty," Andy cooed, watching the horse chomp on the dry grass. He patted the horse's head as

it puffed and snorted. He went back in the shed, fluffed up the hay, and sunk down in it. He took his phone from the pocket and scrolled through his unread emails. There was an email from Misha, from weeks ago, with a file attached: Madeline_thesis_final.pdf.

"Some men know what the ends are," Misha had written. "But they don't know what to do. So they leave."

Andy opened the file. The title read: *Hermits, Monks, Saints, and Sinners: A New History of Russia's Holy Men.*

He began reading.

In his short story "Posthumous Notes of the Elder Fyodor Kuzmich," Leo Tolstoy describes the modest life of a Russian monk by that name who died in 1864 in the Siberian city of Tomsk. The story's twist comes not from the description of the monk's ascetic life, however, but from an attempt to parse his true identity. Some things about him just did not add up. In 1836, Fyodor Kuzmich appeared without any papers in the city of Perm; he spoke foreign languages, possessed good manners, was knowledgeable about the details of the 1812 war, and seemed intimately familiar with St. Petersburg high society. Tolstoy speculates that Fyodor Kuzmich was none other than Alexander I, a Russian tsar who died in 1825 at the age of 47. After Alexander I passed unexpectedly on a visit to a provincial town, he was hastily buried in a sealed coffin. According to rumor, when his tomb in the Peter and Paul Fortress was opened decades later, the coffin was found to be empty; and so the legend of a mysterious and unsettling abdication took root.

Andy stopped reading. He opened the Google app on his phone and started typing the monk's name into the search engine. The phone buzzed, signaling low battery, its screen dimmed, and then it went black. Andy tossed the useless gadget on a hay bale, determined to get back to Fyodor Kuzmich's story at the next opportunity. Seconds later, he was snoring loudly.

In the morning, the mechanical sound of tow-truck hydraulics woke him up. He wondered what it was and decided to walk toward the sound. He was surprised, when, after about three hundred steps through the brush, he found himself on the side of a highway.

A car had crashed into a deer during the night. The deer's mangled carcass lay on the highway shoulder. The tow-truck driver, a black man in work overalls with a name tag that read Moe had just finished loading the smashed car onto the truck's platform.

Andy dusted off the hay, cleared his throat, assumed a casual posture and a friendly smile, and walked toward the driver.

"Can I use your phone, sir?" Andy asked, showing his dead iPhone to the man.

The truck driver looked around, as if searching for Andy's car or any other explainable point of origin.

"Oh," Andy said, sensing the man's unease, "I left my car on the other side." He waved at the line of trees.

Moe guardedly handed Andy his phone. Andy stared at the dial pad for a moment. He then pretended to dial a number, then pretended to speak to someone.

"Oh, yeah, hey!" he said cheerfully into the phone. "I'm in a bit of a bind. Yeah. I need a lift. I'm on the Taconic and, uh, maybe a coupla miles south of East Fishkill?" He looked at Moe, and the man nodded in response. "Oh, good. I owe you one. Yeah. You'll see me. Okay, bye."

He handed the phone back to Moe.

"All good?" the man asked.

"Yeah, man, thanks a lot," Andy said. "Oh, hey!" He dipped into his pocket and pulled out his wallet. He took out the hundred-dollar bill previously rejected by the police officer and tried to hand it to Moe. "For your troubles."

The man held up his hands in stunned refusal. "No need, no need," he said, circumventing Andy at a safe distance to get back into his truck.

"Wait," Andy cried. "Maybe you need more. Here." He took another banknote out of his wallet. His hands shook. Several bills fell out of Andy's open wallet and got picked up by a gust of wind. "Here, buy something nice for your girlfriend," Andy pleaded as the man jumped into his truck, shut the door, and started the engine.

"All good, all good." Moe rolled up the window as Andy tried to shove the bills through the closing crack. The truck roared, issued a puff of black smoke, and was gone.

* * *

A farmer found Andy a day later sleeping in the hay shed and alerted the authorities. After checking his ID and his insurance card, and not wanting to entangle themselves in any potential liability, they sent Andy to a nearby hospital. A nurse in charge, failing to get any next-of-kin information out of Andy, searched his phone with his permission and, out of all people, called Caldera, who rushed to the hospital the same day.

Andy was in good shape, only a bit dehydrated. He said he wasn't lost, just wanted to be alone for a while. He was alert, engaged, answered the hospital staff's questions, but he seemed quieter than usual, not laughing at Caldera's jokes but listening and nodding with a serene smile. Caldera was concerned with this odd new version of Andy and probed around, jumping from topic to topic, trying to induce any interest. When Andy asked him for help finding a cabin to rent, Caldera was relieved and eager to help. There were still things that Andy could want, and that was a good sign. Andy wanted a bare-bones cabin, no amenities, as far upstate as possible. Caldera bristled at the request but promised to find Andy exactly what he was asking for.

"Of course," Caldera said. "Anything you need, bro."

The official legend that went out for public consumption on the Street was that Andy had gone to rehab. Most people bought it at face value out of a desire to move on, to avoid dwelling on the inexcusable, incomprehensible apostasy of one of their own. Exit by addiction warranted more leniency than an exit by choice. A man can only be wheeled away or led away in handcuffs from the trading floor. He can never leave on his own.

* * *

"If he asks, don't tell him that you work for me now. And if he doesn't—don't volunteer anything," Caldera instructed Scotty as they were pulling onto the dirt road that led to Andy's cabin after a three-hour ride from the city in early March, four months after Andy's exodus.

"Understood."

The road got narrower and muddier. They stopped, got out of the car, and walked the rest of the way, about half a mile, to the cabin.

A jubilant mutt puppy greeted them, running alongside until they arrived at the edge of a muddy compound with a log cabin at the center, flanked by stacks of firewood on both sides. In the yard in front of the cabin, Andy had assembled a little woodshop with a worktable, a table saw, a drill, and a pile of two-by-fours nearby in the dirt. A few yards away, a plot of land of about twenty by forty feet was bound by the planks, with several 50-pound sacks of Gromulch planting mix piled up inside the perimeter.

Andy, in gardening gloves and in a weathered, dirty ski jacket, was spreading the rich black compost across the lot with a rake. He had lost weight and had grown a long beard.

"Planting season already?" Caldera greeted him with a luminous smile.

"Oh, that." Andy smiled and stomped his mud-caked rubber boots on the ground. "Had to elevate that plot a few inches. The soil is very acidic here. You know why? Because of all the pines." He leaned on the rake and waved at the thick pine grove surrounding the cabin. "Downstate you're lucky—stick a branch in the ground, and it grows. Not here. Coniferous soil won't grow anything if not treated right. Good for mushrooms though, they say. We'll see in August. You should come again in August."

They hugged.

"Nice digs. Got any girlfriends here?" Scotty giggled. Caldera shot Scotty a quick, impaling glare then grimaced at Andy with an I'm-with-moron scowl.

"No. No one within a ten-mile radius," Andy said, squinting at the low sun that had already begun to set over the tree line. "Wolves come visit from time to time though. Was gonna get some chickens but have to wait till the coop is finished."

"Glad to see you're doing good, man. We got you some treats from Zabar's," Scotty said, hoisting a large brown paper bag in his hand. "There's lox, bagels … I bet you haven't had that in a while, huh?"

"I'll make tea then," Andy offered. "Would you like some tea?"

"You have coffee?" Scotty replied, opening the bag and assembling the foil-wrapped delicacies on the wooden worktable.

Caldera squeezed Scotty's elbow to shut him up. "Yes, Andy. We'd like some tea," he said as warmly as he could. He signaled to Scotty to stay outside and followed Andy toward the cabin.

Scotty stayed behind and began picking on the food, feeding pieces of lox to the puppy. The puppy, a white mix of a pitbull and something shaggier, perhaps a malamute, inhaled the lox, wiggling his tail in gratitude and delight.

Caldera and Andy stepped inside the hut. The single room was small, not more than three hundred square feet, but well-ordered. There were bare necessities: a cot covered with a sleeping bag, a kitchen table, two chairs, one of which was fashioned out of a tree stump. In the deep end of the hut, in the space between the stove and the kitchen table stood several carton boxes filled with canned goods, grains, and pasta. At the foot of the bed, an indulgence—a simple two-tiered bookshelf full of books. The room smelled of pine and burnt oatmeal.

Andy took off his gloves and held his hands over the wood-burning stove.

"How did you survive the winter?" Caldera asked.

"There were some hardships," Andy replied, putting firewood into the pit of the stove. "But, in some way, it was a clarifying experience." He scooped water from a zinc bucket with a ladle and poured it into the aluminum kettle on top of the stove.

Caldera leaned on the kitchen table by the small window and gazed outside through the dusty, sooty glass. On the table lay an open notebook; its pages were filled with hasty handwriting. He hovered and squinted over the scribbles.

Andy came from behind and shut the notebook. "You don't know what you think until you put it all down on paper," he said.

"Ah," Caldera said and moved to the other side of the room to scan the book titles on the bookshelf. "Look at you: Dante, Blake, Spinoza, Kant." He took a tome of Kant into his hands and shuffled through the pages with a pensive look. "What's a good gateway drug?"

"For you? Not this." Andy took Kant out of Caldera's hands. "Let's see." He ran his fingers over the book spines, then picked a weathered copy of Marcus Aurelius's *Meditations* and handed it to Caldera. "Here, start with something light."

The kettle whistled. Andy took it off the stove and poured the hot water into two chipped cups. "I used to ride a bike to town once a week to charge the phone. Just to see what's going on in the world. Then the urge subsided. Last time I went out was a month ago." He brought the cups and a jar of honey to the table. "Try it," he said pointing to the honey jar. "It's local."

"I'm good," Caldera said and sipped his tea.

Andy scooped the honey from the jar with a teaspoon and put it in his tea. "A strange thing happened after a while," he continued. "I began to be able to hold a thought for hours uninterrupted. It's an interesting feeling. It takes you places."

"Yeah." Caldera nodded and glanced at Andy with concern. "That's great. I think you've made your point, Andy. It's a good point. It's a ballsy move, I give you that. But maybe it's time to go back now."

"Why do you want me to go back, Dougie?"

"Why? Look, I don't want you to waste your talent. You were always a smart guy, and now you've become a wise old man. Think about what we can do. Those Arabs, they're still placing their money. I also have some Chinese guys, loaded with cash, begging me to take it. We can team up and open a new shop. I have some ideas. We will crush the competition."

He waited for Andy's reaction, but Andy was quiet. Caldera reached for the honey jar. He scooped the honey with a spoon and put it in his cup. His customary smirk slid off his lips, and Andy thought that he saw signs of distress on Caldera's face.

"Okay." Caldera softened his tone. "Out there they talk about you as if you're dead."

"Oh."

"And it upsets me."

"It does? Why?"

Caldera's face tensed up with a frantic searching. He lifted his eyes, then stared out the window, tapping his fingers on the porcelain surface of his cup. "It's as if you let yourself be defeated. This is not how men like us should end up. We should go out on top, rolling in dough, in a Vegas hotel room, surrounded by beautiful women, spraying champagne all over."

"And all our enemies crushed," Andy continued Caldera's line of thought.

"There!" Caldera exclaimed. "You see? You get it, Andy. Let's go back to that."

"I'll think about it," Andy said, looking languidly out the window.

"Good. Mull it over. Because, Andy," Caldera said, gulping the rest of his tea, "I get it. It's an itch you had to scratch. You showed all of us what cowards we are. But we don't want to have to think about it. We all need you to come back." He paused. "If not for them, then do it for me."

The pale yellow disc of the winter sun was dissolving into multicolored brush strokes behind the trees when Andy walked his guests back to their car.

"Hey, Andy," Scotty said. "You want to know where the ten-year is right now?" He fiddled with his phone. "It's at one-point-five." He giggled.

Andy lifted his head and looked up at the pine tops that rocked gently in the soft wind. "There's a permanent yield in the woods," he said. "It does not require our participation. It is indifferent to us. It's something that just grows. Without intrigue, without hustle. Isn't that beautiful?"

"Yes, Andy," Caldera said. "It is beautiful."

* * *

"What were you guys talking about?" Scotty asked Caldera when they were back in the car. "Hope you didn't let it slip I work for you now."

Caldera didn't respond. They drove in silence.

"I feel sorry for him," Scotty said after a while. "How the mighty have fallen."

Caldera stopped the car on the roadside. He turned off the engine, grunted, and rubbed his forehead. He slumped, squeezed his temples, and covered his eyes with his palm and sat like this for several seconds. Then he turned to Scotty and wagged his finger.

"Now, listen to what I'm telling you," he said. "What you saw here is not for gossip or entertainment. This is for you and me to think about on quiet days. To contemplate our folly. Understand?"

Scotty was quiet, overwhelmed by Caldera's alarming, sobering urgency.

"We just gonna let him be. And if anybody asks about him, tell 'em he retired. Are we clear?" Caldera pressed.

"Yes, Dougie. We're clear."

"Good."

Caldera started the car, and they took off. They did not utter another word all the way back to the city.

Mission Statement

Heresy Press promotes freedom, honesty, openness, dissent, and real diversity in all of its manifestations. We discourage authors from descending into self-censorship, we don't blink at alleged acts of cultural appropriation, and we won't pander to the presumed sensitivities of hypothetical readers. We also don't judge works based on the author's age, gender identity, racial affiliation, political orientation, culture, religion, non-religion, or cancellation status. Heresy Press's ultimate commitment is to enduring quality standards, i.e. literary merit, originality, relevance, courage, humor, and aesthetic appeal.

Other Heresy Press Titles

Nothing Sacred: Outspoken Voices in Contemporary Fiction
edited by Bernard Schweizer & James Morrow

Deadpan by Richard Walter

Animal by Alan Fishbone

Unsettled States by Tom Casey

Devil Take It by Daniel Debs Nossiter

Alice, or The Wild Girl by Michael R. Liska

Newsletter

Don't miss the Heresy Press newsletter SPEAKEASY:
https://heresy-press.com/newsletter/